[Codename] Hannah

[Codename]
Hannah

DANIEL MELLIGAN

Printed in the United States of America
First Printing, 2013

ISBN 978-0-9896850-1-6

Redemption Road Productions, LLC.
1275 Fourth Street #300
Santa Rosa, CA 95404

www.RedemptionRoadProductions.com

Acknowledgements

I'm gratefully indebted to the early and late readers of the manuscript in all its forms; Helen Triolo, Mike Melligan, Dr. Anthony Le Donne, Dr. Alexis Melteff, Teresa Mariani Hendrix and Gina Paisley. Graphic style and form experts Larry Jacobs, Larry Groves, Jared White, and Todd Towner. Publishing operations support by Laura Fowler, Carol Vogt, Jonathan Carr, Caitlin Carr, and Robert McIntosh. To the wonderful fellowship of faith that is the Oakmont Community Church for their support of my artistic interests. And especially to my book shepherds, Deb Carlen and Taylor Melligan.

For Taylor

"Some rise by sin, and some by virtue fall."

William Shakespeare, "Measure for Measure"

CHAPTER ONE

The Gates of Hell

❋ ❋ ❋

Shasta's barking riles up the other dogs, and now there's a riot in the foyer. The nearly blind Golden Retriever, rescued several months earlier, presses his nose to the door and barks through the keyhole. Jackson, a black Lab; Gertie, a German Shepherd; and Todd, the arthritic Border Collie, careen through the house and all crowd behind Shasta, forming a chaotic chorus.

The din notified the Caldwells that someone was at the door before the bell rang. Milo looked at the clock, then at Natalie.

"Are you expecting any visitors?"

She didn't look up from the open refrigerator, where she was focused on finding room for leftover birthday cake from dessert. "I'm hiding from anyone who might know I just turned fifty," she answered.

Milo didn't want the dogs pouncing on whoever had come to call, so he let himself out the side door into the garage.

The Caldwells had just pulled in after returning from dinner. The garage door was still open. The last flush of violet light had washed the Friday night sky, and the suburban evening stillness that hung over Rancho Mirage echoed with the sounds of children playing in nearby neighborhoods, finally cooling down from another scorching summer day. Milo walked the length of the garage and paused when he saw a Cathedral City Police Officer standing on the sidewalk leading to the front door. It startled the officer, who had his back to the garage while he was watching his associate, a Riverside County Sheriff's deputy. The deputy who rang the doorbell stood with his head lowered, listening to the dogs, sizing up the danger that might follow the barking.

"Milo Caldwell?" The police officer asked, taking back the control of the situation. "Yes?"

"I have a warrant for your arrest. I'll need you to put your hands behind your back."

"What's this about?" Milo responded. Feigning casual coolness.

"Hands behind your back, sir." Milo obeyed. He felt the cold steel and bite of the cuffs as the cop keyed the cuffs to lock position. "You have the right to remain silent. Anything you say can and will be used against you in a court of law. You have the right to speak to an attorney, and to have an attorney present during any questioning. If you cannot afford a lawyer, one will be provided for you at government expense."

"I have a lawyer," Milo said. "What's this about?"

The deputy joined the two near the garage and chimed in, "Mr. Caldwell, you're being taken into custody for an extradition warrant issued by the Clerk of the Court, Clark County, Nevada. I'll need to search your pockets." Taking over the arrest process, the deputy turned Milo so he stood between himself and the mouth of the open garage. The police officer had the deputy's back.

"For God's sake." The deputy put his hand into each of Milo's pants pockets, withdrawing his wallet, a ballpoint pen, an empty gum wrapper, and his reading glasses. "You can't take my glasses, I can't read without them."

The police officer positioned himself between the deputy and the front door so he could watch potential movement from the front. At the same time, he took each item from the deputy and placed them in a plastic bag.

The dogs had gone silent inside the house, but at that moment the front door opened and Natalie slipped out, closing the door behind her.

"Milo? Oh my God, what's going on?"

Milo attempted to keep his voice calm, but he heard it shaking as he spoke. "I'm being arrested, Natalie. Something about Clark County in Nevada."

"Arrested? For what?" Natalie's voice had spiraled up an octave.

"I don't know. Call Damon Luce. His card is in the upper left-hand drawer of my desk."

The police officer stepped between Natalie and her husband as he took a small notepad and pen from his breast pocket. He filled in the arrest form with a case number, his name and badge number before handing it to Natalie. "Here's your husband's case number, Mrs. Caldwell."

Natalie took the paper and stared at it without comprehending. She slowly raised her eyes to the officer. "What's he done? Why are you taking him?"

The deputy responded but didn't look at her. He fixed his gaze on Milo, as though he might break free at any moment. "I'm not at liberty to say any more, Mrs. Caldwell. I suggest you contact your husband's attorney."

Natalie couldn't believe what was happening. "You can't just drag my husband from home without telling us why!" Her voice was determined, and she angrily pushed her graying hair out of the way and reached for Milo. "Honey, what do you want me to do?" The deputy held Milo's trapped wrists and firmly began to guide his steps away from Natalie and down the drive and toward the waiting squad car.

"Natalie." Milo tried to turn his head to look back at her, but could only call out over his shoulder. "It's okay. Go inside and call Luce. Then call Cassandra Heller." The deputy steered him to the car while the police officer held the back door open for him. The plastic bench seat was hard and uncomfortable, and the cuffs seemed to seize more tightly with each small movement. The car door slammed with a terrible finality.

She turned on one heel and hurried back up to the house, stopping one last time to watch both agency cars drive away. In the deputy Sheriff's car, Milo's head hung low in the back seat. An evening hush had fallen over the neighborhood. A warm, dry breeze breathed over the rooftops, presaging an approaching Santa Ana. The street emptied, leaving Natalie standing alone, hands on her hips to stop them from trembling. Not knowing whether to slam the door or creep inside like a fugitive, Natalie went inside. "Not the greatest birthday," she gritted her teeth, heading for the phone to call Luce.

It was a ten-minute ride to the station in Indio, but in the backseat of the squad car it stretched infinitely. Milo blinked repeatedly, disoriented. Unable to focus on anything at close range, he instead gazed out the window as far as he could. Night was falling and he was relieved that the darkness obscured him in the back seat, should they pull up to a stoplight and find themselves alongside someone he might know. The deputy had put in an earpiece, and seemed to be informing the station that they were on approach. Milo could hear a low, garbled response coming back over the headset, and he strained to hear what was being said but couldn't quite make it out. After several minutes, he noticed that they were driving past the road that led to his office. He wondered if others were there searching the property.

"Any idea how long it might take for me to clear this up?" he asked the front seat.

"I've just been informed that we're taking you in on a warrant for a bad check you wrote. No telling how long it might take."

"This seems like an awful lot of trouble to go to for a bounced check," Milo scoffed.

"Sounds like it was a pretty big check. Half a million."

Milo was speechless. He exhaled as though the wind had been knocked out of him. After a moment he found his voice. "Half a million dollars?" he croaked. I've never written a check for that amount in my life. Who said that I did?"

"We got a tip about where you were at, Mr. Caldwell," the officer replied, as though that settled the matter.

"A tip? What do you mean? I'm not hiding from anything. What do you mean, a tip?"

"I'm just following protocol," the officer said, a note of exasperation creeping in. "Everything will be set straight in Nevada."

"Do you mean to tell me I'm being taken to Nevada?"

"Just sit back and try to relax as best you can, Mr. Caldwell." It was a command, not an invitation.

Milo was silent for several minutes before venturing again. "Can you at least tell me how much my bail is?"

"Either ten or fourteen million."

"Ten or fourteen million dollars?"

"Yes sir, that's correct."

Milo felt his heart booming inside his chest. His mouth went dry. "For — for a $500,000 check? How is that even possible?"

The officer didn't respond at once. Then he said slowly, "It's certainly the highest I've ever seen. You must have something you're not saying. Usually you get no bail before you get a number like that." The curiosity in his voice barely concealed another tone — one that seemed to say, *you're fucked, man.*

Milo felt himself perspiring beneath his arms and down his back. He wished the patrol car's air conditioning worked more efficiently. Then he wondered in a panic how long he would be in custody, as he didn't have his medication with him. He usually took it in the morning, and he felt a knot in the pit of his stomach when he considered that he might not be free by then. The recently diagnosed tangle of blood vessels in his brain was always at risk for an aneurism, and he knew keeping his hypertension under control was an essential daily requirement.

The officer spoke up from the front seat. "Are you in law enforcement? Or maybe done work for a government agency?"

Milo paused before answering, "Yes."

"Which one?"

"I can't tell you that."

"Well, you're going to have to disclose it at some point."

Milo didn't answer. The rest of the drive to the station was completed in silence.

At 9:00 he still found himself alone, still cuffed, in an eerily quiet interview room. The Indio station had been a flurry of activity when he was pushed through by the arresting officer, but he'd been isolated in this empty room since. He didn't even hear the ticking of a clock. He wished that he could rub his eyes but, his hands remained cuffed behind his back. The overhead fluorescent lights suffused him in alien luminescence and he had to blink repeatedly to clear away the yellow-gray fog that colored the room. After he had been sitting there a long time — perhaps another hour, maybe more — the door opened and a different officer, this one with a grey buzz cut, came in and uncuffed him. He handed Milo his glasses and said in a gruff yet disinterested voice, "You're allowed one phone call."

He stood in front of the door while Milo rose and went to the phone on the wall. He placed a collect call to the first bail bondsman that was listed on the wall next to the phone. The voice at Liberty Bail sounded just as indifferent as the officer guarding the door. Milo gave the voice his name at the bondsman's prompt.

There was a pause on the other end while the voice accessed the Superior Court information site. Then it said, "This looks different than most of the cases I work with. Do you happen to work for a government agency?"

"Yes, I did."

"And what agency would that be?"

"I can't tell you," Milo answered. He swallowed hard and went on, "If you call the Justice Department and ask for one of the two attorneys, they may give me permission to disclose my employer. Roxanne Patriquin or Alberto Correa, those are their names. You just have to speak to one of them."

"Have they told you what your bail is set at?" The voice asked.

"They told me ten to fourteen million. Can that be true?"

A long pause, the bondsman muttered absently, "Let me take a look at this." Milo heard the tapping of a keyboard at the other end of the line. After a moment the voice said. "Can't say I've seen the likes of this before. Ten million is what it's at."

"Well, if you reach the Justice Department – "

The voice cut him off. "It doesn't matter who you work for, there's no way I can do that. It's way out of my league."

Milo swallowed again and looked back at the officer standing by the door. The officer nodded at him once, which he took to mean that it was time to wrap up the call. He spoke urgently into the phone. "Listen, will you at least call my wife? Let her know that I'm okay. I need her to know what's going on, with the bail and everything. Tell her I don't know when I'm getting out. Can you do that?"

"Sure, of course I will. I can at least do that. Why don't you give me her phone number and I'll call her up right now."

Milo gave the bondsman his home number and hung up, grateful for this small instance of human decency. His sense of relief evaporated as he saw the officer by the door advancing on him.

"Come along, Mr. Caldwell. Picture time."

In the next room Milo held up a card with his name and 07162005ABD275 printed on it and was photographed from the front and in profile. He couldn't help but feel like a cliché. He might as well have been acting out a procedural scene from one of Natalie's favorite police dramas. The officer manning the camera asked him to step to the left side of the room where a table held a digital fingerprinting machine. The screen brought up his mug shots and the officer said, "Put your index finger on that black part if you would."

Milo did as he was told.

The mug shots disappeared from the screen but instead of his fingerprint registering in its place: an error message.

"You'll need to press your finger down firmly," the officer snapped, annoyed.

"I am," Milo answered.

The officer pressed a button and the screen went blank, waiting for the new scan. A second passed. Another error message.

"Move over." The officer looked at the screen, punched a few buttons, then said, "Let's try this again." Milo put his finger down and at last the system appeared to accept his print. He repeated this process with the fingers on each hand, then the officer told him to sit down in the chair next to the machine. Milo obeyed. The officer bent over the machine and punched a few more buttons, then muttered to himself, "What now, you piece of shit?"

"What's wrong?" Milo asked.

"Stupid thing won't save the file." The officer punched the same buttons in the same sequence and tried again. Milo heard the machine make an unpromising sound in response. The officer cursed under his breath.

"Goddamn it."

"Do I need to give my prints again?"

"Just sit still and be quiet."

Milo did as he was told and listened to the clicking of the buttons and the digital note struck by the submission button, followed by the sound of the system rejecting the file again. The officer tried half a dozen more times and then said to Milo threateningly, "Don't move." He went to a phone across the room and picked it up. "It's Charlie," he said. "Tell Robertson the print machine has a glitch in it." He stood silent for a moment and tapped his foot impatiently, glaring up at a water spot on the perforated ceiling panels. Then he focused his attention on listening into the phone. "Of course I did. I've tried ten times already." He listened again. "Well just because it worked fine an hour ago doesn't mean it's working fine right now." He shook his head at whatever was said to him. "Yeah, yeah. Okay," and hung up.

He walked back over to the machine and tried again. Rejection. Again. And again. Milo counted twenty attempts in all. Finally, in a fit of frustration, he opened a drawer and took out a piece of paper and an inkpad. Milo pressed each of his fingers into the black pad and then onto the paper. When he was done the officer shoved the paper into a manila file and rammed it into a filing cabinet. "Hands front," he barked, to which Milo complied. The officer cuffed him again roughly. "Either my machine is on the fritz, which isn't too likely, or you…." His voice trailed off.

He was taken to a cramped cell with a thin, dirty mattress and a foul-smelling toilet and locked inside. As the jailer withdrew his keys from the padlock Milo said, "I have a medication that I need to take soon. Will my wife be able to bring it to me?"

The jailer looked as though he couldn't care less. "I don't know anything about that. Just sit still and keep quiet."

He sat on the creaking bed and attempted to gather his thoughts. He wondered if Natalie had been able to reach Luce, and whether she would be able to get his medication to him tonight. He felt his hands trembling and clasped them together, pressing them between his knees to still them. He found himself blinking in the harshness of the overhead lights. It made it difficult to focus his train of thought. Then he heard a voice in his head, low and clear above the din in his brain.

Gordon, it said. This is Gordon's doing.

The lights went out but he continued to sit at the edge of the bed in the dark. At half past midnight there were footsteps at the end of the hall and the lights switched back on in his cell. The jailer unlocked the door and tossed him an orange jumpsuit.

"Put that on," he commanded. "You're being transferred."

Milo stood up, looking at the orange suit in his hands. "Does my wife know?"

"Come on. We don't have all night."

The jailer watched him strip down to his briefs and change into the jumpsuit. Then he said, "Fold up your clothes and place them on the bed. Then turn around and put your hands in front of you." Milo obeyed and watched as he was cuffed again. "Pick up your clothes and walk."

They went the length of the hall and pushed through a back door. Outside the temperature had dropped considerably and Milo shivered. The officer leading him said, "Come on, in back," and he noticed an unmarked van with no windows, save for those in the cab, waiting for them. The officer knocked on the side of the van and went around to unlock the back doors. It was fairly dark inside, but Milo could see another figure in an orange jumpsuit sitting on the bench to one side. At the officer's prodding, he climbed in and sat on the opposite bench. The man across from him had long, greasy black hair and tattoos that extended from the wrists of both arms, disappeared beneath his sleeves, then continued from his collar up both sides of his neck. He had a scar that ran from the left corner of his mouth to his left ear. The man watched the deputies as they closed the van doors, but when he turned his head and saw Milo looking at him, Milo quickly glanced at the floor. He felt himself sweating again, wondering if the man across from him had killed anybody. He swallowed a few times, but the lump in his throat remained.

The van had been idling when there was another sharp knock on the side. They heard the gears shift in the cab and the van lurched forward. Milo tried to avert his eyes from his murderous-looking companion. It wasn't long before the man spoke.

"Don't even give us no fucking seatbelts back here," he said in a whiskey soaked voice. "Wouldn't they be shit-fit happy if there was an accident and we got our fucking heads chopped off. Save the state some money."

Milo tried to say "yeah" but all that came out was an indistinct whisper. He cleared his throat and kept his eyes to the floor.

"Name's Pumpkin Dailey," said the man.

"Milo. Milo Caldwell." He immediately wondered if he should have come up with a fake name.

"Well, Milo Caldwell, what are you in for? Failure to pay alimony?" Pumpkin chuckled at his own joke.

"No, no."

"You don't look like most of the guys I see in here, if you get what I mean."

Milo looked up in spite of himself. "Have you been here before?"

"Sure have. It'll be my second time. Fact this my fourth arrest in eight years."

Before he could stop himself, Milo asked, "What for?"

"Crime of being an Indian." Pumpkin chuckled again. "I'm jerkin' ya. First was arson. Second was assault, then arson, then arson again. They mostly leave us alone at Agua Caliente 'less we really do something to piss 'em off."

"Agua Caliente? You live at the casino?"

"No, I live on the rez the casino was named after." He smiled, showing a gold tooth that glinted feebly in the darkness. "They put in this new pump system out back of the central lodge, not too far from where I live. That thing's been a pain in my ass—makes so much damn racket, 'specially on warm nights when the sound carries. Keeps my ma awake." He chuckled. "So I torched the fucker."

Milo found himself drawn in. "Did the noise stop?"

" 'Fraid not, did some damage to the thing but they fixed it in a day or two. And now here my ass is going back to Smith." The van hit a pothole and they were jostled on their benches. "What'd they get you on?"

"I wrote a bad check."

Pumpkin let out a shout of laughter. "I'll bet you did."

"Or at least, that's what they claim I did."

"You gotta be shittin' me." Pumpkin stared at him incredulously. "You serious?"

"That's what I'm accused of."

Pumpkin shook his head and said, "I'll be damned."

Milo continued, "If you really want to know the truth, I think this might be something my old business partner cooked up. I've never written a check for half a million dollars, like they're saying I have."

"Sure doesn't seem like enough of a reason to send a guy to Blythe," Pumpkin said. "Sure, you got your low-level felons like me in there, but that's where they put the hardcore guys, too. You best watch yourself in there, man."

Milo didn't say anything. He knew that if he spoke his voice would betray the panic rising inside him.

The van was picking up speed now. Pumpkin said, "It's gonna be a long haul out there, man. Six hours or so. And us back here with no seatbelts." He tapped his foot and looked around. "I hate having to just sit still and do nothing, you know? I always try to keep myself occupied. I got a banjo at home, I like to play that. I used to whittle, too, but my ma ain't too keen on me being around knives nowadays. Got in a fight with this punk last year and cut his arm pretty bad. Ever since then my ma tells me I can't be trusted with no knives."

"Were you arrested for cutting him?"

"Naw, man, we mostly try to keep the cops out of our business at

Agua. I don't think he said nothing about the fight when he went to the hospital, or at least he didn't tell 'em it was me that did it. He had it coming to him too 'cause he's the one that started it. You ever been in a fight, man?"

"No, can't say I have."

"I used to fight a lot when I was a kid; I try not to get involved no more unless the other guy's asking for it."

Over the next several hours Pumpkin chronicled a laundry list of his crimes, both major and petty — fights, thefts, arrests, even murders witnessed. Milo listened and spoke only occasionally, interjecting a word here or there to prompt Pumpkin to continue, though Pumpkin didn't need encouragement to keep up his monologue. Milo was secretly grateful to have something to think about other than the van's final destination.

The first light of dawn spread over the horizon when the van finally pulled to a stop. The back doors opened and even though it was still dark, Milo blinked in the harsh floodlights that illuminated their surroundings. An officer with a shotgun stood at the door. "Everybody out," he said.

Pumpkin stood up. "Man, Blythe is a drag, but I'll be happy to get out of this stinking van."

The officer smirked. "Don't get too excited, 'cause you ain't at Blythe."

Milo stepped out behind Pumpkin and saw that they were in a dusty lot filled with buses, presided over by blinding floodlights. Sheriffs armed with shotguns directed a stream of men in orange jumpsuits into a larger bus. Milo asked one of the sheriffs, "Are we going to Calimesa from here?"

The man sized Milo up and seemed to decide he could answer him straight. "Bus is headed to Pressley." They were herded onto the bus.

Sitting down next to him, Pumpkin said, "It's all bullshit, man. The way they keep all us guys in transit all goddamn night. Just wait 'til you get to Pressley, man. It's gonna be packed. But they got this brilliant way of getting around releasing guys if the facility is overcrowded, which it always is. They just shuttle us around. That way they don't have to count us. Keep guys in flux, then it don't matter if they don't have enough beds."

"That seems like a racket," Milo said.

"No kidding, man. The California detention system is the biggest racket there is."

It was eight o'clock in the morning when the bus pulled into the prisoner unloading zone at the Pressley Center of the Riverside County Jail. Each prisoner who stepped off the bus had his handcuffs replaced by a set of shackles binding his wrists and his ankles, with a chain connecting the two. They were then shackled to the man in front of and behind them. The activity was monitored by half a dozen sheriffs, all armed with shotguns. They shuffled in through a waiting set of propped-open double doors, flanked on either side by an armed sheriff.

Through the doors they found themselves directed into a large cell containing several dozen other prisoners. As they went into the cell a waiting officer unshackled them, but their wrists and ankles remained bound. Milo and Pumpkin were pushed through, and before they had a chance to sit down, Pumpkin called out, "Hey, Red!" A short, stocky man with massive arms and shoulder-length black hair shuffled across the cell and greeted them. "Yo, Red, this is Milo. Milo, this here's my friend Indian Red. What did they get you on, man?"

Indian Red answered casually. "Stole some money from a Stop-n-Rob, didn't know there was a cop hiding his car out behind the shop."

Pumpkin laughed. "Man, one of these days they're gonna lock your Indian ass up and throw away the key."

Indian Red shrugged. "I still got options, man."

The two launched into a detailed legal dialogue that Milo struggled to follow. Every now and then a phrase would jump out at him. At one point Pumpkin said something about parole violation and Indian Red responded with something about jumbo pleading - and Milo was struck by the sobering thought that these two seemed to know more about the criminal system than any attorney he knew. He wondered if Natalie had reached Damon Luce.

"Man, they best not put me above two," Pumpkin said.

Milo asked, "What does that mean?"

"Second floor," Pumpkin answered. "The best floor to be on is one. That's where all the DUIs and misdemeanors and shit go. They got plenty of beds and you don't gotta watch your back all the time, if you know what I mean."

"Four is hell," added Indian Red. "Nobody wants four. That's where they put all the murderers and rapists and child molesters."

"He don't need to worry about four," laughed Pumpkin. "His white ass wrote a bad check. He probably won't even be on one for that long, man."

The minutes crawled by. Milo's attention to their conversation wandered. He looked at the men in the cell with them. Many of them had tattoos or scars, like Pumpkin. Many others had powerful arms, like Indian Red. He was struck by the sudden terrible feeling that if any of these men were to pick a fight with him he would go down in an instant. He tried not to make eye contact with anyone.

It wasn't long before the jailer unlocked the door and called out, "Brandon Kennedy, first floor." A young, plump-faced man with blond hair and wide eyes stood up and shuffled out. "DUI for sure," said Indian Red. "Probably a college kid."

"His daddy'll spring him in no time," said Pumpkin.

Every twenty minutes or so, the jailer came back to call out a new name and floor assignment. Indian Red was among the first to go, assigned to the second floor. He pounded fists with Pumpkin and Milo. "Keep your asshole to yourself, man," he told Milo.

There was a clock on the wall outside the cell and Milo found himself keeping track of the time. Four hours after their arrival, the jailer entered and announced, "Milo Caldwell, fourth floor."

Milo felt his heart drop into his stomach. Pumpkin was incredulous, "Must've been some bad check, man."

"Caldwell, let's go!" the jailer yelled. Milo stood and followed him, doing everything in his power not to show his fear.

The next thirty-six hours passed as if in an endless haunted dream. Milo found himself sharing a cell with a child molester who spoke no English. Milo eked out a conversation using his high school-level Spanish, but after the first several painful minutes of attempting to communicate, he gave up and they didn't speak again.

He spent hours pacing the cell, which smelled like stale excrement and vomit. No amount of antibacterial cleaning solution or coats of paint could eliminate the stench of tainted humanity. Every available inch on every wall had the markings or carvings of past citizens of this particular malebolge. Names, initials, names of lovers, and curses at enemies, all carved somehow into the concrete surface. The only personal surface was the paper-thin mattress covered in industrial grade sheets and a dreadfully scratchy woolen blanket.

He was afraid to turn his back on his cellmate and used the urinal standing off to one side where he could keep an eye on the man. His cellmate showed no interest in Milo but he was still unable to relax. Sleep eluded him. He lay awake that night, staring into the darkness and listening to the prisoner down the hall who screamed intermittently after lights out. When at last he began to drift asleep, his snoring woke his cellmate, who kicked his mattress savagely to shut him up. His blood drummed in his veins and his heart pounded in his chest as if trying to escape. He worried about having gone two days without his high blood pressure medication.

His thoughts turned to Gordon Hicks and his political ally, Bob Montefusco, who was currently serving as governor of Nevada. In the darkness on that top bunk with a child molester beneath him and an inmate screaming down the hall, it occurred to him that Gordon and the governor were responsible for putting him here. Could Montefusco have used his political influence to convert Milo's gambling debts in Nevada into felony offenses? It was possible, though Gordon regularly carried debts at those same casinos—he was the one who had taken Milo there and introduced him around. Don't worry about the stakes, just play to your heart's content, Gordon had said, slapping Milo on the back. You're among friends here.

And some friends they had been. Milo found himself wringing his hands in the dark. When he had needed money there was no one to help him. He had waited for a payment from his new business partner, Cassandra Heller, for six months from the last government contract work, planning to pay off the last of the debts with that. And now here he was. He clenched his fists.

In the dead of night there were quiet moments when all he could hear was the breathing of his cellmate. In these moments he found himself praying, which he had not done in many years. *Please, God... holy hell!* It was Milo's first attempt at prayer in years. He realized that he was off to a poor start. "Sorry. I'm so, so sorry. *I'm a damned idiot...* and *poor Natalie.* Milo paused, his thoughts trailing to Natalie. *"Please assure her that I'm ok, God."* It occurred to him then that he might not be ok.

Tears welled up into his bloodshot eyes. *"God please, please. I want to make it all right. Please, just keep me safe in this horrible place."*

The lights clicked on promptly at seven o'clock. The inmate down the hall fell silent. At 7:30 a trapdoor opened and the breakfast trays were pushed through. Milo's cellmate snatched his and retreated to his bunk. Exhausted from his sleepless night, Milo climbed down from his bed in a daze. He picked up the scarred plastic tray. It contained a paper plate that held a grayish, gelatinous substance that he couldn't identify, and a badly bruised apple. There were no utensils. He looked back at his cellmate, who was scooping up the gelatinous stuff with his fingers and slurping it off. "How can you eat this?" Milo asked him. "This isn't food." The man stared back at him and continued to eat, saying nothing. Milo took the apple and set the tray back down on the floor before climbing back into his bunk. He lay back and took a few bites of the apple, which was mushy and tasteless. After several moments his cellmate seemed to comprehend that Milo wouldn't be touching his breakfast, and he heard the man grab the tray off the ground for himself.

Sunday passed just as the previous twelve hours in the Riverside cell had passed — seemingly infinite, dragging hours spent in an exhausted stupor, pacing the cell or lying on the bunk staring at nothing. His guts twisted when he thought of Natalie, and he was flooded with guilt and shame. He tried and failed to control his ragged breathing and racing heart by closing his eyes and visualizing himself somewhere calm, somewhere else, anywhere but here. The daylight hours waned into night and the lunatic screamed again.

Monday morning, after Milo had eaten his tasteless apple and listened to his cellmate eat the rest of his meal, he was startled to hear the cell door being unlocked. He sat up, dazed, and blinked hard in the intense light that rushed in. A corrections officer stood in the doorway, backlit and silhouetted. "Caldwell, time for your hearing," he said.

Hardly daring to believe it, Milo clambered off the bunk and shuffled out after him. All down the row cell doors were being opened and prisoners extracted for the same purpose. He stood passively while the corrections officer shackled him up, and let himself be prodded down the row and downstairs to the ground floor. He found himself directed through the same door he had entered, and waited as he was chained to the inmates ahead of and behind him. As the corrections officer moved away from him further down the line, the inmate in front of him turned around and grinned. It was Pumpkin. "Milo, man, you survived four."

Milo opened his mouth to speak and found that his voice sounded unrecognizable even to himself. He realized he hadn't spoken in more than 24 hours. "I'm half-dead," he answered huskily.

"Yeah man, you look like hell," Pumpkin agreed.

The inmates were herded onto the bus and shuttled to the Riverside County Courthouse. Milo sat and listened to Pumpkin talk the whole way there, but he said almost nothing himself. When they had reached their destination their shackles were replaced by standard handcuffs, and they were separated into groups of fifteen to twenty. The individual groups were directed to various courtrooms, where they were seated in the jury box by the bailiff. They rose *en masse* at the command of the bailiff, who announced the arrival of the Honorable Carlton Bidlack. He told them that they may be seated and they sat.

Judge Bidlack balanced a pair of reading glasses on his nose and peered at the document before him. "Pumpkin Dailey," he called out. "Please approach the bench."

Next to Milo, Pumpkin stood up and moved to the defense table. The good-humored smirk had vanished from his face and instead he wore the same expression that had given Milo a turn several days before — composed and menacing. Judge Bidlack read the charges of arson before him and Pumpkin nodded to each one.

Judge Bidlack removed his glasses and looked at the defendant. "Mr. Dailey, I notice here that you already have two outstanding charges of arson on your record."

"That's right, your Honor."

"Are you able to post bail on these new charges?"

At this, a man in a suit stood up from the audience and moved alongside Dailey. His glossy black hair was pulled back into a neat ponytail. "Your Honor, my name is Samuel Sherman, and I represent the Agua Caliente tribal council. I am here to post Mr. Dailey's bail."

Judge Bidlack motioned to the man. "Please approach the bench, Mr. Sherman."

The matter of the bail was settled and Pumpkin was escorted from the courtroom via the prisoner's entrance. As they walked past Milo,

Pumpkin winked at him and mouthed, "Good luck, man."

Milo hoped that his name would be called next, but in this he was disappointed. He sat through the following arraignment, and the next, and the one after that. After two hours he was the last to be summoned. Judge Bidlack called his name and he stood. At the same moment, a bald man in the back row stood also and identified himself as Mark Thames, the public defender. He hurried to Milo's side and fell into step with him as they approached the defense table. As they walked, Thames queried in Milo's ear, "Just who the hell are you, anyway?"

Milo answered, "I'm just a guy."

"No, you're more than just a guy."

They reached the front of the courtroom and waited as Judge Bidlack pondered the file before him. After a moment he peered at Milo and then directly at the Assistant District Attorney, Roland Boyd.

"Mr. Boyd, I have nothing in the prosecution's folder. No fingerprints, no photo, no history, nothing. Now, that doesn't make sense to me."

Boyd spoke up. "Your Honor, this is just a flight, rather, extradition to Nevada. We really have nothing to do with it."

Judge Bidlack removed his glasses and glared at the prosecution. "What do you mean, nothing to do with it? I don't even have an arrest warrant here." He then looked at Milo. "Mr. Caldwell, do you agree to be extradited to Nevada?"

"No, your Honor." Milo spoke without waiting for Thames to speak on his behalf.

"What do you mean, no?"

"Your Honor, I'm a whistleblower on Governor Montefusco's ethics trial. I'm not interested in going back to Nevada, under his influence, which would put me under his jurisdiction again."

Judge Bidlack scowled, growing visibly irritated with the length of the exchange. "Mr. Thames, I advise you to point out to your client that you are here to protect his interests."

Now looking at both of them, he continued. "You realize, Mr. Caldwell, that you can stay incarcerated for up to one hundred-twenty days if you don't accept this extradition."

"I do, your Honor," Caldwell interjected.

Thames dropped his head in astonishment and disdain.

"Mr. Thames," Bidlack growled, "you would make life much easier for all of us if you were on the same page as the defendant." Thames remained silent. Judge Bidlack continued, "Mr. Caldwell, I really must encourage you to consent to extradition."

Milo recovered his composure and whispered his concerns into Thames' ear.

Thames responded, "Your Honor, my client will agree to the extradition provided that once he obtains private legal counsel, he may then exercise his option to rescind the agreement."

"That sounds reasonable enough," snapped Judge Bidlack. He knocked his gavel once against the desktop. "Mr. Caldwell, you have seven days to arrange for counsel. You'll remain here until either bail is posted or you agree to extradition. Otherwise, this court is adjourned for the day."

The bailiff escorted Milo from the courtroom to a waiting deputy, who shackled him and led him back to the bus. The number of passengers had dwindled considerably since their arrival, as many posted bail. He was almost sorry to not be riding back with Pumpkin. The bus ferried them back to Pressley Center and Milo found himself again in the cell with the child molester.

Another grueling 24 hours passed. Nervous, exhausted, and sleep deprived, Milo lay on his bunk, staring at the ceiling above him, unable to focus his thoughts or what little energy he had on anything in particular. The hours crawled and occasionally he would doze off, skimming the surface of sleep but never quite going under. The night passed in a similar fashion to the two that preceded it: screaming down the hall, Milo drifting off and snoring, his cellmate delivering a swift kick to the underside of his mattress.

Finally, on Tuesday, the cell door opened and the jailer announced that he had a visitor. He was escorted to the visiting hall where he found Natalie seated on the other side of a glass barrier. She forced a smile when he sat down, but her lovely face could not conceal the hours of worry and wear that weighed on her since he'd been arrested. Her light blonde hair had been pulled back in a bun and under the glare of the lights in the visitor's hall it almost looked white. There were shadows beneath her hazel eyes that she had attempted to cover with makeup. They each picked up a receiver.

"Hi, honey," he said.

She choked out a sob and sat for a moment, trying to collect herself. "Milo, you look awful," she said at last.

Milo tried to contain himself. He felt as though he were on the brink of tears as well, but struggled to maintain his composure. "It's been hard to get my beauty rest in here."

She nodded and wiped her eyes. "I've been doing everything I can to get the bail together," she said. "I talked to Luce, I talked to almost a dozen bail bonds places. I even tried to cash out the rest of our 401k. It's no use."

"So we're broke."

Her face showed nothing but sorrow and misery. "My sister has contact with an attorney in L.A., and she called him yesterday. He said he might be able to look into the case."

"What would he be able to do, exactly?"

She paused before answering. "I don't know. I don't know, but it's the best we've got at this point." They both fell silent. Eventually she continued, "I know this is a stupid question, but are you doing okay?"

"I'm okay, sweetie. I haven't been sleeping or eating a whole lot, but I'm holding up."

She broke down once more. "Oh God, Milo. You look like you've aged ten years in the last few days."

At that moment someone tapped Milo on the shoulder. It was the corrections officer who had brought him to the visiting hall. "Time's almost up," he said. "You got two minutes."

"How are the kids doing?" Milo asked.

"They're worried sick, of course. They wanted to come."

"Natalie." Milo's voice suddenly broke. "I don't want them to see me like this. Please."

Her eyes welled with fresh tears. "I know, I know. I knew you would feel that way. Carrie's in hysterics. Jeremy's just clammed up, you know how he is. But I can tell he's upset."

"Tell them I'm sorry. For all of this."

Natalie withdrew a tissue from her purse and blew her nose. "I don't know how, but we'll get through this. Maybe the lawyer can help."

Milo's reply was unenthusiastic. "Maybe." They looked at each other through the glass, their eyes reflecting one another's wretchedness.

"Natalie, I know this sounds crazy, but since I've been in here I've been praying again."

She smiled sadly. "It doesn't sound crazy. I've been praying too."

"Whenever I get out of here, I'd like to start going to church again."

"Time's up, buddy," interjected the corrections officer.

Milo said, "I love you," and blew Natalie a kiss. Natalie reciprocated, then put a hand to her mouth to stifle the sound of her weeping. They hung up the receivers, and Milo was led from the room back to his cell.

On Wednesday, the attorney from Los Angeles paid him a visit. He was a short, paunchy man in a brown suit. They were seated on either side of the glass and the attorney, who identified himself as John Carson, began speaking as soon as they picked up the receivers.

"Now listen to me, Milo. Just listen and don't say anything. Your family is working on obtaining a defense attorney in Nevada because these casino debts are a very complex legal matter. Arrangements need to be made, and we're working as fast as we can. Only a very few lawyers have the skills to navigate the complexities of state licensed gambling debt. I have to ask you to be patient on this. We've got a guy on the line, David Abram, and we think he'll agree to take your case. Abram runs a litigation firm in partnership with Principio Olveira, who was formerly the mayor of Las Vegas. Everyone called him Prince. These are important guys to have on your side. They defend all the high-profile cases in Vegas, a lot of the politician and celebrity gambling debts and whatnot. They are known as the "King and Prince of the Strip." Abram just needs to agree to a retainer amount and then we're set. He says he also may be able to knock a couple million off your bail." He paused and took a breath. "I can't stay long. Is there anything you need in there?"

Milo said, "I haven't had my high blood-pressure medication in almost a week. I really need it."

Carson almost hit the ceiling. "Are you kidding me? They haven't even given you your medication? They will once I'm through raising a little hell on this side."

He was evidently successful. Later that evening, in addition to his inedible meal, Milo was given a small paper cup with one of his blood pressure pills.

⊕ ⊕ ⊕

Thursday afternoon Milo anxiously awaited Natalie's next scheduled visit. But the hour approached, lingered, and then passed by. Two hours after the designated time, he signaled a guard to ask why he had not been released for the visiting hour and whether his wife had come. "Everyone's on lockdown right now, pal," was the answer. "There's been a murder on this floor, and visiting hours are suspended indefinitely."

That night, for the first time in five days, there was no screaming from the inmate down the hall. Although it had set Milo's teeth on edge to hear it every night, the absence of sound after lights off was eerie.

Friday came and went. Then, on Friday night, he heard the door unlocking. He wondered if the mealtime had been altered for some reason.

The guard said, "Caldwell, let's go. You're leaving."

Milo sat up. "To another cell? Or Nevada? What do you mean?"

"You posted bail. Let's get a move on."

Hardly daring to believe it, Milo clambered off his bunk and followed. He felt himself quaking from head to toe as he walked down the hall. The arduous release process - four more hours - tempered his joy. While he waited he was permitted to make a phone call to David Abram. "How did I post bail?" he asked.

"The ten million dollar bail was based on a belief that you had fled the state of Nevada to avoid the casino debts," Abram replied. "To hold up in court the notices of debt must be certified. We've done some digging around and we couldn't find any evidence that your notices were ever sent, much less certified. On this basis your bail was reduced to $100,000."

"If the notices were never sent then how could they even get a warrant to arrest me?"

Abram answered, "You must have some powerful enemies."

Then, at long last, they gave Milo his clothes and he was free to go.

It was 5 o'clock in the morning when he stepped outside. The air was cool, and felt sharp to inhale after the stale and fetid oxygen trapped in his cell. He walked to the sidewalk and looked around. There was no one to greet him, save for a handful of idling cabs. He realized no one would have any way of knowing he'd been released.

He approached the first cab. An elderly driver folded his newspaper and looked at the disheveled figure peering through his passenger window. Milo said, "I'll give you $200 to take me to Rancho Mirage."

The driver thought it over, then answered. "Get in."

Milo stayed put. "Only I don't have the money on me. When we get to Rancho Mirage I'll be able to pay you."

The driver looked doubtful at first, but considered the man before him and seemed to decide he was on the level. "All right." Milo slid into the backseat. The driver turned around. "Anybody know you're coming?"

"No, I don't think my wife knows I've been released."

The driver nodded. He said, "You look like you've had a rough time of it, son."

"Yes, sir. I don't mind saying it's been one of the worst weeks of my life."

The driver nodded again. He handed Milo his cell phone. "Give your wife a call and let her know we should be there in about an hour and a half. There's a Taco Bell about twenty minutes away. We'll make a stop there first."

Milo took the phone. "I don't even have a few dollars on me, I'm afraid."

The driver faced forward and started the engine. "Don't worry about it, I can spare you a few bucks for a meal."

Milo felt tears stinging his eyes. He said, "Thank you," very quietly, to which the driver made no answer. He dialed his home number and Natalie picked up on the second ring. When he told her the news she said, "Oh, thank God," and began to weep on the other end.

The first light of day had begun to peek over the mountains. Milo sat back as they moved swiftly down the freeway. The slightly stale crunch of the taco tasted better than anything he had ever eaten. He ran a hand through his hair, which felt thinner than it had only weeks before. As the cab headed south and he began to doze, he turned his thoughts toward paying a visit to Gordon. In half sleep, he took stock about how the two of them even found each other.

CHAPTER TWO

1999

John Stagnaro could always spot a business opportunity when it came through the doors of the El Dorado Casino. In the high-stakes casino world of Reno, there's not enough money in just getting paid to reel in the big fish. The serious return was in going above and beyond for a high-profile guest. Most hosts were little more than errand boys or girls Friday for big spenders with big egos to match, spending most of their time running around tending to the whims of those egos.

But a smart host pins a prominent guest from across the floor. They ingratiate themselves to the guest; make themselves indispensable. They establish a relationship with the guest, and through this relationship the host ceases to be a servant and becomes instead a trusted associate who operates within the delicate ecosystem of the casino. And a smart host uses that contact as a means to other ends. Stagnaro spent most nights meeting and greeting and watching greedy suburbanites get drunk and lose their money. But if the situation was right, and a guest had that certain quality that he looked for – well-made but not attention-grabbing clothes, good posture even when he or she was losing, confidence, and above all a sense of calm control, whatever the outcome of the game – he would introduce them to his other employer, Gordon Hicks.

In the casino world, everything works both ways. To establish a working relationship, it had to be mutually beneficial for both parties. Johnny Staggs, as he was known around Reno, split his time between the Peppermill two nights a week and the El Dorado three nights a week as Gordon's dedicated casino host. Whatever Gordon wanted, Stagnaro got for him. Gordon only drank when he gambled, and he gambled a great deal. If Gordon should show up at the casino while Stagnaro was at the Peppermill or had the day off, he would immediately receive the call and find a way to be on the El Dorado floor in twenty minutes or less. The more he drank, the higher the stakes. So whether Gordon won or lost, the casino won big every night that he made an appearance.

Stagnaro, too, won big. Through casual conversation he learned about his clients' interests and business. If a client had interests in common with Gordon, Stagnaro made certain to arrange an introductory meeting between the two. These meetings almost always led Gordon to new opportunities for wealth. John Stagnaro had an eye for it. "Johnny Staggs, you're my golden goose," Gordon was fond of saying after a few drinks, on nights when he was playing good hands. He would slap Stagnaro on the back, his red face sufficiently swollen with gin and tonic. "You got a business sense about you, you know that? You should go into finance." He would take a drink. "No, don't you go anywhere. You're too valuable to me."

"Don't worry, Mr. Hicks," Johnny Staggs would answer. "I'm not going anywhere."

It was a slow Tuesday night at the El Dorado the week after Thanksgiving. The host slouched in the chair behind his desk and gazed out over the casino floor. It had been a dull week, and he'd been forced to run errands for several high-rolling but otherwise unimportant Chinese tourists, who were the majority of the visitors that time of year. It grated on Stagnaro, who thought it below his pay grade. His manager walked by and hissed at him, "Mr. Stagnaro, please button your jacket." The host complied begrudgingly.

It was at that moment that he spotted a solitary figure sitting at one of the blackjack slot machines at the edge of the non-smoking section. The man appeared to be in his late forties, with rimless glasses and neatly combed dark hair peppered with a hint of grey. Although he was dressed simply, in charcoal slacks and a light grey button-down oxford, he was well put-together in a way that immediately made Stagnaro take notice. A briefcase leaned against the blackjack machine at his feet. He didn't have the look of decrepitude or desperation that characterized so many guests on the floor. He also wasn't too flashy. He was somewhere in the middle between the polar opposites of the majority of El Dorado guests. He was inconspicuous, easy to miss.

Normally Stagnaro would've passed him over for someone more important-looking. But it was a slow night and there was something about the man's appearance that pushed the host to approach him.

He did so with an ingratiating smile. "How are we doing this evening?" he asked.

The man looked up at him and grinned timidly. "Fine, thank you."

"I'm John Stagnaro, one of the casino hosts. I wanted to introduce myself and let you know that I'm available, should you need anything this evening. Will you be with us long?"

"Thank you, no," the man answered. "I'm just here for a few hours. I live in Lodi and come out here sometimes just to get away for a bit."

The host nodded emphatically. "I understand completely. A little alone time to clear the head."

"That's right. I work from home and I've got two teenagers in the house. It can be difficult to concentrate when they're blasting the TV and their dance music."

"It sounds to me like you've earned a little bit of a break," Stagnaro agreed. "Can I get you a drink or some dinner?"

"I don't drink, but I suppose I could go for a Coke." He looked at his watch. "A steak doesn't sound too bad either."

"Very good, Mr. – "

"Caldwell. Milo Caldwell." They shook hands.

Stagnaro looked in on Milo throughout the rest of the night. He treated him like an old friend, and encouraged him to move from the blackjack slot machines to the tables.

He introduced Milo to the dealers and instructed them to take good care of him. They all promised to do so.

Against his better judgment, and as the evening wore on, Milo found himself confiding in Stagnaro about his line of work. He explained that he was in the process of pioneering a new technique for colorizing black and white movie film. He had partnered with a producer in Hollywood who shared his love of classic movies, and together they were in the process of creating software to restore and colorize older films that had not aged well.

"You see, a lot of the earliest feature-length can never be fully restored because parts of the film reels were lost or damaged," Milo explained. "Many of the movies that we think of as classics today just sat around in warehouses or storage closets getting moldy or water-damaged – for decades. Now that there's a resurgence of interest in restoration and preservation, I'm working on software that uses digital graphics to fill in some of the blank spots. At this point, for a black and white film to be colorized, it has to be essentially painted in by hand. But this software uses the same digital techniques to colorize the film as it does to add the graphics."

Johnny Staggs listened attentively. He seemed genuinely interested. "Have you created any samples yet?"

Milo patted his briefcase. "We're working on *Gunga Din* right now. I should have a few test strips completed within the next two months."

With an air of confidence the host said, "I would love to see them when they're done."

Over the next two months, Milo increased his visits to Reno. Each time he went, Stagnaro greeted him warmly. He made it known that anything Milo desired could be easily obtained. He also went to great lengths to assure Milo that as a professional host, he handled matters with the utmost discretion. "Should you be interested in any female companionship during your stay with us, Mr. Caldwell, just say the word."

Milo was embarrassed. "I'm married, you know."

"I understand, Mr. Caldwell." Stagnaro looked him in the eye. "I assure you that if you would like any companionship, we will be very discreet."

"It's not like that. I'm sure there are plenty of married men who think that what they do here is separate from their home lives. But my marriage is sacred to me. I try not to get into potentially compromising situations."

The host smiled deferentially. "If the world were filled with husbands like you, Mr. Caldwell, I'm sure it would be a better place."

In January, Milo shared a sample of the colored test strips from *Gunga Din* with Stagnaro. Johnny Staggs now had Milo's complete confidence. "I know someone who will be very interested in this. Very interested indeed. Would you mind if I told him about your project? I'm sure he would like to meet you."

"Sure," said Milo. "Who is he?"

Stagnaro answered, "Someone with very deep pockets."

Three days later, Milo received a phone call at home from his host. He had spoken with one of his contacts, a regular guest at El Dorado, about the colorization software, and the gentleman was very interested to meet with him. Would he be free to meet with Mr. Gordon Hicks at his home office in Incline Village the following evening?

Milo frowned into the phone. "Tomorrow won't work for me. It's my daughter's eighteenth birthday and we have plans to celebrate as a family. Isn't there another night?"

"I'm afraid Mr. Hicks is a very busy man, and after this week he won't be returning to Reno for several months." Stagnaro paused on the other end. "I can ask him whether he would be willing to postpone the meeting until a later date, but I must caution you that the opportunity could fall by the wayside in that time."

Milo sighed while the host waited patiently for his answer. Finally he said, "Okay. I'll find a way to be there."

The following afternoon he sent Carrie flowers and balloons at school and told Natalie that he wouldn't be able to join them for dinner. She was visibly disappointed but when he stressed the meeting's importance to his business venture, she said she understood.

At one o'clock he set out for Tahoe. It was unseasonably warm and the late afternoon sun shone on the snow-frosted trees along the lake. As he neared Incline Village, a light rain began to fall, despite the sunshine. The melting snow at the edges of the road turned to grey sludge, sticking to Milo's shoes. He parked in front of the house with the address Stagnaro had given him.

It was an opulent mansion in the guise of a rustic log cabin set on an expansive stretch along the north shore of the lake. From the street, Milo turned down a private road that led a winding half-mile to the house. A yellow Corvette sat in the driveway in front of the garage. Milo pulled up behind it to park. A flagstone pathway curved down the hill from the driveway to a set of steps that descended to the front door and as he followed this, he paused to look up at the place. It was three stories tall, constructed in a Swiss chalet style, but had clearly been built recently. It looked almost brand new and well cared for. The reflective glass of the front windows showed nothing of the interior, instead mirroring the image of the world before it. Milo watched a reflection of himself approach the front door. He rang the bell. To one side of the yard a gardener stood atop a ladder, trimming the evergreens. After watching him for a moment, Milo looked back to the entryway in which he stood. He noticed that there were two cameras set above either side of the front door, both aimed inward at him.

The door was answered by a slim man about ten years Milo's senior, with a receding hairline and a pencil-thin mustache. He was extremely tan and had icy blue eyes that startled with their sharpness. He said, "Mr. Caldwell?"

"Please, call me Milo."

"Gordon Hicks." They shook hands. "Thank you for making the drive to meet me here. Please come in. We'll talk in my office." Milo stepped inside and followed Gordon to his study. Walking behind him, Milo realized that he was almost a full head taller than his host. He felt himself oddly self-conscious, as though his stature merited an apology.

The study was at the end of a long hallway lined with photographs. Milo's eyes flickered across these as they walked while he answered Gordon's innocuous questions about his drive from Lodi. The photographs, by and large, showed his host relaxed and smiling with what Milo assumed were various business associates. Some even looked as though they might be political figures. All of these framed pictures seemed to be of business functions—he did not see any personal photographs.

They settled into a pair of comfortable green leather armchairs in the book-lined study. The walls not taken up by books were filled with framed awards of merit. Gordon saw Milo noticing these and said, "I'm not generally one to brag, Mr. Caldwell. I don't keep these mementos around to revel in a former glory. Rather, they serve to motivate me to continually push the boundaries of my success. There are many people who do well for themselves and are content to rest on their laurels, as long as they have acquired the trappings of success. But it is my belief that success is a journey, not a destination."

"It certainly looks as though you've been doing well for yourself in that respect," Milo replied good-naturedly.

Gordon smiled. "My fiancée says that I'm never satisfied. But to me, satisfaction is only a matter of achievement for a fraction of the moment. I get far more satisfaction from crafting strategy than from the endgame." He looked at his watch. "Can I offer you anything to drink?" Milo thanked him but declined. Gordon nodded as though he approved of the answer. "I never drink at home myself. I'll allow myself to have a nip when I'm in Reno or Vegas, but otherwise I prefer to keep a clear head. I'm also a strict Catholic, so I like to keep my conscience clean. Now then – Mr. Stagnaro tells me you're in the midst of developing quite an impressive product."

Milo smiled and withdrew a disk from his briefcase. He handed this to Gordon, and briefly explained the colorization and digitization software. He also described how he had been led to this project as a result of his 15-year background in medical software. As he listened, Gordon held the disc in one hand and turned it over slowly several times, nodding periodically. When Milo was finished he said, " 'Course I'm computer illiterate, myself. But it sounds like a damn interesting venture. I'm a great fan of classic film." He gestured to one wall of the study that Milo hadn't seen upon their arrival. It was filled with framed movie posters, each featuring personalized autographs. "My prized possession is the one of *Lawrence of Arabia* signed by both O'Toole and Alec Guinness. I had the pleasure of meeting them in 1978. And then there's that *Citizen Kane* one signed by Orson Welles, whom I met in '83, just a couple of years before he died. Hollywood doesn't produce that type of *auteur* any more. It seems as though the film industry is tanking."

"I agree," said Milo. "We are desperately in need of a twenty-first century Cecil B. DeMille."

Gordon nodded appreciatively. "Right you are. Now, tell me a bit about yourself, Mr. Caldwell. You sound to me like a self-made man."

"I've been very fortunate in many ways," Milo answered modestly. "I started out as an emergency room technician in Fresno. I got my associates' degree and started working at the hospital while I was pursuing a bachelor's. But within my first year they introduced a new software in the ER that nobody knew how to use. I essentially had to teach myself, which led to developing further software for the hospital, and I wound up not finishing school. I worked in the medical field for fifteen years, developing compression software. And I was struck by the inspiration to use those same techniques for classic film within the last few years. So, it's been a lot of hard work but also a lot of luck."

"Luck has very little to do with it, Mr. Caldwell. You worked your way up, just as I have. I came from nothing – I was raised by a single mother who nearly worked herself to death to put me through school. My father never paid a dime of child support and I never saw him after my tenth birthday. I went to Princeton on scholarships, and when I entered the business world, I found myself working alongside the sons of real estate tycoons and senators. I told myself that I owed it to my mother to be better than all of them; not to let them beat me just because they'd been given a running start in life. I was determined to not only catch up with them, but to surpass them." He paused and looked out the window at the lake, which was grey and churning, suggestive of an approaching storm. Waves lapped the sandbar at the foot of the property and churned beneath the boat tied to the dock. "As you can see, I've built quite a lot from nothing. I could have retired years ago if I'd wanted to, and live in the utmost comfort. But I've got to keep moving. Like a shark, I suppose. You know what they say about sharks."

"What's that, exactly?"

"If a shark stops moving it dies. I don't much care for thinking of myself as a shark. But better a shark than a minnow." He broke his gaze from the window and looked back at Milo. "I'd like to do business with you, Mr. Caldwell."

"I would be very interested in that, Mr. Hicks. But please, call me Milo."

Gordon nodded. "As long as you call me Gordon. Now, as far as the partnership is concerned, I'd like to propose a 50/50 arrangement. It strikes me that this software you've got has many uses both within Hollywood and beyond."

"That's what I've envisioned," Milo answered. "I don't know quite what its uses outside of Hollywood might be, but I know they've got to be out there."

"Does the producer you've been working with have any claim to this software?"

Milo thought a moment. "He shouldn't. It was my concept originally and I've been the one developing it. He's been on the other end trying to drum up interest among his contacts in the film industry."

"I'll have my lawyer draw something up that gives us protection, just in case," Gordon said. "Now, are you amenable to the 50/50 split?"

"Yes."

"And what type of investment are we talking here?"

Milo took a deep breath. "Well, I've gotten some advice on this from an attorney. First you've got the compression software. I'm told that should be worth $1.5 million. Then you've got the object tracking and the anomaly detection software, which will require an additional $10 million." He paused, steadying himself to look Gordon in the eye. "So, eleven point five million for both."

Gordon considered this for a moment, never breaking their eye contact. Milo felt himself growing fidgety in the silence, but didn't allow himself to look away. At last Gordon nodded. "Okay," he said. "You've got yourself a deal. We'll start with the compression possibilities. I will personally put in the $1.5 million and we'll go from there." He put his hand out and Milo shook it. His grip was firm and controlled.

They rose from their seats in unison. "Let's take a walk across the street," Gordon suggested. "There are a few people I'd like you to meet."

Up the street half a block from the house was North Shore Realty. When Gordon entered, the staff halted what they were doing and greeted him enthusiastically. He introduced Milo around, and he was warmly received. Gordon put an arm around Milo's shoulders. "These folks are the lifeblood of my operations. They're the ones who let me sleep at night by making me money when I'm not awake to do it myself." The staff of half a dozen had gathered in a semi-circle, and there was a collective chuckle at Gordon's statement. Still holding onto Milo, Gordon addressed the group. "This is my new business associate, Milo Caldwell. He's a brilliant software developer and he's going to make me even richer than I am." Another polite chuckle from the group. "You'll all probably be seeing him on a regular basis from now on, so let's make him feel welcome. Milo, my boy, when you're here you're like family. And we know how to take care of one of our own. Anything you need when you're in town, you just let one of these good people know." Milo grinned shyly and nodded. The employees beamed at him in unison. Gordon turned and addressed a single member of the group, a woman in her thirties with chin-length brown hair. "Sue, we're starting out with a $250,000 commitment on my part. The big picture is a million-five. Milo here is also going to be drawing a monthly salary of $20,000. I want you to see to it that a check gets cut before the weekend."

"I'll get right on it," Sue answered, nodding.

Gordon turned back to Milo. "Now that that's all settled, can I interest you in some dinner? There's a great little steakhouse down the road. The chef is a personal friend of mine."

Milo felt slightly uncomfortable, having to give an answer in front of the staff. "That's a very tempting offer, Gordon. Unfortunately it's my daughter's eighteenth birthday, and I was hoping to be back in time for cake."

Gordon smiled and patted him on the back. "A brilliant mind and a family man to boot! Your wife is a very lucky woman."

Milo returned to Lodi at nine o'clock with a bottle of champagne that Gordon had sent for Natalie. She balked when he handed it to her and looked at him sideways. "Where did you get this?" she asked. "This stuff is probably $200 a bottle on sale."

Milo kissed her on the cheek. "It was a gift from my new business partner. He just pulled something out of his wine cellar—looked like he had a lot of expensive stuff down there. He told me he has around six thousand bottles in his private reserve at any given time."

Natalie stared at him. "Who is this guy, anyway?"

Milo smiled. "Someone with very deep pockets."

CHAPTER THREE

Two weeks after his meeting with Gordon, Natalie handed Milo an engraved invitation that had just arrived in the mail. It read:

You are cordially invited
to celebrate the union of
Gordon Thomas Hicks
and Julip Celine Harris
September 1, 1999 at 4 pm
Santa Monica Catholic Church
RSVP

"You must have really made some impression to merit a wedding invitation from a guy you just met," Natalie said.

"It'll probably just be us and 300 of Gordon's closest friends," Milo answered.

On this score he wasn't far off. Gordon called him three days later to ask if he had received the invitation. He hoped they could make it. "We added your name to the list the same day we handed it over to have the invitations printed," he said. "We already have almost 400 on the list, so we figured we could squeeze in two more. I've put Julip in charge of the whole thing. I just sign on the dotted line when she brings me a receipt. She's got an eye for these types of things, you know. She fancies herself an interior decorator, though I don't know if she's ever decorated so much as a birthday cake. The wedding is her guinea pig. Can we count the two of you in?"

"We'd be honored to attend."

"Good, good. Of course, it's strictly an invite for the ceremony and the reception, you understand." Milo didn't understand. What else could it be an invitation to? Gordon clarified this immediately, adding, "We've got a group of about 250 on a chartered jet to Miami after the reception. From there we'll be getting on a cruise. It's my second marriage. I intend to go all out this time." He paused, then continued with a touch of pride. "Whole thing should end up carrying a price tag of about four and a half million."

Milo groped for an appropriate response. "It's sure to be a fun party, then," he said at last.

"Anything for Julip," Gordon rumbled affectionately.

Milo spent the next several months hard at work on the digitization and compression software. The visits to Reno temporarily ceased, and he holed himself up in his office for ten and twelve hours a day. The appearance of a regular $20,000 check each month had a remarkably uplifting effect on the whole household. Natalie began to make regular appointments at the beauty parlor and spa, pampering herself with massages, manicures, trips to the sauna, hair appointments, and eventually a Botox injection or two. Carrie, who had just graduated high school and was supposed to be looking for a summer job, instead spent much of her time at the mall, and after coming home with arms laden with shopping bags, she always made sure to kiss her father on the cheek. Jeremy, who was two years younger than Carrie, cemented the respect of his friends by always possessing the latest video game. Nobody argued or complained at dinner anymore. Instead, everyone conversed happily, did their chores without being asked, and went to great lengths to give Milo the peace and quiet he needed to work on his project.

Summer came and went, and the day of the wedding approached. Natalie had bought a new dress for the occasion, and had Milo's best blue suit pressed and his black shoes shined. She navigated as they made the drive down to Santa Monica.

"How much did you say he told you the wedding was going to be again?" She asked as they made their way south on Interstate 5.

"Four point five million," Milo replied. "But that includes the cost of flying 250 people on a private jet to Miami afterwards so they can join the bride and groom on their honeymoon cruise."

Natalie shook her head in wonder. "The kind of money this guy has. How did he make his fortune?"

"I don't know too many of the details. I know he was a Wall Street guy. I'm sure we'll find out a lot here at the wedding." In truth, Milo had begun to research Gordon Hicks as soon as he had learned his name. What he found had given him second thoughts about going into business with Gordon, but he had decided to keep their meeting. He learned that Gordon had been once been one of the top traders at Grant McKinley Wilson, the Wall Street investment firm that had been so highly esteemed in the 1980s before it was discovered that the firm's value was built entirely on junk bonds. This strategy had caused the company to collapse, wiping out the life savings of millions of investors and turning its top shareholders virtually overnight from Wall Street power players into objects of public outrage and scorn. Gordon hadn't been one of the big heavy hitters in the firm, but he had been in the top ranks and had paid mightily for his position through fines and legal action. Milo recalled that his grandparents on his mother's side, as well as many of their friends, had lost a great deal of money through the scam.

Milo's initial reaction had been to forego even the potential of doing business with Gordon, but he had talked the matter over with a friend who worked in finance. He had convinced Milo that there was no way to know whether Gordon had knowingly participated in the charade, and that there were many talented finance guys at Grant McKinley who got punished unjustly for the greed of a few. He suggested that Milo at least meet with Gordon and decide for himself, and Milo moved with caution. Once the money started to flow, Milo's initial scruples began to fall away. However, he wasn't ready to share any of this with Natalie just yet. "The way Gordon tosses money around, though — clearly it's no problem for him."

"Clearly," Natalie echoed. She placed a hand tenderly on the back of his neck. "But let's play it safe for a while."

Milo jabbed back in guilt. "That's a nice dress you've got on there."

She held her ground. "Hey, bud, this was on sale!"

Milo sighed. "It does seem to make things a little easier, though. I suppose we should be saving at least some of it."

"Let's start by slowing it down with the kids. Sometimes Carrie gets you wrapped around her little finger." They were quiet for a moment, Milo ruminating on the truth. Then she said slowly, "Honey, if this business with Gordon doesn't work out you can always go back to the medical technology field if you need to. We were doing OK weren't we?"

Milo looked at her. "Why shouldn't it work out?" There was a slight edge in his voice.

"I'm not saying that it won't. But I'm saying 'just in case'…"

He smiled at her. "So you do love me for my looks?" he asked.

She pulled down the visor to check her make-up, "Well, I used to before you became a smart ass."

●　●　●

They arrived at the Saint Monica Catholic Church at 3:30 p.m. It was a large, grey, stone building with a belfry topped with orange terracotta tiles. Milo thought it looked familiar. "I feel I've seen this place somewhere before. In a movie, maybe."

"Didn't you say Gordon loves movies?" Natalie asked. "It makes sense that he'd have the wedding somewhere that was featured in a movie."

The ceremony began at 4 o'clock on the dot. The interior of the church was decorated lavishly, and the train of the wedding dress stretched nearly ten feet down the aisle behind the bride. Natalie raised an eyebrow at the dress, a riotous collection of lace, organza, silk, and tulle that nearly drowned the woman wearing it. She leaned into Milo and whispered, "The flowers alone are probably enough for a down payment on a house. The dress could have put the kids through college." Milo smirked.

The priest conducted much of the ceremony in Latin. Milo gazed around at the other guests in attendance. He recognized several from the offices at North Shore, but by and large the men appeared to be in their late fifties and early sixties, in clean-cut Gucci and Armani suits and expensive-looking ties. The women generally seemed to be in their mid-thirties to early forties, some with outlandishly decadent hats that looked as if they'd come from the derby scene in *My Fair Lady*.

As they turned to one another to exchange vows, Gordon lifted the exquisite veil from the face of his bride and everyone sighed in a collective acknowledgment of her radiance. The sounds of cameras clicking echoed throughout the cathedral. Milo thought she had to be at least twenty years her future husband's junior. Gordon slipped a shimmering diamond band, likely visible all the way from the back row, onto her finger. They both said "I do" and the audience responded with polite applause.

"No one sounds particularly enthusiastic," Natalie whispered.

"I'm guessing that these are mostly business associates, rather than friends," Milo answered.

At the end of the ceremony the guests filed out to watch the bride and groom climb into a black and cream 1937 Rolls Royce Phantom III. Ushers in tuxedos showered the wedding party with white rose petals. A pair of photographers dashed around, capturing the couple from every angle as they descended the steps from the cathedral.

The reception took place at the Loew's Hotel on Ocean Avenue. The first sight to greet them as they entered the ballroom was a six-foot tall version of Sleeping Beauty's castle at Disneyland, reproduced as a wedding cake. It towered over them atop a table at the entry to the dance floor, surrounded on all sides by a cascade of gifts wrapped in a variety of candy colors. The perimeter of the ballroom had been decorated to replicate the floor of a casino, complete with craps tables, slot machines, and cocktail waitresses in tight, sparkly dresses. At the head of the room was a long stage, currently occupied by a twenty-piece Big Band era orchestra.

After dinner was served and the cake had been cut, the newlyweds moved to the center of the dance floor for their first dance while the band played "At Last." Milo noticed as they moved around the floor that Gordon seemed to be directing his wife's attention to various guests in attendance. When the song had ended the band struck up a medley of Frank Sinatra songs, and the guests moved to the floor.

With the conclusion of the medley, the orchestra was replaced by a rock band, prompting some of the more hesitant guests to abandon their tables and come to the dance floor. Between acts, the main stage opened up in the middle and another, smaller stage floated into the dance floor. This smaller stage soon filled with belly dancers, each with a full-grown snake wrapped around her. It was as though they had suddenly stepped into a scene from *The Ten Commandments*. After the belly dancers had undulated, a magician swallowed swords and then sawed a beautiful assistant in half.

As they watched the elaborate rounds of entertainment progress and the attendees grow increasingly intoxicated, Milo ventured, "It feels a little bit less like a wedding reception and a bit more like a Vegas floorshow."

"You can say that again," Natalie agreed. "I can't really say I'm too disappointed we weren't invited to the cruise. I don't think I could handle another day of this, much less six months."

Soon, Gordon and his new bride began to make the rounds. When they reached Milo and Natalie, Gordon hugged them like long-lost friends.

"Julip, I'd like you to meet my new business partner," Gordon introduced them. Milo shook her hand. She was a slender, athletic woman with short bleached blond hair, long red fingernails, bright red lipstick, and a flirtatious smile. She purred, "Gordon has told me so much about you. He simply thinks you're a genius!"

"That's right, he's my genius!" Gordon positively shouted. He had clearly drunk a fair amount. His face was red and swollen. "Ladies, if you'll excuse us, I'd like to introduce my new pal around." Taking Milo firmly by the arm, he steered him across the room, stumbling a few times, and abandoning his bride to Natalie.

"Say, Gordon, have I seen your wedding church in a movie or something?" Milo asked.

Gordon nodded. "It was used in *Going My Way,* the Bing Crosby picture from '44. It was damaged pretty bad in the Northridge quake and a whole group of celebrities contributed to the renovation." He grinned. "As a matter of fact, I exceeded all of 'em with my own single donation. Wrote a check for five million. In fact the archbishop officiated the wedding." He pointed to the edge of the dance floor and said, "Someone special I'd like to introduce you to." They came to a group of about thirty people congregated near one of the blackjack tables. They were gathered around a balding man with a broad smile. He was in the middle of telling a story and when he finished, the group laughed boisterously in unison. Some of the more enthusiastic listeners slapped their knees and wiped tears from their eyes. Over the ruckus, Gordon called, "JJ!"

The man waved at him and shouted back, "There's the lucky bastard!" and began making his way toward them through a crow of admirers. When he reached them, he embraced Gordon and shook Milo's hand heartily.

"Milo, I'd like you to meet Jacob Singer. J.J. and I used to work together at Grant McKinley."

" 'Work together' is the understatement of the century," Singer countered with a laugh. "Gordon was like a limb to me. My top trader, the best! I wouldn't have been able to function without him."

"Now we're neighbors in Incline Village," Gordon added.

Singer laughed again and put an arm around Gordon. "He can't get rid of me!" The crowd that had been gathered around Singer had now reformed nearby, watching this exchange and laughing along with him as if on cue. It was immediately apparent that his larger than life persona and gregarious nature was something Gordon coveted. While Singer appeared outgoing and comfortable, Gordon became suddenly subdued and introverted before the crowd of admirers. His voice grew quieter and he seemed to look to Singer for permission to continue the conversation. Milo wondered if he coveted or despised Singer's obvious cult of personality.

After exchanging a few pleasantries, Gordon shook Singer's hand and said in a tone of voice that could only be considered reverent, "I'm so thankful you were able to make it, JJ. I know how busy you are."

"I wouldn't have missed it for the world," Singer responded with genuine warmth. "I'm only sorry I can't join you for the cruise."

"Think nothing of it," said Gordon. "Maybe next time. We're taking a trip to Ibiza next year. We would love to have you if your schedule permits."

"Have your secretary call my secretary," Singer answered. "She's the keeper of my schedule. Off the top of my head I'd say next year is going to be pretty full for me from start to finish. It's difficult to imagine I'll have time to get away. But it sure sounds like a great offer."

Singer moved away, and Gordon's expression darkened. Gordon leaned into Milo and said, "That son of a bitch. Thinks he can look down his nose at me while he drinks my champagne. Like he's above all of us just because he walked out the door with the most money in the bag. Even after his jail time he still thinks he's invincible, the smug piece of shit." They continued around the edge of the room, Gordon introducing him to various former colleagues from Grant McKinley JX Wilson. They all struck Milo as slightly stiff and wooden, as though they weren't entirely enjoying themselves. Their wives and dates were drunk, for the most part, several of them nagging the men to join them on the dance floor. After a round of introductions lasting fifteen minutes or so, Gordon said, "Go get your wife. There's some folks here I think she'd be interested in meeting."

With Natalie in tow, Gordon introduced them to various Broadway actors, directors, and producers. They learned that he was a principal investor in several on and off-Broadway musicals, including *Romp* and *Eyes of Esther*. He also introduced them to Patrick Swayze and his wife Lisa, who were in attendance. Swayze shook their hands warmly and made amicable conversation. As they walked back to their table Natalie put a hand to her chest and said, "Be still, my heart."

They sat down and Gordon pointed out a group of relatives from Long Island and New Jersey congregating in one corner. They appeared to be keeping to themselves. Many of them wore dark glasses indoors. "They don't go much for all the ballyhoo," Gordon explained. "Several of my aunts have given me an earful already this evening about how I spend my money."

At this point Julip approached Gordon and whispered something into his ear with a giggle. He gave her a playful swat on the rump. He turned to them and said, "Duty calls. Got to get a few more meet-and-greets in before we take this party to the airport. Milo, I won't be back until June of next year. All communications will go through Sue at the North Shore office."

Milo stood up and shook his hand. "Thank you for inviting us, Gordon. We had a great time. Enjoy your honeymoon." They said their goodbyes. The couple moved away and Milo sat back down. From the dance floor, a man stumbled to their table and sat down heavily. He had introduced himself earlier, but Milo failed to recall his name. He was now clearly very drunk. His eyes were bloodshot and his tie was unknotted, hanging askew around his neck like an oversized noose. He sat, weaving unsteadily into his chair, watching Gordon and Julip as they departed. Then he said loudly, "Once a whore, always a whore." Milo and Natalie looked at each other and decided not to respond. They each took a sip of wine and averted their eyes from the drunkard. He spoke up again. "She thinks that just because she married up, nobody will remember what she really is. I'll bet most of these jerks don't even know. But I know."

Milo said gently, "Can I get you some water?"

The man shook his head violently. "Do you know about the blushing bride? I'll bet you don't have any clue what she is."

Milo said, "Maybe it's time to take a little break, pal."

The man continued as though no one had spoken. "She's a cheap stripper Gordon picked up in Reno two years ago. Now she thinks she's fucking Princess Diana just because he bought her some new clothes and put a ring on it. Really she's nothing but a common trailer trash bitch in a $20,000 wedding dress." Milo and Natalie both sat frozen in uncomfortable silence. The man slouched back in his chair and stared at a half-empty glass of white wine on the table that somebody else had left behind. Then he picked it up and downed it in one gulp. He said, "I gotta wish her well, though. She's my goddamn sister, after all." With this he rose unsteadily to his feet and wandered off toward the restroom.

The dance floor was now an impenetrable bacchanalian mass of flailing arms and legs. One particularly inebriated man at the edge of the crowd who was dancing a sloppy foxtrot with his date reeled her in by one arm and then flung her back into the crowd, knocking several laughing people off their feet. Another man barreled past them carrying his date over one shoulder, while she screeched with delight.

Natalie said, "This is starting to resemble *The Great Gatsby*."

Milo took a bite of the remaining piece of cake on his plate. "Are you ready to go?"

She was already on her feet. "Really? I thought you'd never ask."

They claimed their belongings from the coat check and waited in the lobby while a valet went to fetch their car. Another couple stumbled out of the ballroom and through the front doors to their waiting limousine. The chauffeur held the door open for them and they tumbled into the backseat, the woman leaving one of her shoes behind on the pavement in the process. The chauffeur picked up the shoe gingerly, and handed it in to her. After a moment the valet returned with Milo and Natalie's minivan and Milo tipped him.

They drove in silence for the first thirty minutes. After careful consideration Natalie spoke up. "Gordon seems like an interesting character."

Milo considered his response. "He is. I'm not sure if he's acting or if he's genuine. The whole wedding and reception seemed rather contrived. As if he were trying to impress everyone with the amount of money he was able to blow on the thing."

Natalie glanced at him. "Are you sure that's really the kind of person you want to do business with?"

Milo didn't answer at once. Then he said "How can you ask me that question now, Nat?"

"Now, don't get worked up. I just want to make sure you've thought this through before you throw everything into a business venture with him." A tense silence followed.

They were nearing an exit on the freeway, and Milo took it with an unexpected jerk of the wheel. They pulled into a gas station and sat idling. Milo looked at her.

"Gordon has already put more than half a million dollars of investment money into the project. He's already paid me almost $200,000 in salary. I can't just back out. And what for? Because you don't like the way he spends his money?"

"It's not that," Natalie protested. "I'm not saying you should pull out. I just want to know that you're in business with someone honorable. Someone you can trust. Does he strike you as a trustworthy partner?"

"What is that supposed to mean?"

"You saw his associates. All those people from Grant McKinley – how do you know he didn't make all his money ripping off senior citizens like the rest of them?"

"It's irrelevant now. It's all in the past, and frankly it's none of my business. Or yours, for that matter. It doesn't matter what he used to do, it matters what we do together going forward."

"And what that man said about Julip?"

"We have no reason to believe that guy was telling the truth. You saw how drunk he was."

"But – "

"Christ, Natalie!" Milo hammered a hand on the steering wheel. "Why are you treating me like a child? Do you think I'm incapable of judging someone's character? Of course I think Gordon is trustworthy, or I never would have gone into business with him in the first place!"

Neither of them spoke for several moments. Then Natalie said, "I'm sorry." She wasn't, really, but she knew Milo's temper made him a crazy man behind the wheel when he was worked up. She'd save the discussion for when their lives weren't in the balance. "Can we just go home?"

Milo looked out the driver's side window to where cars flew past on the darkening freeway. "I want this, Natalie. I want to be able to provide you and the kids with the kind of life you deserve. And I want to do something important and worthwhile with my life. I want to leave my mark on the world somehow. This looks like the best chance, so far. I have the feeling it could lead to something big. Maybe Gordon isn't the perfect business partner. I know it's a risk... but everything in life is a risk. I have to take this chance to do something significant, or I might not get another shot. And I need you to support me in this."

Natalie nodded. "You're right. It is a risk worth taking. I am on your side. Let's just forget that I said anything, okay?"

They sat that way, not speaking for several moments. Milo felt a knot forming in the pit of his stomach, a result of the guilt that was overtaking him for having exploded at Natalie, when in truth he worried that she might be right about Gordon. After all, hadn't he himself had the same thoughts on learning of Gordon's past? But he couldn't admit this now, not after causing such a scene. And then there was the money... he tried to put these thoughts from his mind and put the car into gear. They pulled out of the gas station, heading back toward the freeway. The moon had begun to rise over the hills in the east. The city of Los Angeles shimmered in the gathering darkness, a million pinpoints of light glinting from the hills and valleys, stretched out along the coastline. The Pacific Ocean beyond became an infinite black plain that stretched as far as the eye could see.

CHAPTER FOUR

For the next six months, Milo rarely left his home office. He slept four or five hours a night, got up before everyone else, went into his study, and remained there until after everyone else had gone to sleep. Natalie brought him coffee, toast and eggs in the morning and a sandwich in the afternoon, and he ate these meals with one hand while typing with the other, his eyes glued to the computer screen. She insisted that he at least join them for dinner, but he could only be pried away from his desk with the third or fourth knock on the office door. The dogs tended to gather at the closed door, whining and scratching in the evenings when they knew he was about to emerge, and when he came out for dinner they exploded into a joyous frenzy of barks and slobber and wagging tails. He often tripped trying to wade through them, and while at first he might laugh and affectionately shoo them, as time went on he grew increasingly annoyed with the predictably riotous behavior that awaited on the other side of his office door. His thoughts were often somewhere else at the dinner table, and if someone spoke to him he had to be jolted from his reverie to respond. As the kids were clearing the table, he rose and went back to his office. Natalie watched him go and said nothing.

For the first two months he shut his computer off every Friday evening, and they went out to dinner or to see a movie as a family. Carrie was in the middle of applying to colleges and he often helped her with her application essays, or took Jeremy to the golf course to play nine holes. On Saturday nights he took Natalie out to dinner, or they took the dogs for a walk by the creek that ran behind their house. On Sundays they went to church, and had lunch with friends afterwards. But as the weeks wore on, Milo began to work late into Saturday evenings as well. He told Natalie that he was falling behind, and that he just needed an extra day to catch up. Then he began to work Sundays as well. Some nights he never came out of his office for dinner.

In early March he received a call from Gordon. The ship was docked in Bali and the honeymoon party had rented an entire luxury hotel and secluded beachfront. "It's a goddamn paradise here," he told Milo. "Have you and your wife been to Eastern Asia before?"

"I'm afraid not," Milo answered.

"Well, we'll have to do something about that. Now, down to business. Sue sending you your checks on time?"

"Yes, no problems with that."

"Good, good. And everything's going smoothly?"

"So far. I'll look forward to meeting with you when you get back next month to go over everything."

Gordon paused on the other end. "Well, Milo, it's looking like we won't actually be back until end of July. We've decided to make a detour to Italy on our way back, and Julip's never been there before, so she's got a whole list of things she wants to do, so you know how that goes."

Milo removed his glasses and massaged the bridge of his nose between his thumb and forefinger. "Okay, that's not a problem. I'll just keep doing what I've been doing."

"Good man. The Pope has agreed to see us in May, and of course that's not the type of chance a guy gets every day."

"Are you serious? The Pope?"

"Quite an honor, of course. The Vatican has agreed to allow Julip and me an audience with His Holiness to bless our union."

Milo was dumbfounded. "How is that possible?"

"Well, we've got to pay for it, of course. A million and a half for five minutes' time. Seems like quite a value for a lifetime of happiness, wouldn't you say?"

Milo worked through the first months of summer, resuming occasional weekend trips to Reno. His face grew drawn from the long work hours and he began to lose weight, imperceptibly at first and gradually more noticeably. His clothes hung off him awkwardly, and one afternoon as he walked through the kitchen to reach the bathroom, his hair standing straight up from where he had run his hands through it in frustration, Carrie turned to Natalie and asked, "What the heck is going on with Dad?" With the kids out of school, the house always seemed to be filled with noise and distraction, and he found himself itching to get away from his family. He was beset by a tinge of guilt for his lack of participation in the daily affairs of the household, and left one Saturday morning without telling anyone where he was going. He returned with a black Labrador puppy some hours later, and the other three fell to fawning over the new addition at once. He watched as the puppy took a few tottering steps around the backyard while everyone laughed with delight, then he went back inside and shut himself in his office for the rest of the day. Natalie watched him go and chose not to tell him that a dog was not a substitute for his presence. He must have sensed her angst, but not the reasoning behind it: the following weekend he presented her with a gift of a new gold necklace from which an amethyst stone hung. She accepted the gift with her own mixed feelings. It was her favorite gem.

By August, Gordon had returned and asked Milo to pay him a visit at Incline Village, so they could review the work he had done in the past year and formulate their future plans. They met again at Gordon's home office, and after spending some time discussing the progress of the compression software, Gordon revealed his plan to pursue sales of the software to various entertainment and media companies. Especially where his former Grant McKinley colleagues were now involved.

"The goal is to quickly get some high-profile interest and investment," he said. "Kirk Courson is a big fish that we're going to want to reel in. He's president of Constar Entertainment, and we've also got to court Alex Melrose, who's the CEO of Constar Gaming. Those meetings will have the potential to yield some big results. I'll also set up meetings with Steve Wynn, Leon Black, and Gary Winnick from Global Crossing. That should give us a good running start."

"These are all people you worked with?" Milo asked.

Gordon nodded. "And they all know it's in their best interests to take my calls. Now then. I think the next step is to set up an office in Reno, near the airport. We fly them in, show them around, let them play a few hands. Show them a good time, in other words. Then we seal the deal. Of course, for you this means more trips up here. I would imagine that drive is going to be a pain in the neck if you have to make it twice, three times a week." Milo said he didn't mind, but Gordon waved him away dismissively. "I think it would be best if you relocated here to be close to the business. Give the wife and kids a change of scenery. Tell you what—" He pulled open a desk drawer and removed a checkbook. He wrote a check out and ripped it free, handing it to Milo. It was for $25,000. "This will be your down payment. I've got a realtor here who's the best in the business. He'll find you something phenomenal in less than a week, I guarantee you."

Milo sat looking at the check in his hands. "This is very generous of you, Gordon. But I'm not sure I can accept it."

Gordon waved him away again, this time impatiently. "Nonsense. Let's not waste any more time discussing it. I'll have my realtor get in touch with you tomorrow."

Milo continued looking at the check, trying to find the right words. "Of course, I'll have to discuss it with Natalie. We've been in our home for five years."

Gordon leaned back in his chair and regarded his partner, unspeaking, for several moments. Finally he said, "Tell me, Milo. What is it that you want out of life?"

The question caught Milo off guard. He answered slowly, "The same things as anybody else, I suppose. A happy, healthy family that I can provide for. A comfortable place to live. Enough food on the table."

"There's something else you're leaving out," Gordon said. "I've sensed it in you since the first time we met. Now don't do me the disservice of being dishonest with me. Call a spade a spade, for God's sake. Why did you decide to go into business with me?"

"I suppose I want to do something significant. Something that will make an impact on the world."

Gordon snapped his fingers and leaned forward. "That, right there. That's what I've known about you since our first meeting. You have a drive, an itch, a desire to change the world. To leave your mark so that when you're gone you'll be more than just a name on a headstone. Isn't that right?"

"Yes, but – "

"But nothing. That is man's most fundamental longing. It is our universal goal. That's all there is to it. Don't try to justify it, or take its power away by apologizing for it. Embrace your need to do something worthwhile with the miniscule amount of time you've got on this planet. Now, do you want to be rich?"

Milo faltered, "I– I suppose – "

"Answer the question. It's a yes or a no. Do you want to become rich while you change the world?"

Milo looked out the window to the lake. It was a mild, sunny day and the waves gently lapped the sandy shore. He said, "Yes."

"Then let's get one thing straight right now. If there's one thing I know and understand in this world, it's how to make money. You've got the idea, the expertise, the technical know-how. But without my vision, without my fundamental guidance, you're going to end up peddling your wares to some small-minded nobody who will waste your talent and your hard work on a pathetic low-level enterprise that you don't even want associated with your name. If you stick with me, you're going to make a difference in this life, and you're going to become fabulously wealthy because of it. It's as simple as that. But it's all or nothing with me. You're either all in, and you follow my advice, and you trust me to lead the way, and you don't second-guess me and think that you know more than I do about what it takes to be an entrepreneur, or you walk away right now. For Christ's sake, you've seen my house. You came to my wedding. You've become acquainted with my lifestyle. Can you possibly doubt that I know what I'm talking about?" He sat back in his chair and ran his hands through his hair. "Believe me, I understand that not everyone has got what it takes. If you're going to strike out on your own, if you're going to take a risk, if you're going to do anything of worth in this lifetime; you've got to have courage. You've got to have balls of steel. And from the time we come into this world, we're taught to play it safe. To make smart decisions. You've got to be a half-lunatic to do anything daring. It takes the type of guts that most men just aren't raised to have. But I sense you've got them, even if they've been buried under years of playing it safe. So it's up to you. Either you trust me, and put all your cards in, or you cash out and walk away before the game has even begun."

Milo was silent. The clock on the wall ticked quietly. Outside a speed boat raced by, splitting the placid surface of the lake with its wake. The sound built and built as the boat came closer, then it was past and all was peaceful once more. At last he said, "I'm in."

Gordon smiled and handed him the check. They both rose and shook hands. Gordon put an arm around him. "You haven't any idea how far we'll go, my boy. You can't even imagine. But soon you'll see. Now, how about we celebrate with a little trip into Reno and some dinner." It was a statement, rather than a question, leaving Milo no room to refuse.

They made the thirty-seven minute drive to Reno in Gordon's Corvette in thirty-two. It was a clear, chilly evening and Gordon drove with the top down, taking the curves through the Sierra at breakneck speed. Milo was silently thankful when they arrived at the El Dorado in one piece. As soon as they pulled up to the curb in front of the casino, a man in a suit hurried out to meet them. "Mr. Hicks, how wonderful to see you again," he said, shaking Gordon's hand emphatically. Gordon handed him the keys to the car.

As soon as they pushed through the casino doors, John Stagnaro was at their side. "Mr. Hicks! Mr. Caldwell! What a delight. What can I get for you gentlemen this evening to make your stay a comfortable one?"

Gordon answered while leading the way to the blackjack tables. "Just get a couple of steaks delivered to the blackjack table. I'll also take a double Macallan on the rocks. Milo, what's your poison?"

"Nothing for me, thanks," Milo replied, dodging cocktail waitresses and oblivious tourists wandering the floor.

Gordon stopped in his tracks and turned to face him. He clapped a hand heavily on Milo's shoulder. Stagnaro skidded to a halt behind them. "Come on, my boy. Tonight's a night for celebration. Loosen up a little! Anything you want" He snapped his fingers in the air and pointed to Johnny Staggs. "This guy's the best host in Reno. Anything you want is at your fingertips." Stagnaro beamed proudly. Seeing Milo's hesitation, Gordon continued, "One drink won't kill you. You're wound too tight, my friend." He gripped his companion's shoulder tighter.

Milo said, "I suppose I'll take a Budweiser."

Gordon patted him on the back. "Good man," he said, and resumed his purposeful trek forward. The host disappeared to fill their order.

Upon reaching the area where the blackjack tables were situated, dealers paused whatever they were doing to greet Gordon, including several who were in the middle of dealing cards. Gordon seemed focused on one dealer in particular, a beautiful young redheaded woman with a bright smile. She cooed in a Southern accent, "Why hello, Mr. Hicks, what a treat," as Gordon kissed her on the cheek. He slid one hand down her back and let it rest on her behind. "Milo Caldwell, meet Misty Simmons, my personal favorite blackjack dealer. On Tuesday nights, that is."

Misty giggled. "Oh, you."

Gordon gave her buttocks a squeeze and took a seat across the table. Johnny Staggs was already at their side with drinks in hand. Gordon proposed a toast before the game began. "To the future," he said loftily, chinking his glass against Milo's bottle. He downed the Scotch in one gulp and handed the empty tumbler back to Stagnaro. "Give me a Lagavulin this time," he commanded, and the host turned and ordered a waitress to fulfill the errand.

While Misty shuffled the cards, Gordon reached into his pocket and withdrew a handful of red chips. He handed these to Milo and pulled out a second handful for himself. "A thousand dollars apiece on these," he said. "Go wild. Bet it all on one hand if you want."

"I thought there was a $10,000 table limit on blackjack."

"Well, they make an exception for my friends and me. Don't they, Misty?" Gordon asked her.

She smiled. "We sure do, Mr. Hicks."

The waitress returned with a second double scotch, and Gordon promptly downed this as well. Misty dealt their cards and said, "Gentlemen, place your bets."

Milo set his pile of red chips on the table and sat looking at them. When he had made a mental note of the number in front of them he picked one up and handed it back to Gordon, saying, "You can have this one back."

"Something wrong with it?"

"Nothing's wrong with it. But you gave me thirteen."

Gordon smirked. "Ah, so you fall for all the superstitious mumbo jumbo."

Milo shrugged. "I try not to tempt bad luck." He put forward a single chip, and won. Gordon put down three, which he lost.

They remained at the blackjack table for a good while, pausing only occasionally to eat their steaks. Gordon grew increasingly drunker, and his bets and losses became astronomical. By Milo's count, he had lost $300,000 after two and a half hours of play. The dealers switched out half a dozen times, and each time it was a young woman prettier than the one she replaced. Gordon joked lewdly with each of them and made no effort to keep his hands to himself. By the beginning of their fourth hour at the table, he had lost $400,000 and could barely remain upright in his seat.

Milo, who had only had two beers, steadied his partner as he swayed in his chair and dropped several chips on the floor. "Gordon, maybe we'd better get you a room so that you can lie down," he suggested gently.

"Nonsense!" Gordon barked. "This is petty cash. My luck's gonna turn any minute now." He blinked and gazed unevenly around the casino floor. "All this shit you see here — none of this would exist if it weren't for Grant McKinley. You know that? All these losers would have nowhere to go to part with their money." He gestured wildly toward a row of slot machines occupied by various people. "I'm not proud of what we did. You think I wanted all those people to lose their life savings? I think about them every day. But I've repaid my debt to society. Do you know I always give money to people on the streets? And I donate to charity. That's more than Singer can say!" He said these last words with a shout, then calmed down. "I may have royally fucked up, I'll grant you that. But I'm not as bad as that piece of shit. That human parasite walked away with $300 million. And now he thinks he's some kind of fucking saint because he did a little jail time in a Club Fed and because he's re-branded himself as a philanthropist?" Milo noticed that the blackjack dealer had quietly packed up her things and moved away, leaving them alone at the table. Gordon seemed to be lost in a reverie, and spoke as if to no one in particular. His words slurred. "I know I'm a sinner. I know that. But at least I have the goddamn balls to admit it. At least I've worked hard for everything I've got. My poor mother, God rest her soul. She worked in a Laundromat by day and a diner at night. She had to retire at fifty because she could barely walk." He quit talking abruptly and choked back a sob. "I lied about going to Princeton. I tell everybody that because it sounds better than the truth. You wanna know the truth? I never went to college. I worked my way up through the rackets. My first job was for the Falcone family. I worked for them from the time I was seventeen until I was twenty-five. And I ain't ashamed about it, because I took care of my mother with the money I made." He slammed his fist on the table, startling several people nearby. "I've clawed my way up to where I am right now. And fucking Singer walks around like can't anybody touch him. Do you know what that scumbag is up to right now?" He swiveled around and fixed his gaze directly on Milo with bloodshot eyes. "He's in the middle of trying to buy a pardon from the White House. He bragged about spending twelve million so far to get his name cleared. At my goddamn wedding, he bragged about it. The worthless piece of trash." He picked up his glass and found it empty. He looked at it a long time, as though more scotch would suddenly appear in it.

Milo looked around the floor for Stagnaro, who he finally noticed at the edge of the floor, talking to the blackjack dealer who had left them moments before. She was pointing at Gordon, and the host's gaze followed. Milo gestured for him to come over.

"I'll tell you one thing, though." Gordon reached out suddenly and caught Milo by the lapel of his jacket. "I'm going to best that bastard, one way or another. I'm going to show him that he can't step on me. I'm gonna make him lick the bottom of my shoes."

Stagnaro arrived and gently put his hands on Gordon's shoulders. Gordon loosened his grip on Milo. "We've got the Tower Suite all made up for you, Mr. Hicks," he said soothingly. "Why don't you let me help you up to your room?"

At first Gordon seemed reluctant to obey, but after a moment he surrendered and let himself be propped up between Milo and Stagnaro. They navigated him across the floor and to the elevator. The Tower Suite was on the top floor. By the time the elevator reached it, Gordon had begun to sag against them as if falling asleep. The host flicked the lights and they guided their charge across the room, laying him on the bed. Stagnaro whispered to Milo, "We've set you up in one of the suites a few floors down, Mr. Caldwell. You can leave the rest up to me." He began removing Gordon's shoes.

"Maybe you should call his wife and let her know he's staying," Milo whispered.

Stagnaro smiled grimly. "I believe Mr. and Mrs. Hicks have an understanding about this type of thing." Milo took this to mean that it wasn't the first time this had happened.

"Do you think he'll be okay?"

"Mr. Hicks always bounces back. He has quite a strong

constitution." He reached into his jacket pocket and pulled out a key card and handed to Milo. "Suite 1200. Just put your key card in the slot after you punch in the floor number, and the elevator will take you right there."

Milo thanked him and went to the elevator. The last thing he saw as the doors closed before him was the host pulling the comforter over Gordon as he began to snore.

Milo's suite was less luxuriant than Gordon's, but far exceeded the grandeur of any hotel room he'd stayed in before. From the floor-to-ceiling windows, he stood overlooking the dazzling array of lights below. Loosening his tie, he went to the phone and called Natalie. She didn't sound particularly surprised when he told her about what happened.

He had difficulty falling asleep that night. After tossing and turning for two hours, he sat up and turned on the television. There weren't many good options in the vast wasteland of late night television, so he settled into a documentary about the Great Depression. Images flashed by: despondent, dusty people with weathered faces living in tents or driving down a dirt road, with all their earthly possessions piled atop their trucks. Barefooted children in still photographs gazed at the camera with large, haunted eyes. Men in overalls who couldn't have been older than he was, yet were stooped over from years of backbreaking labor without respite. He thought of his father with his long, drawn face and world-weary eyes.

In the morning he called up to Gordon's room. Gordon began talking before the phone got to his mouth. He sounded extraordinarily chipper, considering his state last evening. "Come up for some coffee and breakfast, my boy!" he chirped. "The chef here makes the best omelet on the strip!"

Gordon answered the door in a terrycloth robe, and as they crossed the suite, he returned to an easy chair by the window where he had been reading the newspaper. Several others were spread out at his feet. "Beautiful day, isn't it," he proclaimed robustly when Milo took a seat across from him.

Milo poured himself a cup of coffee. "Are you feeling all right this morning?"

"Never better." Gordon stood and went to the phone at the bedside. "Get Joe Worthington on the line. Tell him he's got to come up with a few houses for my partner to take a look at next week." He hung up and walked back over to the window. He looked over the city spread out below them, awash in morning light. "It's a damn fine town," he said. "Your family will love it here." Milo reached into his pocket to find his watch, and discovered that he still had several of Gordon's red chips. He put these on the table. At the sound of them clattering one by one on the wood, Gordon turned and looked at them sharply. He looked at Milo. "You'd better hang onto those for me," he said. "You never know when you might need a little back-up."

Milo protested. "But there's almost $100,000 here."

Gordon turned to face the window once more and declared, "Like I said, back-up."

CHAPTER FIVE

The new house sat on a quiet suburban street that could have been anywhere in America, were it not for the snowcapped mountains in the background and tumbleweeds that were loosened from their moorings toppling down the road. The stoplights bounced in the high desert wind as they drove down their new street. It seemed exceptionally blustery on move-in day, and the men from the moving company had to clap their hats to their heads with their free hands. Eventually, as their hands were filled and their arms heavily laden with boxes containing family portraits, books, kitchen wares, tightly bubble-wrapped glass and porcelain trinkets, Natalie's quilting supplies, and various other household bric-a-brac, the movers took off their hats and stowed them in the cab of the van.

The single-story house on Whispering Creek Way was the same color as the desert dust from which it rose. Though it was only marginally distinguishable from the hundreds of houses in the subdivision surrounding it, the Caldwells had nonetheless fallen in love with it when the realtor, Joe Worthington, showed it to them. It had five bedrooms (one of which was turned into a guestroom and one of which became Natalie's sewing room), three bathrooms, an office, a swimming pool and a hot tub, a massive kitchen, a three-car garage, and enough floor space for the dogs to run around without constantly getting underfoot. After the moving crew filled the house with boxes and left, Milo and Natalie sat on the back patio and took in the view. "It may be a McMansion, but at least it's our McMansion," Natalie said, sipping a glass of white wine. In the distance, a wall of clouds perched atop the snow-dusted peaks of the Sierra. The wind had died down, and the sudden silence of the surrounding desert was stark. Not even a cricket chirped.

Three days after the move, Hicks Limited had leased and begun to operate from a commercial warehouse space in an anonymous-looking building near the airport. At first it was just Gordon and Milo, their desks joined, facing outwards, in the middle of the cavernous empty space. Milo noticed that the top of Gordon's desk bore a black X made of electrical tape. He asked what it meant. "It reminds me of my desk at Grant McKinley," was Gordon's answer. He did not elaborate.

Milo spent several days in the new office drawing up a business plan for Hicks Limited, in addition to continuing his work writing the compression software. His already long workdays began to stretch to fourteen and fifteen hours. Meanwhile, Gordon worked with his contacts to drum up interest in their burgeoning enterprise. Within the first two weeks of moving into their new space, they'd secured meetings with all of the potential investors that Gordon had been courting. These meetings took place over the course of a month in Las Vegas, Los Angeles, Dallas, and New York. Milo discovered that Gordon only traveled on a privately chartered jet kept at the airport exclusively for his use, and rented out at a rate of $3,000 per hour. In the meetings Gordon was polite, firm, and deliberate; but always in control. Milo saw right away that he had no interest in doing business anyone's way but his own. Several potential investors offered to buy the technology, or to turn the venture into a manufacturing company, of which Gordon would be the head. Gordon cordially refused each of these offers. On their flights to and from these meetings, he told Milo that he had no interest in owning a company that produced or sold things in volume. His singular goal was that the business should make a technology that could be licensed to somebody else for a profit. "I'm not going to be put in the position of being the public whipping boy anymore," he declared. Milo learned that Gordon's name had come up unfavorably several times in an exposé book about JJ Singer and Grant McKinley written by a New York Times journalist, and that this was a constant source of vexation for him. One afternoon, searching for a pen, Milo came across a copy of the book, titled *In the Lair,* in the upper right-hand drawer of Gordon's desk. Cursorily flipping through it, he noticed that Gordon highlighted in yellow all mentions or allusions to his name.

Their highest profile meeting took place in Los Angeles, with Dinetel. Gordon secured a meeting with Kathy White, an upper-level executive in the company, and one of Gordon's ex-employees. Together, he and Milo presented a series of tests on their technology and compression software, which resulted in Dinetel making an offer to purchase the technology at a fixed price. The offer also included a cap on the earnings that Hicks Limited could make, a provision at which Gordon balked. In the end they walked away from the deal. When Milo asked Gordon why, he said, "They know that the technology is worth a lot more than they're offering. If they buy it from us, they get to keep the profits, and believe me, there will be profits. If they license it from us, we make money on a continual basis."

It didn't seem to matter to Gordon that the Dinetel deal would have put them in the black, repaying all of the operating expenses they had put into the business and securing them financially for the foreseeable future. "Trust me, kid," he said, looking out the window as the jet took off from the LAX runway. "There are bigger fish in the sea waiting to be caught. We just have to be patient."

Milo wondered if he ought to be concerned that they hadn't started to turn a profit. It had been eighteen months since they'd gone into business together, and so far the cash infusions into the business came directly out of Gordon's pocket. Gordon wasn't worried in the least. He was perfectly confident that things would turn around soon. In the meantime, he continued to dump millions of dollars into the business. Milo's salary, the rental on their warehouse workspace, the travel expenses, the equipment, the security cameras and utility bills — all paid for directly by Gordon. He also revealed to Milo that he had negotiated a lease on the private jet, to the tune of $975,000.

This was the way things went for a while. Gordon would deposit his money, and just as quickly dish it out. Like the money laundering days of his past, the company became a source of financing a vast array of Gordon's interests. It was the same way with his non-profit charity Rainbowz. He set up the nonprofit to benefit children's services in the Reno area. Each year, Rainbowz hosted a lavish three-day event at the El Dorado casino that included a celebrity golf tournament, an auction, and a posh dinner affair that attracted hundreds of real estate barons and wealthy contractors from California and Arizona. Hundreds of thousands of dollars went into the charity, and quite a bit of the money raised made its way toward worthwhile endeavors in the Reno area. But in the course of this event, one thing remained true: Gordon was paid from the proceeds. He always found a way to wrap a benefit into his beneficence. Milo and Natalie attended one of these functions with Gordon and Julip, at which Gordon became extremely drunk and lost a great deal of money at baccarat. After the event ended, Gordon simply wrote himself a check from the proceeds.

Milo was increasingly troubled by his partner's erratic behavior, but he put it out of his mind. He told himself that as long as he received a steady paycheck, he wouldn't be overly concerned about the cash position of the company, which he left to Gordon. However, on more than one occasion, it was clear to him that he didn't actually have the luxury of detaching himself completely. One evening, after an eighteen-hour work day, he arrived at home exhausted and ready to tumble into bed. He had just pulled his car into the garage and killed the engine when his cell phone rang. It was Julip.

"Is Gordon with you?" she asked quickly, not bothering with any polite conversational formalities. He told her that Gordon had left the office several hours earlier to get some dinner. She sighed in exasperation on the other end and asked bluntly, "Has he been gambling?"

"I honestly don't know," Milo answered. "We don't talk very much about that sort of thing."

"Well, he's been losing big lately from what I can get out of him," Julip said. "I had to go pick him up a few weeks ago because he blacked out at the craps table. He told me he lost $1 million that night alone. Honestly, the things I put up with! I just don't know what to do with that man sometimes."

Milo shifted uncomfortably in his seat. Though he never would've admitted it to anyone, Julip made him terribly uneasy. He never told Gordon what the man at the wedding had said about her, and there was no quiet way of knowing whether or not it was true. But there was something in the way she conducted herself that suggested she was not to be trusted. Gordon told him there were times she disappeared for days at a time. He never seemed upset by her disappearance, and only mentioned it to Milo very casually. At other times, she called Milo on his cell phone repeatedly, demanding to speak with Gordon about the most trivial things. Or, if Milo wasn't with Gordon, she tried to learn where he might be or what he might be up to. Gordon didn't carry a cell phone of his own, as a result of his residual paranoia over the government's wiretap of him during his tenure at Grant McKinley. Therefore, if Julip wanted information about his whereabouts, she almost always had to go through Milo. Now he said, "Well, you know

Gordon. He seems to always end up on top."

She ignored this and continued breezily, "When you see him, just let him know that I'm leaving tonight to drive to San Diego. I should be gone for about a week." Milo said he would be sure to relay the message.

The work went on for a year without significant product. Milo and Gordon continued to pursue their respective paths—Milo spending upwards of twelve to fourteen hours a day at work, Gordon going on the wagon for a month or two at a time before spectacularly falling off. He seemed to possess a keen intuition towards Milo's discomfort for the ways things unfolded at times, though Milo never spoke of his feelings openly. At one point, he was on the brink of expressing his concern to Gordon for the sake of the business, but before he could say anything, Gordon told him that he wanted to upgrade Milo's lifestyle. They had recently attracted a new investor, and as a result Milo received an unexpected $50,000 bonus. He put Natalie in charge of using a portion of this for decorating their new house, and put the remainder towards helping his children through college.

Several months later, a new investor by the name of Wade Price provided them with another cash infusion. Gordon instructed Milo to sell 1.5 million dollars' worth of his own shares in the company. He then put $980,000 back into the company at Gordon's direction, and netted $100,000 himself as a result.

With input from Wade Price, the compression software was re-configured to provide options in the security and surveillance environment. Bandwidth was an ongoing concern for any large scale transmission of signal, and new ways of compressing data could always pique the interest of those in that industry. Six months after the re-configuration, Versatronix awarded them a three-year contract to license the software for use in their surveillance system at $1.5 million per year. Versatronix paid the amount up front. It was the first large sale they'd made on a licensing deal as a company, and they celebrated with champagne in the warehouse. Gordon put his arm around Milo's shoulders. "It may be less than Dinetel offered us, but mark my words—it's a gateway to bigger and better things," he said. "The digital surveillance industry is where the real money is. I predict it won't be six months before the casinos hear of it, want it, and hell, even demand it."

❀ ❀ ❀

In fact, his prediction came to pass much sooner. At the closing of the Versatronix deal, Gordon got in touch with one of the executives at Constar Gaming. Milo had taken to reading *In the Lair* on the sly, when Gordon had left for the day and wouldn't catch him. He knew Gordon had worked with Kirk Courson in the days when Constar was building casinos using junk bond products from Grant McKinley. At present Gordon's other acquaintance at Constar, Alex Melrose, oversaw both the Constar studios and the gaming properties. They flew to Los Angeles to meet with Melrose at Constar Studios.

Melrose was a compact man with inky black hair and dark, penetrating eyes. When he turned his attention to whoever was speaking to him, he focused an intense gaze on the listener and leaned forward, tensed, as if listening with his whole body. He didn't say a word during their presentation, but sat with elbows resting on his knees and his hands clasped together. When they finished, he leaned back in his chair and smiled. He looked immensely pleased. He gestured for the pair to take seats across the table from him.

"I can't tell you how much potential there is for this technology in our casino," he said. "It's a dirty little secret in the industry that the surveillance technology is far less advanced than one would suppose. I know people envision a high-tech operation, but in reality what we've got are six thousand cameras on the floor, each one connected to its own VCR machine in the basement."

"Do you mean the surveillance isn't already digital?" Milo didn't hide his surprise well.

Melrose nodded. "That's correct. At this time, videotape is the only admissible form of forensic evidence for prosecuting fraud, so everything has to be captured in tape form. And all six thousand of those video recorders are watched by only three people. It's a spit-and-glue operation, but until now we haven't had much of a choice." He pointed to the projector screen behind him, where the final slide of their presentation lingered. "I see this as an opportunity to change that. This would allow us to compress all that data so we don't have to dedicate whole rooms to the tape storage of past footage. Until the law changes on forensic evidence, we can still upgrade the system and be ready for the future in security."

He ended the meeting by ordering 100 computers to take the place of 100 VCRs, as a trial run. They shook hands and boarded the plane to head back to Reno. The following week, Hicks Limited installed surveillance equipment in the highest-risk areas of the casino. Melrose set up a live-streaming feed of the footage directly to his home in Los Angeles, so he could watch casino activity unfold in real time from five hundred miles away.

Soon thereafter, Gordon was struck by an idea that he proposed to Melrose. In attempting to combat theft, he reasoned, the tracking software they had created could be greatly useful to the casino. Gordon knew from his many years in the casino system that serious instances of theft were perpetrated by casino employees. If the tracking software could identify and track individual visible chips, this would give the casino management a way of keeping tabs on chips that didn't remain on the table. If the tracking followed the chips into the hands or pockets of employees, the movement would be captured, and eventually security would pick up on the unauthorized placement of the high value chips. Melrose was enthusiastic about the idea. Gordon offered to upload the software into the computers that they'd already installed, so that Melrose might see the tracking capabilities in action for himself. Within a week, they were ready to sign a $10 million contract with Constar.

They installed another 100 computers at the casino, each with the tracking software ready to go. High value chips were the one thousand dollar chips and above. It was understood that the easiest chips to steal were the thousand dollar chips that were red and traditionally called "tomatoes." All other chips of higher value were more easily tabulated on the casino floor, since there were fewer to count.

In September, Gordon and Milo flew to Las Vegas to tour the casino and see how their technology was doing in action. They were in the basement with Melrose, watching the night's events unfold via live feed on the wall of video screens, when a security guard entered and told them that a Colonel Marks from the Air Force had requested to meet with them. He was waiting in the lobby.

Gordon didn't budge. "What does he want?" he demanded.

"I believe he's interested in your technology, sir."

Gordon didn't react at first. Then a grin spread slowly over his face. He gripped Milo by the shoulder and said gleefully, "I told you there were bigger fish out there, my boy."

CHAPTER SIX

They met Colonel Pete Marks in the lobby. He was an extremely tall man, with steel grey hair and grey eyes. He stood stiffly in his uniform amid the hustle and bustle of the casino, cradling his hat under one arm. Gordon approached him with a hand extended. "Colonel Marks. Gordon Hicks." His grin had disappeared and he looked suddenly solemn and almost imposing, despite being much shorter than the colonel. They shook hands and Gordon introduced Milo as well.

Colonel Marks said, "Gentleman, we've heard about a technology you created that has generated a great deal of interest at the Pentagon. I'm here to inquire whether I might take a look at this creation of yours."

Gordon looked around the casino floor and rocked back and forth on his heels, as if considering whether to grant permission. At last he said, "Come with us, and see for yourself."

As they descended into the basement, Milo asked the colonel how the Air Force had come to hear about the tracking software. "We're always on the lookout for new endeavors that might be useful to the United States Government," the colonel answered. Milo decided not to pursue the line of questioning further. In the basement, they stood before the wall of monitors and Milo explained how the technology worked.

Colonel Marks turned to him. "So, if I were to carry these chips, would you be able to follow me all around the casino floor?"

Milo nodded. "Each and every little movement."

Colonel Marks looked back up at the monitors. "I would like to test it, with your permission."

Gordon handed him a red chip. The colonel placed the "tomato" in his right hand and positioned his palm up and open, the chip in full view. He ascended the stairs leading up from the basement, and once on the main casino floor kept an open hand, exposing the red chip to every conceivable security camera. He then began to move about the floor. For the next twenty minutes they tracked the movement of his chip as he traversed the casino, going up several flights of stairs at one point and performing other evasive movements. When he was finished walking the floor, they together watched the digital file of his walk around the property. The computer-generated brackets superimposed themselves on the video image of the colonel's hand moving throughout the test. He listened as Milo interpreted the software's capacities while watching the digital monitor. By the time they finished, he was visibly excited. "Shit, I'm interested," he said.

Gordon nodded, as though he had expected that response. "Why don't we all go have a drink upstairs."

They retired to a private cocktail lounge, and Gordon ordered a round of gin and tonics. The colonel sipped on his. "Mighty nice place this is. I can see why folks have a difficult time leaving." He set down his drink and pulled two business cards out of his pocket. He handed one to Gordon and one to Milo. "Gentlemen, I'm a member of the Air Force Battlelab unit that operates out of Eglin Air Force Base in Florida. This is where we test fly Unmanned Aerial Vehicles, or drones, as the public knows them. I would very much like to use this tracking technology you've created as part of a series of tests with our UAVs. I wonder if you could be persuaded to bring the necessary equipment and materials down to Florida next week for the purposes of a trial run."

Gordon said, "I'm sure we could work something out."

The colonel nodded. "I'm glad to hear you say that, Mr. Hicks."

"Of course, there is the matter of our fee for the tests."

"And what is your fee, Mr. Hicks?"

Gordon leaned back in his seat. "One hundred fifty thousand, non-contingent upon whether or not you decide to do business with us afterwards."

"It's a deal." They shook hands. "But based on what I've seen today, gentlemen, I would be mighty surprised if we weren't ultimately interested in doing business with you."

Gordon replied coolly, "We'll see where we stand after the tests."

The colonel took his leave and Gordon ordered another round. He sipped his gin and tonic in silence for some time. Milo could tell that there was something on his mind. Presently he ventured to ask, "What do you think about the possibility of doing business with the

Pentagon? Seems like the type of opportunity we've been waiting for."

Gordon said nothing at first. He finished his drink and ordered two more. When the waitress brought them he took both drinks for himself. Then he spoke up. "We've got Pentagon on the line, right where we want them. We're not going to reel them in too quickly. We'll let them drag with the hook in their mouth for as long as it takes."

"As long as what takes?"

"For as long as it takes for me to decide on a sufficient payback." He downed one of the gin and tonics in a single swift motion and a dark flush crept up his neck and spread over his face. "The government hunted me like a dog in the last days at Grant McKinley. And I'm going to make them pay for it. Do you know what it cost me?" He started in on the next drink. "Twenty-five million in fines that I had to pay to my own government, as if I were some sort of traitor. As if I had to buy my way back into citizenship. Another two million to defend myself against their efforts to permanently besmirch my name. It's going to cost them at least that much to get my business. And they'll have to pay a lot more than that before I call it even." He finished his fourth gin and tonic and snapped his fingers at the waitress in the other room. When she brought two more, he drank half of one and set it down before him. Then he slammed his fist on the table so hard that the drinks sloshed out of their glasses. "They robbed me of ten years of my life, goddammit! And I'll see to it that they pay through the nose for it."

Milo said gently that he should be getting back to his room so that he could rest. Gordon hardly seemed to hear him, lost as he was in his reverie of revenge. Milo slipped away and rode the elevator to his suite.

In his room, he sat on the foot of the bed. His hands trembled. He removed his glasses and rubbed his eyes with the heels of his hands. He was overcome by a great longing to speak to his father, and turned to look at the phone on the bedside table. The blindness of his urge subsided slowly, and he remembered that his father was still in the hospital. Ardell Caldwell had slipped into a coma three months before, following steady deterioration of his health, and from this coma he was not expected to emerge. Milo's mother had told him that if nothing changed by the end of the month, she was going to do what Ardell would have wished her to do long ago: have the doctors pull the plug. Milo realized miserably that in some twisted way, it would be a relief that there was no possibility of his father learning about his going into business with the government. He continued to stare at the phone, as if willing it to ring so that he might receive the final news, as if the act of the phone ringing could change the direction of the events that had been set in motion. But the phone didn't ring. It sat there passively, unobtrusively, as silent as a stone.

CHAPTER SEVEN

As a young boy growing up in Waukegan, Illinois, Ardell Caldwell watched his two older brothers and the older boys in his neighborhood, as well as the brothers and neighbors of his friends, enlist in the army and go to war. He longed to join them, but was frustrated that his dreams of manhood seemed always just beyond his reach. In the summer of 1942, he and his friends spent their afternoons playing games hunting for Nazis, or capturing Japanese spies hiding behind their mothers' rosebushes.

When Ardell's eldest brother Paul was discharged the following year, Ardell watched with a mixture of anticipation and impatience as his father's car pulled up in front of the house one afternoon. Paul stepped out of the car and stood, hesitating, on the sidewalk. Ardell could see that Paul was staring up at the house, but he didn't understand why his brother wore an expression of fear. It was as though he were afraid to enter, afraid even to move toward the house. Ardell had promised his parents that he'd wait for his brother to settle in before he began pestering him with questions about his time away. But he began to wonder why his brother was acting so scared to take a single step up the walkway to his childhood home. Their father climbed out of the driver's seat and came around to where Paul stood, frozen in place. Their father retrieved Paul's suitcase from the trunk, and as the trunk lid slammed shut, Paul flinched, startled. Ardell saw his father put an arm around his son, and at that moment Paul's eyes dropped from the house to the pavement. The scene bewildered Ardell, who grew increasingly fidgety waiting for his brother to come inside. When he couldn't take it any longer, he ran to the front door and burst out onto the porch, yelling, "Hey, Paul! What are ya doin' out here? What's takin' so long?" His father gave him a warning look that seemed to suggest he had done something wrong. His normally gregarious brother, who at any time before would've jogged to the porch, laughing, and ruffled Ardell's hair affectionately, instead looked as though he'd seen a ghost.

The color drained from his face, and he began to shake from head to toe.

Ardell struggled to make sense of the following weeks. Before his brothers joined the army, they had been a devilish pair, always filling the house with laughter and music from the upright piano in the parlor. Paul and Clint had specialized in pulling pranks on their mother, like the time they snuck a dead fish from the grocery store into the kitchen sink, which was filled with soap and water. While she was washing the dishes, she reached in and grabbed the slimy thing, and her screams could be heard clear down the street. The boys were only a few months apart in age, so all the trouble they got into was gotten into together. They were virtually inseparable from the time they could walk. Ardell was almost eight years younger than Clint, and idolized his two older brothers. He had been heartbroken that he couldn't join them when they both volunteered for enlistment in the army, and had solemnly kept his promise to them that he would look after their parents while they were away. Now Clint was fighting in Italy, and his father explained that there was no way of knowing when he would return. When Ardell asked why Paul had come home already, his father grew uneasy and struggled for the right words. "Paul had a difficult time over there, son," he answered vaguely. "It's tough for everyone over there. But it's harder on some than others." Ardell had nodded as though he understood what his father meant, though really he didn't understand at all.

When Paul returned, the laugher and music of former days ceased. Ardell often didn't see his brother all day: Paul locked himself in his room and asked to be left alone when anyone knocked. At dinner he ate little, and seemed not to hear when he was spoken to. His cheerful, lively face now looked drawn and haggard, and Ardell noticed that his brother's once rosy cheeks had become sunken and pale. Sometimes he screamed in his sleep, a blood-curdling sound that echoed through the house, and Ardell curled up in his bed, terrified, until he heard his father enter Paul's room and quiet his son. When Clint returned six months after his brother, it was as though Paul hardly knew his former partner in crime. Ardell overheard his parents talking with Clint one night about Paul's condition. His father confessed he had hoped Clint's coming home would improve Paul's outlook. On the contrary, as the months passed he seemed to be worsening. One evening Ardell came home from baseball practice to find Paul cowering in one corner of the kitchen, a small knife in his hand. Clint stood several feet away, trying to coax his brother to give him the knife. Paul shook his head miserably. Tears streamed down his face. "I don't want to live anymore," he sobbed. "I want to die. I'm already practically dead. What difference could it make?" The standoff ended after an hour with Clint slowly moving closer to his brother and finally taking the knife gingerly from his hand. Paul collapsed on the floor in defeat. Later that night an ambulance came and took him away. It was to be the last time Ardell saw his eldest brother.

At the age of twenty, Ardell got a job at a printing press warehouse in Chicago and married a local girl named Sarah White. His dream of going to college had fallen apart after Paul's breakdown. Their father began to drink and eventually lost his job. The money they had saved for Ardell's education drained away, and by the time his father found a new job at lower pay, there was nothing left. His father died of an internal hemorrhage at 59 and not long after, his mother returned to live with her parents in Scotland. Ardell had worked from the time he was fourteen, and by the time he got married, he was spending whatever extra money he had on liquor. He had wanted to be a newspaper reporter, but without a college education, working at a printing press seemed to be as close as he could get. When he was twenty-one, his left hand got caught in the press one day and was crushed beyond use. He was right-handed, so he was able to keep his job, though the accident slowed down his ability to execute tasks. The memory of his brother's condition after the war lingered with him, and as he matured into adulthood he tried to better understand what had happened, but everything seemed initially connected to what Paul went through. He never doubted for a moment that the war had been for a just cause, but was nevertheless angry that it had cost him his brother, and eventually his father's job, as well as his own college aspirations. The frustrations of his life built up one by one, and turned him into a bitter man at a young age. He often grew enraged while discussing politics at the neighborhood tavern, starting long, drunken tirades against the government.

Because of his interest in world affairs, he followed the news hungrily, reading the paper on the train to and from Chicago each day, and watching television news in the evening while Sarah fixed dinner. In 1953, his wife was six months pregnant when he turned on the news one evening to find an Edward Murrow program about a U. S. Air Force lieutenant named Milo Radulovich. Radulovich, a seemingly ordinary man from Michigan, was being accused by Senator McCarthy and the House Unamerican Activities Committee of being a Communist sympathizer. He'd been discharged from the Air Force as a result. The reason given by HUAC was that Radulovich's father and sister were suspected of being communist spies. However, all purported evidence against him was sealed in an envelope, and the contents were never seen by anyone beyond McCarthy's inner circle. Radulovich challenged his discharge from the Air Force, but after a protracted legal battle, the discharge stood.

Over dinner, Ardell spoke of the subject vehemently. "Our government has the power to pick out any Tom, Dick, or Harry at will and ruin their lives, to crush them completely! Look what they are doing in Hollywood. Blacklisting people. Guilty, til proven innocent!" He fumed, hammering his fist on the table for emphasis. "This is what happens when the government gets too much power. It overreaches, it destroys people. We're trying to fight the Communists, yet Washington employs the same oppressive tactics against its own people!"

"I wish you'd lower your voice, dear," his wife said quietly, a fearful look in her eyes. "If anyone should hear you, they might get the wrong impression."

"It's gotten so a man can't freely speak his mind in his own home," Ardell grumbled, settling in to spoon some mashed potatoes onto his plate. "It's not right." They ate their dinner in silence, Sarah with one hand resting on her stomach. Her pregnancy had only recently begun to show. She could see that her husband was in a dark mood... usual for him when he watched the news. After dinner she cleared the plates, and he moved to the sitting room and mixed himself a drink with his one good hand. The other hung at his side uselessly, like a crumpled piece of paper. "It's not right," he said again, to himself. He sat in the easy chair and sipped his whiskey soda, thinking.

After a second and third drink, he accosted his wife in the kitchen, where she was cleaning up the remains of their meal. "We're going to name the boy Milo," he declared, his eyes filled with a fiery passion.

His wife stopped scrubbing the stovetop and looked at him. "I thought we had agreed on Charles, after my father," she said timidly, but unable to conceal a note of dismay.

"Sarah, I don't expect you to understand how important this is," Ardell answered, adopting a patronizing tone. "This man could have been our neighbor; he could have been me — it could have been anybody. He was just an ordinary person whose parents were immigrants, like my grandparents or your parents. His family came to this country to escape oppression, and now they face oppression here. We can never forget what extraordinary times we live in, and how we must continue our fight for life and liberty. Sometimes we have to fight for liberty against our own government!"

"Please, keep your voice down," Sarah pleaded, shooting a nervous glance toward the slightly ajar kitchen window.

"Dammit Sarah, stop hushing me!" he yelled. "I have the right to speak freely on my own property! We're naming my son Milo whether you like it or not!"

With this, he stormed out of the house, snatching his coat and hat on his way to the door. His wife sighed and returned to the stovetop. She resented her husband's oft-repeated assertions that she was dull-witted or simpleminded simply because she didn't always agree with his way of thinking. She had been the valedictorian of her high school class. When she had met him in a dance hall on her eighteenth birthday, she had fallen hopelessly in love. She'd always thought she would marry a man at least six-foot-two, though Ardell barely cleared 5'10." He was a fantastic dancer and looked deeply into her eyes while he spoke of his interests in history and economics. There had been something slightly wounded in him, that showed in the way he talked and the way he carried himself. She had wanted to save him as soon as she met him, though she didn't know from what he needed saving.

She didn't find out about his brother until a year after they were married, following the accident at the printing press. His veins coursed with a potent mixture of Scottish and Norwegian blood. He was predisposed to drink, but following the accident, began to drink more frequently, and sometimes, in a melancholy state of mind, he told her about the troubles of his family life following the war. How his father had died violently, coughing up blood, and how his mother struggled to pay the hospital bills before fleeing to Scotland, where the creditors could not pursue her. How his brother Paul had been taken to a mental institution in southern Illinois, and refused to see his family each time they came to visit. How his brother Clint had married his high school sweetheart, only to lose her to a fatal car crash two years later. At times when Ardell spoke of these things, he put his head on Sarah's lap and cried. But as he grew more accustomed to living without one of his hands, something gradually hardened in him. Now when he drank he became angry, not sorrowful. He flew into a fury at Sarah over insignificant things, like the way she made the bed or folded the towels. He sometimes told her that she was stupid and that he wished he had married someone with brains rather than good looks. When she became pregnant, he lamented that now she would lose her good looks as well.

Their son Milo was born in February of 1954. Ardell fell in love with the boy and eased up on his drinking. He spent his every free moment with his son, building him a treehouse and teaching him how to fish and how to make animal calls: all the things a young boy should know. When Milo was six, his mother became pregnant again. However, in the seventh month of pregnancy Sarah slipped on the icy front step one winter morning and fell to the sidewalk. She miscarried that afternoon, and in the hospital it was discovered that the baby had been a girl.

Ardell was inconsolable. He took up drinking again and began to miss work. After a year had passed, he made up his mind that they were moving to Los Angeles, where it never snowed. He quit his job and moved his family to California. But it was more difficult finding work there, and he drank more heavily. At last he found a job working nights for the railroad as a switch operator. In the daytime, he supplemented his income by working at a gas station. The years of manual labor and drink began to wear him down. His temper grew worse, and at times it was unmanageable. Once in an argument with Sarah, he broke nearly every dish in the house on the kitchen floor. When Milo was old enough to understand such things, he recognized that his father's greatest fear had been to waste his life and intelligence. Ardell had been an exceptionally bright young man with a promising future, and in his own mind he had frittered away this potential; in his own eyes and heart he'd become a failure, and this fact haunted him always.

Milo, on the other hand, was a competent but hardly gifted student. He did not excel at anything in particular, but managed to do passably well in everything. Ardell often said to him over the dinner table, "You have to find your true calling, son. You've got to make yourself stand out in some way. You can't be content to do only as much work as you need to in order to get by – you should work hard at what you love so that you don't end up wasting your talents."

Milo knew better than to counter his father when he began this familiar lecture, so he simply nodded and said nothing. If his father had listened, he would've told him that he didn't know what he loved. He felt he could do anything he put his mind to, but there was nothing that stirred a sense of ambition in him. To that end, he graduated from high school without applying to any college, and for this his father lectured him endlessly. Milo grew to feel the incessant pressure from Ardell was counterproductive to finding his "true calling," so on his eighteenth birthday, two days after high school graduation, he moved out of his parents' house and into a studio apartment of his own.

For two years he lived in the studio apartment, and worked at the hospital as an emergency room technician. When he married Natalie, his high school sweetheart, he knew he'd better start thinking of his future, and began taking courses at the local community college. His relationship with his father had become strained over the years. Ardell watched in frustration while his son seemed to move through life without any sense of urgency, taking his time about finding his path. Dinners at his parents' house were always a tense affair for Milo. His father talked of nothing but Milo's wasted potential. "You have so much talent, son, and such a fine mind, and it doesn't seem to concern you in the least that you're going to wake up one morning and realize that you've never done anything worth a damn." Ardell had recently been diagnosed with an ulcer, and temporarily forbidden to drink alcohol. Instead, he drank glass after glass of water, as though his thirst could not be slaked. "I don't think you properly appreciate the many advantages you've had," he would continue. "When I was young, I wanted more than anything to be a college man. But college was expensive, and only the brightest and most privileged were able to go. Now it's open to anyone, and affordable! And here you make the ludicrous choice to not go!"

"It's not all that affordable, Pop," Milo said quietly. "I couldn't pay for it with what I make at the hospital. I would have to take out loans and I don't want to do that."

Ardell snorted contemptuously. "They say thrift is a virtue," he grumbled. "But it's possible to be thrifty to a fault. You're robbing yourself of a golden opportunity." Even when Milo enrolled in community college, his father was not placated. "You belong at Stanford or USC. Not some second-rate joke school that accepts anyone with a pulse."

Then they had their first true argument, a screaming match over the phone, when Milo told his father that he wouldn't be taking any further college courses and would instead continue his work in medical technology. Ardell said that he was going to waste his life away working for someone else instead of having people work for him, or working for himself. "I suppose you're content to be somebody else's slave instead of your own master!" He roared into the phone. The call ended with Milo hanging up on his father. They didn't speak for nearly a year after that.

As Ardell aged, his years of drinking began to catch up with him. At age sixty-three, he suffered a mild stroke that left him with occasional tremors in his good hand. He was forced to retire early as a result, and against his doctor's express orders, started drinking once more. Following Milo and Natalie's move to Reno, he suffered a severe stroke that resulted in a coma lasting three months.

Milo received a tearful call from his mother after he returned from his Las Vegas trip. His father had awakened. He told Gordon that he needed some time off, and flew to San Diego. Though his father had emerged from the coma, it was nevertheless difficult for him to speak or move his arms. Milo's mother warned him that the doctors had said Ardell might not make it through the following weeks.

Milo arrived at the hospital carrying a bouquet of flowers on a drizzly October morning. He knew that flowers were the sort of thing his father would hate to see in his room, standing as they did for his ill health and mortality. Nevertheless, Milo felt helpless in the face of tradition, powerless to do anything but to follow the proscribed paths of someone confronting the death of a family member. And maybe they would cheer his mother. He checked in with the front desk; and was directed to Ardell's room on the fifth floor. The elevator was a ponderously slow machine whose halting ascent caused Milo to wonder if there was some greater force at work attempting to prevent his meeting with his father. They hadn't seen one another in more than two years.

Ardell was propped up on a pillow, staring out the window when Milo arrived. He turned his eyes toward the door at his son's entrance, and smiled feebly. A thin rubber tube ran into each nostril, supplying oxygen. His arms rested lank and lifeless on either side of him, much thinner than Milo remembered. He leaned over and kissed his father on the forehead before realizing that he'd never made such an intimate gesture. "Hey, Pop," he said, and set the flowers down on the bedside table. His eyes quickly scanned the stack of paperbacks sitting there – *1984, All the King's Men, The Manchurian Candidate*: Ardell's holy trinity of literature, a trifecta that summed up his life's paranoiac philosophy. Milo wondered if his father had had the presence of mind to bring these to the hospital with him, or if someone had given him copies. Milo drew a chair next to the bed and sat.

"How are you feeling, Pop?" he asked.

Ardell swallowed and managed to croak out the word, "Shit."

Milo smiled in spite of himself. "At least you're in good hands."

Because of the tubes coming out of his nose, Ardell was unable to snort contemptuously, but he managed to make a face that conveyed the same sentiment. He swallowed and said laboriously, "Bunch...of... quacks."

Milo found himself at a loss for what to say to his father. He never imagined, in his many years of navigating their difficult relationship, how it might feel watching him die. Now that the time had come, he felt no increased sense of clarity or revelation, but instead found himself feeling as ambivalent and uncomfortable as ever. So he said the first thing that came into his mind. "I started a new company, Dad. We've got some big time clients."

As soon as he saw the look that Ardell gave him, he realized his mistake. Ardell said slowly, "Your.... mother.... told me." He swallowed hard. "Working... for... Big Brother."

Instinctively, Milo went on the defensive. "The Air Force approached us only very recently. We are doing some tests for them in Florida, but that doesn't mean anything will come of it. And anyhow it's a great opportunity, it could be a game-changer for us."

He stopped speaking when he became aware that Ardell was shaking his head. His eyes were closed. He managed to say, "Be... careful." Milo didn't answer. He suddenly felt ashamed of himself for trying to argue with his severely debilitated father as he lay incapacitated and dying in his hospital bed. Milo looked down at the ground. Then he heard his father speak again. He said only one word, and he said it very softly. Milo wasn't even entirely sure he heard it correctly. But it sounded like, "Proud." He looked up and found that Ardell's eyes had closed and he had turned his head away, exhausted from his contribution to their meager conversation.

Milo remained at his father's bedside for several hours while the old man slept. Presently, he picked up the copy of 1984 and began to read it. It was a novel he was supposed to read in high school English but never had. Instead, he had relied on the Cliff's Notes version, and still managed to get a "B" on his response essay.

In the early afternoon he began to doze, awakening only when the book slipped off his lap and landed with a soft thud on the floor next to him.

He remained in San Diego for the rest of the week, visiting his father several more times. But the old man seemed to have used up all his energy in the brief exchange with Milo, and spoke no more. Remarkably, though the doctor had predicted Ardell wouldn't last much longer, his health began to improve incrementally. Though he continued to have difficulty speaking, he was eventually able to move his limbs slightly. With the assistance of a wheelchair, he left the hospital one week after Milo's arrival. Milo helped his mother get Ardell set up at home before returning to Reno.

As soon as he walked through the door, Natalie told him that Gordon had instructed her to have him call the second he got in. "It sounds pretty urgent," she said.

He called Gordon at the office. The voice on the other end was filled with mirth. "I just got word from Colonel Marks and the Air Force," he said. "They want in. You leave for Florida in three days."

The following day, a man in a suit arrived at the offices of Hicks Limited and announced that he was a representative of a security wing of the military, the Defense Intelligence Agency. His card introduced him as Paul Heron. "Gentlemen, for the upcoming tests we'll need you to pass several background checks to obtain top security clearance." He balanced a pair of reading glasses on the end of his nose and withdrew a stack of papers from his briefcase. "First I must ask if either of you have dealings with foreign governments or their employees, either in the past or currently." Gordon said that he did, with one of his smaller business ventures, but didn't go into much detail. Heron nodded. "In that case, I'm afraid only Mr. Caldwell would qualify for the background check, and therefore, the clearance."

"What if we hired another employee who could pass the background check?" Gordon wanted to know. "Would that individual be able to accompany Mr. Caldwell in my place?"

"As long as that person passes the check," Heron answered.

By the end of the day, Gordon had made a phone call to Kathy White at Dinitel that succeeded in convincing her to leave her position and come to work for him instead. Kathy would manage the contract relationship, payment schedules and control of sensitive documents. Kathy had worked with Gordon in New York for the investment firm Hallofax, which had taught Gordon everything he needed to know to succeed at Grant McKinley. Kathy had moved to the West Coast following the birth of her son, and gotten into the software business at the dawn of the personal computer era. She was an extremely tall woman with thick glasses and a loud, nervous laugh. Milo found her to be very quiet and reserved, so her sudden shouts of laughter at times never failed to startle him. He and Kathy both passed their background checks within twenty-four hours, and the following day boarded the jet bound for Eglin.

Colonel Marks met them, and as they drove in a large black SUV to the testing site, he explained that the purpose of the tests was to determine whether a drone equipped with the tracking software could locate and identify predetermined objects. Once the object was identified, they hoped the drone would follow the target and provide its exact coordinates as it moved through various terrain. "If your software does what we want it to do, this will be an invaluable tool in combating international terrorism," Marks said.

They arrived at an unremarkable-looking beige building, not much different from the one Hicks Limited occupied. Inside, Marks directed them to a desk station containing three laptops. As he looked over the laptops, Milo realized that their technology was not much more advanced than his home computer. The Air Force had arranged for him to upload the computers with the tracking software, which would be used to identify pre-selected people and objects. Once this was done, military personnel took the laptops into the field to remotely validate the tracking as the elements were imaged from drones more than a thousand feet in the air.

The tests lasted several days, and Colonel Marks appeared to be exceptionally pleased with the results. However, he said he was unable to authorize the licensing of the technology himself; it needed to be run by his superiors first. Milo and Kathy returned to Reno and apprised Gordon of the results of their trip.

Gordon smiled as he listened. "They think they're going to play hard-to-get," he said. "But they don't realize who they're bargaining with."

Before long, the holidays rolled around, and Gordon invited Milo and Natalie to a spectacular Christmas party at Incline Village. They encountered many of the same friends and associates who attended the wedding, with the notable exception of JJ Singer. "He's in Washington, making one last plea for a presidential pardon," Gordon told Milo while pouring himself a drink. "He was angry when Clinton wouldn't come through for him and now watching that son of a bitch fall flat on his face is the only thing I want for Christmas this year."

He introduced them to his personal attorney, Tony Frye. Frye politely asked them how business was going, but seemed shocked to learn about their tests with the Air Force.

"I'm surprised that you would even put a toe in those waters, Gordon," he said, clearly concerned. "After the mess at Grant McKinley, I'd think you'd want to give the government a wide berth."

"If I did that I couldn't get back all the money they took from me,"

Gordon answered succinctly, finishing his fourth martini.

Frye looked at Milo, as if to ask what he thought about it. Receiving no indication one way or the other, the lawyer turned back to Gordon. "I'll say this as both your attorney and your friend, Gordon – I think you're making a big mistake." Gordon signaled to one of the servers to bring him another martini. "You dodged a bullet after the Grant fallout."

"What are you talking about? I lost millions!"

"You avoided jail time. Should I remind you that there are plenty of people in Washington who would love to see you locked up for life? Why on Earth would you risk getting into bed with them again?"

Gordon's drink arrived and he took it eagerly. "You sure know how to brighten a party, Anthony," he said, finishing it almost as quickly as it had arrived.

CHAPTER EIGHT

January 2003

The tests at Eglin left Gordon, Milo, and Kathy feeling confident that there would be a positive outcome for Hicks Limited. They anticipated a rich offer from Battlelabs, and they were not disappointed. In the early part of January the reports began to roll in, and the independent evaluators for the Air Force called the results exemplary. The software had maintained a high number of objects identified in the field tests and the false positives that object tracking inevitably produced were negligible. The Air Force had used other products in similar ways, but in the words of Colonel Marks, none of them came even remotely close to pinpointing the objects that Hicks Limited's software identified and followed. They specifically said they'd assigned a blue car as one of the "valued objects." In the test, the Air Force ran several automobiles of the same model onto the tracking field and intentionally ran them in a scramble pattern. They did the same thing with weapons, and people who looked and dressed similarly. Each time the tracking maintained the correct identification. That, according to the report, was phenomenal.

January and February rolled by as they awaited final word on a possible Air Force contract. Gordon became increasingly impatient with their slow response. Then he hit on an idea. "It's like taking a woman on a date," he told Milo. "You've got to wine her and dine her before she'll put out." He called Colonel Marks and extended an invitation to the other colonels at Eglin to spend a night on the town in Reno. It didn't take much arm-twisting before accepting his invitation.

The four colonels arrived in the privately chartered plane, which had been flown to Florida just to pick them up at six o'clock on a Friday evening. By nine that evening, west coast time, Gordon treated them to dinner at Le Rollande, followed by a private party at the Atlantis Hotel.

"Wait until you see this," he promised, leading them through a backdoor entrance held open by a smiling security guard. They found themselves ascending a nondescript staircase that was clearly accessible only by the door they had used. The faint, muted sounds of the casino came through the walls, and as they continued upward the sound was drowned out entirely. An imposing security guard wearing a gray suit held open a door at the top of the stairs for them. Through the door lay a smaller, private casino entirely at their disposal. The security guard closed the door behind them, at which point Milo realized the room had no windows and not a security camera in sight. He also realized with a start that the cocktail waitresses were all topless. He fidgeted uncomfortably as Gordon said, "Gentlemen, welcome to Reno. Don't ever let it be said that we don't know how to treat our guests."

There was a cocktail waitress for each member of the party. Milo nervously shrugged his off immediately by saying, "I don't want anything to drink tonight. Please take care of these other gentlemen." She smiled and looked slightly confused.

It was clear from the get-go that the colonels were thrilled by the "anything goes" nature of their private gambling room. They had no qualms about pawing the unclothed cocktail waitresses or running up the bar tab. Gordon handed out poker chips as if they were candy while Milo watched with growing alarm. Pulling Gordon to one side he asked, "Where did you get such a *lame brained* idea?"

Gordon was growing visibly drunk by the minute, and he was irritated that Milo would interrupt his good time. "Don't you know me by now?" he asked loudly. "I own this town. They give me whatever I want. Besides, these guys make less than you do, they are going to eat this stuff up!" This point inspired an idea and he yelled, "Who wants a steak?" The colonels all cried out in the affirmative.

Milo stuck around for as long as he could stand it so he wouldn't look like a bad sport. But by 1:00 a.m., he was restless and tired of watching the debauchery of the men in uniform. Before slipping out, he paused at the bar and asked the bartender, "Where's our tab at so far?"

The bartender consulted his record. "One hundred and counting," he answered. Milo shook his head, resigned to the bacchanalian nature of doing business Gordon-style.

Milo drove himself home and went to bed. When he arrived back at the office at 6:00 a.m. he was surprised to see Gordon already there, albeit slumped over his desk and snoring. He gently tapped Gordon on the shoulder. Gordon sat up, reeking of alcohol. He looked dazed. Milo asked him, "Where's your entourage?"

"Hotel – hotel," Gordon muttered in response.

"Why don't you go home and get some sleep?"

"Don't be a jackass. Get me some coffee."

Milo microwaved enough day-old coffee to give the fresh pot time to brew and brought it to Gordon. While Gordon drank it down he asked, "Do you think your little trick worked?"

Gordon grinned drunkenly and said, "That Battlelabs contract is ours, or my name isn't Gordon-fucking-Hicks."

They received word in the early afternoon that the groggy officers had boarded the jet and were en route back to Florida. It wasn't a week before Colonel Marks was flying back to Reno to sign the contract.

APRIL 2003

A month passed, and they dove into their work for the Air Force. They were surprised one Monday morning when a black SUV carrying a CIA agent arrived at the warehouse. He was a slight, quiet man dressed in khakis, golf shirt and sports jacket – despite the warming weather – who identified himself as Rhys Wilson. He said he'd heard about the object tracking software and the way the compression made it work, and was interested in reviewing the system. Gordon leaned back in his chair and said, "Good news travels fast between Langley and the Pentagon."

Milo and Kathy exchanged glances. They had been expecting this, though they hadn't told Gordon; they'd decided to wait to see what happened overall. While at Eglin, they conducted their tests from an Air Force trailer sitting in an open field that housed all the computer and monitoring validators. There was a second trailer next to it. One day, the Air Force personnel asked them to try the software on the drones being monitored in the trailer next door. When they arrived, they discovered that the workers were tech staff from the Agency, performing and developing similar technologies.

Wilson said, "I'd like to propose an arrangement: $150,000 to lease ten laptops for a period of one year from your company, with this software uploaded on them. You purchase the laptops, we direct you from there. How does that sound?"

Gordon didn't blink. "$200,000 and we'll think about it."

Wilson was equally unflinching. "Two hundred fifty thousand and we close the deal today."

Gordon seemed to consider the offer for a moment, then nodded. "We're ready to start when you are," he said.

Wilson opened his black briefcase and withdrew a manilla envelope containing twenty different headshots. Milo and Kathy peered over Gordon's shoulder as he leafed through them. They were startled to recognize several high-profile faces from the evening news: Osama Bin Laden, Ayman al-Zawahiri, Abu Musab al-Zarqawi. Kathy looked up at Wilson. "Do you mean to say these are the targets we'll be tracking?"

Wilson smiled, and this time it was genuine. "Are you folks ready to do your country a great service?"

Milo spoke up. "You do understand that the software has to have facial recognition protocols built into the system," he explained. "You know the differences between tracking weapons and automobiles and human targets are enormous. The tracking software will take hundreds of hours of programming to gear it to specific facial recognition. It can be done, but it will take several weeks to build in the permutations."

"We recognize that it'll take some time, but your work seems way ahead of other products in the field. It could be immeasurably useful in the War on Terror."

Wilson gave them a slate colored credit card and instructed them to phone the requisition agent listed on the back as Big Safari with all the equipment they needed up to ten workstations. They were to use the authorization codes on the card and whatever they needed would be delivered within 24 hours.

The equipment did, in fact, arrive the next day, and Milo immediately began the work building the algorithms for compression and facial recognition. Even though the military purchased more satellite bandwidth than all other companies worldwide, the Hicks compression software was essential for transmitting this kind of information quickly. Milo's workdays began to increase from fifteen hours a day to eighteen or twenty. He often left the office last, drove four miles to his house, slept for three hours, then was back at his desk before the others. He finished the work in July, at which point Wilson paid him a second visit and gave him several DVDs to scan and use as ingredients for the image recognition. It wasn't long before he realized that the video capture, unlike static images he'd previously been analyzing, presented a different type of challenge. The movement in the video captures contained angles of the tracked faces, and changed continually. Each angle had to be registered as a single capture.

One afternoon, he was in the middle of scanning a single video frame from an Al-Jazeera newscast using the software. During such scans, the software regularly performed a series of forensic tests on the image to determine whether it had been altered in any way. This was necessary in video, because often the original capture from camera had been edited by studio equipment. Milo's tracking detection software would signal when a manmade change had altered the footage. In this particular case, a large number of the forensic detectors were sending signals verifying changes to the image.

So many flags went off on this particular tape that at first Milo thought someone had intentionally tampered with it to test him. He put a call in to Wilson.

"If you purposefully embedded elements in the frames, I would appreciate knowing why," he said. "I don't know what to do with this information, so I don't want to spend time trying to decode the signal." Wilson didn't say anything. Milo continued, "This isn't our forte, and if I spend time trying to decode it, it's going to slow down the task at hand. With your permission, I'd like to get back to doing what I was hired to do."

Wilson took a deep breath and answered slowly. "Mr. Caldwell, I don't know anything about any embedded signals."

They were mutually silent for a full minute. Then Milo said, "Then where did it come from?"

"Frankly, I don't know."

"Could another agent have planted it?"

"They would have had to run it by me first; it seems an unlikely explanation." He paused, thinking. "I know it's not part of our original agreement, Mr. Caldwell, but I need you to analyze those signals for me. We need to know what it says to understand where it may have come from."

"That could take weeks."

"Let's not worry about how long it takes," Wilson replied.

In all, it took Milo a month to determine that the signals he detected appeared to be a barcode. He recognized the type of bar code as the kind used in medical delivery information. He shared this with Gordon, who asked plenty of questions but had no idea what to do. Milo didn't have an answer, either, so he decided to keep scanning the frames. Soon he discovered that the code began to repeat. In all, they were embedded four times in the frame. He discovered that the barcode contained a second set of numbers that looked familiar. In that strange, mathematically oriented brain of his, he wondered if it was a Julian calendar date. Julian calendars keep a running count of days from the first day of the year, but do not add days for leap years; therefore, the running total is different from the Gregorian calendar. If it was a Julian date, then it curiously coincided with—November 8, 2003, three weeks from the present. He immediately sent the information to Wilson.

On the morning of November 8, he picked up the newspaper from his front porch on the way out the door at 6:00 a.m. Once he arrived at the office, he made himself a cup of coffee and opened the paper at his desk. The headline read:

CAR BOMB KILLS 17, WOUNDS 120 IN SAUDI ARABIA

He read on with trembling hands. The incident had taken place in Riyadh, Saudi Arabia. On a hunch, he turned on his computer and did an internet search for the numbers he had found embedded in the barcode. Nothing showed up by the numbers themselves. Then he had a thought: what if they were longitudes and latitudes? He tried first with typing the numbers that were listed left to right, no geographical match. He tried again with the numbers right to left — as they'd be in Arabic — and there was a match. - Riyadh, Saudi Arabia.

All that day, he waited in nervous anticipation to hear from Wilson. The call never came. The following morning, however, when he arrived at the office at five in the morning, there were several black SUVs waiting in the parking lot. Milo walked to the front door and watched while the passenger-side doors of two of the SUVs opened.

A guy with salt and pepper hair and dressed casually in slacks and a sports jacket exited one. His face was slightly pockmarked, as though his teenage acne had left scars. A woman in her early thirties, with dark skin and black hair tied in a low bun at the nape of her neck stepped out of the other car. She wore a pantsuit and sunglasses, despite the weak early morning light. They approached simultaneously.

The man spoke first. "Milo Caldwell?"

"Yes, that's me."

"I'm special agent Walt Dirkes. This is special agent Kyla Taylouni." She removed her glasses to reveal startling green eyes. They both presented their credentials. "May we step inside?"

When Gordon arrived, an hour later, he found Milo sitting across the table from two strangers. He shook hands with them while Milo introduced them.

Walt Dirkes spoke first. "Please have a seat. Mr. Caldwell was just explaining to us how this software of yours works."

Gordon remained standing. "It seems to have everyone in your world pretty excited."

The agents exchanged looks. Dirkes continued, "Frankly, gentlemen, we're going to need a bit of an explanation as to how your software was able to predict the events of yesterday morning in Riyadh."

"We didn't 'predict' anything," Milo insisted. "I already told you, the only information our software uncovered was a barcode, repeated several times, and another number that looked to be a date. I forwarded my findings to Wilson three weeks ago, and that was that."

"But surely you must have had a theory as to what these numbers could have meant," Dirkes pressed him.

Milo was growing irritated, having dealt with Dirkes' needling all morning. Since their arrival, Kyla Taylouni had hardly said a word. "I'm not an analyst, I'm a programmer," Milo answered. "I didn't know what this information meant, nor did I think it was my business to know. I didn't even consider them to be coordinates until I saw the paper this morning."

Dirkes pounced on this, saying, "So you had absolutely no feeling of duty to look into the matter further? You can see what the outcome was — lives could have been spared had someone like yourself taken just a moment to look at the bigger picture and try to figure out what was going on."

"Now wait just a minute," Gordon interrupted. "You can't seriously expect us to do your job for you. We design software, not educated guesses on matters of national security."

Dirkes glared at him, momentarily at a loss. Then he said irritably, "Fine. Just get to work analyzing these." He pulled several DVDs out of his briefcase and shoved them roughly across the table. "Is there anywhere to get a decent coffee around here?"

Milo said, "We have a coffee maker."

"I said a decent coffee," Dirkes snapped.

After listening impatiently to their directions to the nearest Starbucks, Dirkes asked Kyla if she wanted anything, and left in a huff. Gordon went to his desk, leaving Milo and Kyla sitting alone at the table. Milo waited to see if there were any further directions on the new assignment. At last she spoke. "I apologize for my partner's rudeness," she said, her voice surprisingly deep. "He's a college soccer referee and he's upset about missing matches this week. He was supposed to officiate the national college semi-finals, and now he's ticked."

"Do you mean the two of you will be here all this week?" Milo asked.

"Not just us." She looked at her watch. "The NSA deputy director should be along shortly."

Milo sighed. With this interruption, it was shaping up to be an even longer day than usual. He asked, "Do you enjoy what you do?"

The question caught her off guard. "Excuse me?"

"Do you enjoy working for the CIA?"

She looked over the floor of the mostly empty warehouse. "It has its rewards and challenges, just like any other job."

At ten o'clock the National Security Administration deputy director, a man by the name of Stuart Jackson, entered the warehouse with half a dozen CIA technology personnel in tow. Walt Dirkes and Kyla Taylouni rose to meet him, and they conferred just out of earshot as Milo watched from his desk. Several moments later, the newly arrived CIA personnel began to set up tables and computer equipment. They re-swept the warehouse for bugs and other forms of eavesdropping equipment. They checked the security cameras the Air Force had installed.

Seeing this, Milo and Gordon stood in unison. Gordon demanded,

"What's going on here?"

Jackson turned to see who had addressed him, then looked back to Kyla and Dirkes. Dirkes said something in a low voice and Jackson nodded. He came to where Gordon and Milo stood behind their desks. He said, "Do you gentlemen make up this entire operation?"

"Kathy White is our government contract compliance expert. She's out with a sick child," Gordon answered. "Now would you mind explaining what you are doing without our permission?"

"This equipment should help expedite your scanning process," Jackson answered, gesturing toward the laptops and desk top workstations that were being set up. "We need things to move a little faster than they have been." He pulled a stack of papers from his briefcase. "Now then — there's the matter of price. What are your monthly operating costs?"

Gordon considered for a moment before answering, "$200,000."

That was twice the actual operating costs. Milo waited to see if the deputy director would balk. But it didn't faze him in the least. He said, "Fine, fine. We'll draw up a long-term contract in the near future. For the time being, you've got four weeks to decode the tapes you've been given."

By Saturday, November 15, the first month's check arrived by courier, and immediately Gordon put himself on payroll for $40,000 monthly. Milo, however, was kept at $20,000. Milo was miffed at the move, but he decided Gordon's negotiation would lead to better things. Besides, he needed Gordon's help leading the bureaucratic meetings with all these government guys. Milo hated that part.

Over the weekend, there was plenty of work to do overseeing the set-up of the new equipment and stepping up the work flow. Though the drive was only four miles to his house, both nights he slept in his car for an hour or two in the parking lot before going back inside. He had already kept several changes of clothes in his desk drawers. He brushed his teeth in the office bathroom and ate cereal at his desk while he worked. He did the best he could at answering calls from the kids and Natalie by way of text messages. By Monday, the set-up team had the additional computers up and running, and Dirkes began to push for the work to progress more quickly. Milo tried to explain that even with the advanced computing support, anomaly detection was a laborious task. Deciphering a single frame often took hours, but Dirkes insisted that Milo complete ten frames per day. Gordon and Dirkes got into regular shouting matches, with Dirkes insisting that the Agency was under the gun and needed them to work faster. Gordon retaliated by saying that the only way they could work at all was if everyone in the warehouse backed off. The Agency staff would retreat to their cubicles or meet as a group in the conference room. Gordon and Milo couldn't really figure out what they were doing there at all, but it was apparent that for the while, they were stuck with each other.

Meanwhile, Gordon began to follow Milo around like a needy pet. "I'm sure I could learn the algorithms," he said hopefully. "If I could learn the market metrics of Wall Street when I was twenty, then surely I could learn this." Milo attempted to explain it to him several times, but Gordon failed to grasp the lessons. Eventually Milo gave up, but Gordon continued to stick by his side as though he were protecting his prized golden goose.

Being in the mix of this chaotic warehouse, Gordon had increased his smoking to three packs of cigarettes per day. One day Walt Dirkes asked him for one, and after that they began to take regular smoke breaks together. This led to a reduction in the strain between them, and a formation of what could almost be called a friendship. On Friday, the twenty-first, Gordon invited Dirkes to join him for dinner. After they'd left, Kyla spoke up suddenly. She asked Milo, "Why don't we order a pizza?"

She and Dirkes had set up at a pair of desks across the floor from Milo and Gordon, and both were in triangle with Kathy's workstation at the front of the warehouse. Kyla hadn't spoken much to any of them in the two weeks she'd been there, and Milo assumed that she, like Dirkes, was unhappy to be stuck in Reno. He left her alone and made no attempt to strike up a conversation, so her suggestion surprised Milo. He said hesitantly, "I've got a lot of work to do, I'm not sure I could take a break..."

She stood up and came to where he sat. When she reached his

desk, she crossed her arms. "I've been here for the last twelve days straight. I've never seen you not working in all that time. I think you've earned an hour lunch break. Come on, I'm buying."

Twenty minutes later they sat across from one another at Milo's desk, with a Hawaiian pizza and a couple of Cokes. Kyla said, "I take it that Gordon is the brains of the operation, and you are the brawn?"

Milo finished his slice and reached for another. "Gordon is more the executive of the operation. I'm the labor," he offered sarcastically.

"And you're okay with that arrangement?"

Milo was defensive. "I knew what I was getting myself into."

Kyla sighed and leaned back in her chair. "I wish I could say the same about my job."

He softened, "How does someone get hired by the CIA anyway?"

"I was recruited," she answered. "I did my doctoral work at Columbia in Psychology, after studying International Relations as an undergrad in Toronto. My dad's a banker, and my mother's a therapist, so they pushed me to do well in school. When I was growing up, I got grounded if I ever brought home grades that weren't As. So I did well, and the Agency recruited me for the Behavioral division directly out of graduate school."

"And it's not what you thought it would be?"

"I wouldn't say that." She smiled crookedly. "But you've seen what my partner can be like to deal with."

Milo grinned. "Gordon and Dirkes, twin sons of different mothers. It's probably why they butted heads so much at first." They ate in silence for a while. Then Milo said, "So is this the type of thing you normally do? Watch over government contractors to make sure they do their jobs correctly?"

Kyla sighed. "I'm afraid that's not too far off the mark."

"Doesn't that get boring?"

She thought about it, then said, "Most of the time I'm confident that what we're doing is necessary, even if I don't know the exact reason. But my husband, whose whole family is in finance, doesn't agree. He seems to think I'm wasting my talents."

"If it's normal for you to spend weeks watching other people work, I'd have to agree."

"It sounds like you don't appreciate having us here."

"I'm sorry to sound rude," Milo said. "But I just don't see the point of it. Your being here isn't going to enable us to work any faster."

"Perhaps not," Kyla responded. "But hopefully it will help you grasp the seriousness of what you're dealing with."

CHAPTER NINE

If she'd been really honest about it, Kyla didn't much see the point, either. In fact, there were a number of things about working for the CIA that didn't sit well with her. Of course she never spoke of them to anyone but her husband. And yet, she couldn't tell even him everything, because he needed no further ammunition to support his crusade to get her to quit.

For starters, there was really no way to have been prepared for the immense and frustrating amount of bureaucracy she encountered once she signed on. Far from the spy movies that she grew up watching as a child in Toronto and upstate New York, there was little about her position within the Agency that was thrilling. Most of the time, she felt as though she was a glorified paper pusher, albeit a covert paper pusher. The field assignments she did go on, including the one that landed her in the warehouse at Hicks Limited, were by and large dull and tedious.

Then there was the matter of being a young woman of color in a field dominated by older white men. Despite the fact that it was no longer the 1970s, you might never know it from the way some of the men in the Agency acted. Discrimination was everywhere. In the mildest of scenarios, she was treated like a subtle joke, an uppity nuisance. In the worst cases she was treated with outright hostility, like a secretary who had forgotten her place. At Toronto University and at Columbia, she'd graduated at the top of her class. The fact that she was born of an Indian father and English mother, had dual citizenship in Canada and the US, lived in London for several years as a child, and traveled extensively before she was old enough to drive had all been part of a worldliness that made the CIA take notice. The fact that she spoke four languages didn't hurt either. It was part of the reason they recruited her. But once she had joined the ranks of the Behavioral division, none of that seemed to matter to her colleagues.

She was further troubled, after the events of September 11, 2001, to serve a government that pursued such a nakedly aggressive foreign policy in the name of national security, and by the swift tidal wave of hysteria that swept the country thereafter. An atmosphere of fear and paranoia had gripped both Washington and the nation at large, leading to injustices perpetrated against innocent people because they might look a certain way (usually not so different from how she looked), or come from a foreign land. There was tension all around, and one unfounded suggestion that you were not entirely in support of the unilateral military action in the Middle East could arouse suspicions about your sympathies – not unlike the Red Scare she had studied with fascination in her undergraduate history classes. Of course, she could speak of this to no one without being labeled a radical, and endangering her job. The past two years had been a troubling time for anyone with dark skin, whether or not they were a government employee. She'd already been stopped and searched at more airport security checkpoints than she could count. When field assignments took her and Walt outside of Washington, especially to non-urban areas, she always let him drive. When she didn't, she got pulled over and had her driver's license inspected almost every time.

As she settled into her hotel room at nine o'clock on a Friday night, she couldn't help feeling a mounting frustration. After pizza with Milo, she had turned down a cellphone offer to join Dirkes and Gordon at a club near the El Dorado. It struck her that the CIA was placing an unconscionable amount of faith in a spit-and-glue operation, which presented itself as comprised of three people, but in reality was clearly functioning as a result of the efforts of one person. She was incredibly concerned about Gordon, and she failed to understand why the agency allowed him to spend time at the warehouse at all. He didn't much contribute to the day-to-day operations of the enterprise, and was just the money behind things. Had it not been for what seemed to be a unique code written by Milo Caldwell, Gordon Hicks would never get that close to an operation.

Milo on the other hand, seemed to be so engulfed in a tunnel-vision state of mind about screening the data that he hardly seemed capable of parting with his computer. She couldn't tell if he had a home he went to at the end of the day. He was always there before she arrived, and was still working when she returned to her hotel. She would've felt sorry for him, had he not been so blatantly oblivious to how much his partner took advantage of him. But then, it wasn't her affair to get involved in these matters. She mostly observed (or, as her husband archly called it during their nightly phone calls, "babysat") and let Dirkes act out his alpha male showdowns with Gordon.

When everyone came into work on Saturday morning, a call from counterterror sources reported that there was new evidence pointing to another terror attack, but no one was giving any details. The only directive was to work the team faster. At first, Milo and Gordon acquiesced as much as possible, but by late morning they began to push back. Gordon, who never shied away from a good fight, led the charge. He told the Dirkes that even with enhanced computing capabilities, the most they could be expected to process effectively was seven or eight frames per day, as opposed to the ten the agency expected. As it was, they were going to be spending the week of Thanksgiving working twenty hours a day.

By Monday, November 24, four counterterrorism agents joined the group, and immediately set up a cluster of cubicles in the warehouse. Almost every hour, one of them received a phone call from an agency superior instructing them to push harder on the guys responsible for the processing. Three of the four new agents had PhDs, a fact that they immediately made known, along with their skepticism that Milo and Gordon actually knew what they were doing.

They told Gordon and Kathy White that their assignment was to vet the data that Milo was generating. Gordon made it clear that it was a colossal waste of time, because he was not giving them access to the room where Milo performed the processing. But the agents insisted that it was within the parameters of the licensing agreement to remain on the property, and that was that.

However, it soon became clear that maybe there was another reason for their presence. At one point, one of the agents disengaged from their desk cluster and strolled casually over to Milo. He asked offhandedly, "So, I understand that you only have an associate degree."

Milo didn't even look up from what he was doing. "That's right," he answered.

"You must've taken quite a lot of math at your community college."

"Some."

The agent nodded. "Then you must have a natural gift for it."

"I suppose I do."

"That would be one explanation."

This gave Milo pause. He met the agent's gaze. "I beg your pardon?"

The agent didn't blink. "We've just all been wondering how someone with, if you'll excuse the phrasing, such a limited education could have such an astute grasp of higher mathematics."

By this time Gordon too had begun to take notice. "What are you going on about?" The challenging note in his voice was obvious.

Milo said, "Are you suggesting that I've somehow fabricated these results?"

The agent put his hands up defensively. "No one's suggesting anything. It's just very unusual for someone of your background to have accomplished something of this magnitude." There was a barely-concealed smirk on his face as he said this.

Gordon stood up, his expression livid. The agent had clearly struck a nerve. "You've got some gall!" he barked. "You come in here and disturb the work we've been asked to do by your Agency, then you question our ability to do it? Why don't you go sit the fuck back down."

This roused the attention of the other agents, who made their way to their colleague. One of them asked, "What's going on here, Jerry?"

"I'll tell you what's going on!" Gordon yelled. "This son of a bitch is trying to tell us that we don't know how to do our job!"

"I simply asked about Mr. Caldwell's background," the first agent explained to the others.

Another agent spoke up. This one was less passive-aggressive and more openly aggressive than the first. "I still don't see how a guy with an AS degree is making all this happen," he said.

Gordon was nearly purple with rage. "No one has asked you to be here, so just get the fuck out."

The agent responded smugly, "In fact, the people who are cutting your goddamn paychecks asked us to be here."

Milo tried to make peace. "Let's all just calm down, it's tough on all of us to be here like this during Thanksgiving…" he said, doing his best to appease, though the accusations against him made his blood boil.

The second agent sneered. "Yeah, let's let the snake oil salesman get back to his work."

At this, Gordon went ballistic. "All right, you fucking eggheads," he yelled. "You think you're so much goddamned smarter than us? There – " He pointed to a whiteboard on the far wall. "Put a problem on the fucking board. If my guy solves it, then will you shut the fuck up?"

The agents considered, then agreed. After arguing amongst themselves for several minutes, they put a calculus problem on the board. Within minutes, Milo had solved it. The PhDs returned to their desks, muttering to themselves. Milo waited until their backs were turned and, wrote beneath the equation "Not bad for a guy with an AS degree."

Milo, still angry at the interchange, saw his opportunity and asked Gordon to join him outside. Gordon complied.

"I want my salary doubled, Gordon, I've got just as much invested in this project as you do. And now with all these clowns here… It isn't about the money, Gordon, it's about professional pride. You, of all people, should be able to appreciate that."

Gordon smiled and then snorted out a laugh. "Goddamn, my boy! I was half expecting you to offer me your resignation. Of course; consider it doubled." Gordon paused and then added, "You know, it's a relief to know that you're thinking like a killer, Milo. I always knew you had it in you."

The day finally ended and, though the agents were none too pleased to be away from home during Thanksgiving, it was agreed that the warehouse would be closed. Everyone went their own way, which meant that most of the counterterror guys arranged with an escort service to set up a party at one of the few high end dance clubs on Reno's strip. Kyla returned to her room at the El Dorado and spent Thursday watching the Macy's Thanksgiving parade, then Woody Allen's *Hannah and Her Sisters* and finally *Planes, Trains and Automobiles*. Walt would tell her later that he watched all three NFL games from a sports bar, and admitted to losing two grand on wagers.

Milo spent the day with his family somewhat flushed with the pleasure of seeing how he had leveraged his stakes on the day before. But as the day progressed, he became tired of the social etiquette required to be in a room full of loved ones. Inevitably, he began to think of work. He had hoped that he'd proven himself before both Gordon and the agents. He replayed the math showdown in his head, and imagined a scene on Friday morning where the educated agents would first apologize *en masse*, and then promise to leave him alone so he could do his job.

But when Friday morning rolled around, it was obvious that Wednesday's challenge had the opposite effect. They began to harass him even more. The lead bully of the group, Greg Richmond, came to Milo's desk twice an hour to goad him into working faster. After three days and six hours of watching the baiting, Kyla suddenly accosted him in front of the group. "What the hell is your problem, Richmond?" she demanded. "Why don't you stop micromanaging and let them do their job?"

She hadn't said much during her time in the warehouse, so the outburst caught everyone by surprise. There was a tense moment of silence while Richmond exchanged looks with his colleagues. "I'm under orders, same as you, Taylouni," he sputtered in response.

"Your actions are impeding the progress of their work," she said, her voice rising. "I will not sit idly by and watch you bully them when they're already under a tremendous amount of pressure."

One of the other agents said to Dirkes, "You better get your partner under control, Walt. Sounds like she's forgetting who signs her paychecks."

Dirkes, surprised as anyone else's by Kyla's strong reaction, said softly, "They're just following orders, Taylouni."

Kyla retorted, "Orders to hassle a government contractor?"

"Whose side are you on, anyway, maybe it's your time of the month?" Richmond turned vile and moved toward Kyla. An obvious attempt at intimidation.

"First, Richmond, grow up and second, 'side?' I repeat: I will not sit here and watch you interfere with the work of these people."

"Work? You call this work?" Richmond gestured wildly around the room. "Look at this two-bit joke of an operation! Do you actually believe they're doing anything worth a shit here?"

Gordon and Milo watched it all go down from across the room, and this latest insult drew Gordon's ire. He shouted from across the floor. "What are you suggesting now, asshole?"

Just then the security door signaled, and Kathy White appeared. She had returned from seeing to her once again sick child. "What am I missing now?" she joked.

Richmond returned to Gordon's provocation. "You know exactly what I'm talking about. This phony set-up you've got here. You expect us to believe that you and that college dropout partner of yours have actually created software that somehow detects code in television broadcasts? – something no one in the counterterrorism unit has been able to achieve? This is a farce, is what this is. A sham. And you know it!"

Gordon yelled back, "You're nothing but an impotent, frustrated middle-level bureaucrat who can't even dream of achieving what we've done here."

Richmond went red in the face. "You're bilking the government out of millions of dollars, you filthy fucking liar! I know who you are, we all know who you are! You're one of those Grant McKinley bastards who ripped off innocent citizens who trusted you and now you're trying to rip off the U.S. government!"

"Sit down!" Gordon screamed. "You have no idea who you're dealing with! I'll have you fucking fired!"

As they traded insults, each man had advanced on the other until they met in the middle of the floor. The screaming match continued for the better part of an hour. Finally, spent, they retreated to their respective sides of the warehouse to rest. Dirkes came to the middle of the floor and proposed that everyone call it a day. "We'll meet in the morning," he said, "at 9:00 a.m. Hopefully that will give us all the opportunity to cool down, so we can come to the table peacefully and work all this out."

Kathy chuckled and said quietly, "These other nuts almost make this guy look reasonable."

The agents left in a huff. Kyla and Dirkes followed shortly thereafter. Gordon, whose blood pressure had yet to subside, muttered, "I need a drink. Anyone else feel the same?" Kathy said she would join him. Milo declined, insisting he had a few things to finish up.

Gordon stood over him, looking drained for the first time since Milo had met him. He said, "Son, I'm not normally one to make this type of suggestion, but for your own good I really think you should call it a day."

"I won't be too long," Milo insisted. "It'll take me thirty minutes tops to finish up. I'll be out of here by three, three-thirty at the latest." He felt a headache coming on and he needed to be by himself for a while.

Gordon shook his head but said nothing further. He and Kathy left. With all the shouting in previous days, the silence in the warehouse was noticeable in its fullness. Milo leaned back in his chair for some time, his head tilted at an angle, his face covered by his hands. He remained that way for several minutes. He considered the presence of all of the Agency staff, calculated the possible reasons for why, on one hand, they would sign such a large contract, and then do almost everything to provoke animosity. He considered the possibility that they indeed needed to challenge everything. That there might be something brewing on the terrorism front, and that this was their way of weeding out confirmation bias.

The other possibility that he didn't want to consider was that they were there to glean whatever they could in the prospect of surreptitiously securing the software. Were they trying to look for clues and ways they could reverse engineer the framework? They sure asked a lot of questions in that regard. The only reasonable tactic he had was to continue to keep the software proprietary. Every process, every day's output had to be safeguarded. God, now his head was really hurting and he realized he'd become as paranoid as his father. Then, with a squeak of his chair, he leaned forward and got back to work. For a long while, the only sound was the clicking of his fingers over the keyboard.

The phone at his desk rang so suddenly that it made him jump. This was a phone that was never used, never got calls. It rang twice, three times. He peered down at the caller ID. It was a blocked number. He sat deciding whether or not to answer it, when at last he reached for it and the ringing stopped.

Thirty seconds later it rang again. He picked it up. "This is Milo," he said.

At first there was no answer, just a few quiet pops on the other end. Then a low whirring noise. He responded, "Hello?"

A voice that was more machine than human said, "The raid is tomorrow."

"Who is this?"

"Early morning, tomorrow." The voice was low and distorted, mechanical. "The CIA raid on the warehouse is tomorrow."

"Who is this?" Milo demanded.

"Don't ask questions," the voice rebuked him. "Just listen. All the computing equipment will be confiscated. Your business with the government will be terminated. You will be blacklisted. Everything you've worked for will be gone."

Milo looked around him, as if there might be agents lurking in the shadows. His heart was suddenly pounding in his chest, and he could've sworn that the sound echoed through the warehouse. He lowered his voice and spoke into the phone. "Why are you telling me this? What should I do?"

"Disassemble the software. Download the data from everything, including the backup. Wipe it clean and then hide the source code."

"But what if they find it? Where am I supposed to hide it?"

There was no answer.

"Hello?"

Whoever had been on the other end was gone.

CHAPTER TEN

Friday night, November 28, 2003

❖ ❖ ❖

Gordon and Kathy hustled back to the warehouse when they received Milo's frantic phone call. He wouldn't go into details over the phone, but told them that they needed to return immediately. When they arrived he relayed the warning he'd been given, and they sprang into action.

"Pull the hard drives from your server," Kathy suggested in a panic. "Then remove the back-ups."

Once Milo had finished, he grabbed other encrypted disks that contained portions of the source code on them and he asked, "Where am I supposed to hide this stuff?"

It was Gordon's who took charge. "You leave that up to me," he answered, taking the disks and hard drives from Milo. He left the warehouse and returned forty-five minutes later, smoking a cigarette. "Now, let's try not to get jumpy," he instructed the other two. "Everyone go home and have a nice dinner, drink a glass of wine, take a soak in the hot tub. Take a goddamn sleeping pill if you need to. We all want to be rested and have our wits about us in the morning."

Milo did as he was told, though he had difficulty falling asleep. At 4:00 AM, after a fitful night's slumber, he dressed and made himself some coffee for his thermos mug before driving to the warehouse. Gordon and Kathy were there when he pulled up.

Kathy kept watch from the window near the back door. At 5:30, she reported that half a dozen black SUVs had pulled up in the adjacent open field, and were all pointed at the warehouse. Winter exhaust poured from each running vehicle. Gordon smelled like he'd been chain smoking non-stop since the previous afternoon. Without thought, he stubbed out his cigarette in the overflowing ashtray on his desk and lit another one. "Everybody cool, calm and collected?" he asked cryptically.

It took an hour for the CIA team to finally come through the doors. Kyla and Dirkes were among them, as were the four counterterrorism agents who had taken up residence. Richmond led the group. "Gentlemen, Ms. White, please step away from your desks."

Gordon didn't budge, didn't even look up from his desk. "Go fuck yourself, Richmond," he answered, loud enough for all to hear. "You can't act like this on US soil. Where's your FBI counterpart? You can't execute squat without them."

Richmond went white. "This is a Federal raid!" he shouted. "Step away from your goddamn desk! It's not a suggestion!"

Milo and Kathy had stood and moved away the first time they'd been told. At length, Gordon rose with a dramatic roll of the eyes and followed suit. Richmond ordered several of the agents onto the computers that the three had occupied. While they busied themselves Gordon baited them, "Can I offer anyone some coffee while you're here? Doughnuts?"

"Just be quiet," Richmond told him.

"Any idea how long this is going to take?" Gordon continued. "We're really quite busy and you're interrupting our work."

"I said 'keep your goddamn mouth shut'!" Richmond bellowed. Several moments passed. Then he growled impatiently at the men navigating the computers. "What's taking so long?"

The agent at Milo's desk looked up uncertainly. "The hard drives don't have anything on them," he answered.

At this, both Richmond and Dirkes lost their composure, shouting, "What?!"

"There's nothing on this one either," another at Gordon's desk reported.

Richmond turned on the three standing innocently by. "What did you do with it?"

Gordon savored his answer. "I guess that's none of your business, now is it? The software is our property. You're paying us for operations and output. You don't have any claim to it."

Richmond's eyes glowered. "Now you listen to me, Hicks, what we are doing here is a matter of national security. You just don't get it, we can do whatever it takes to keep this work in play. And you know that what we are beginning to work on here is something that neither of us want the FBI to know about. They will take these secret payments we've been making to you and turn them over to the Department of Treasury. You don't want the IRS looking into your books."

Gordon cut him off. "No, you listen. This ends here. We've put up with all the meddling we're going to take from you and your band of cocksuckers. Either you get your precious Deputy Director Welding out here immediately and have him ask us nicely to continue, or we shut this whole thing down today."

Richmond gritted his teeth, "Look, I'm certain the two of you are the con artists of the fucking century, but I got orders and those orders are to take this down today."

"You want to try, motherfucker?" Gordon shot back.

Dirkes detached from the group and came to Richmond's side. "Let's let Welding deal with this."

It was as though he were trying to split up a dogfight between canines with locked jaws and indefatigable resolve. At length, Richmond came away unwillingly. He shook visibly with anger from head to toe. Dirkes put in a phone call, and after conversing for several minutes announced that the CIA deputy director would board a plane from Washington that afternoon.

Gordon had another trick up his sleeve. From the very beginning when Colonel Marks and the Air Force had first made contact with them, Hicks had stayed in touch with his friend Bob Montefusco, the US House Representative for the Reno area.

Montefusco was currently serving on the House Intelligence Committee, and it so happened that he was at home in Reno during Thanksgiving/Christmas adjournment. Before the deputy director's arrival, Gordon put in a call to the Representative and asked him to join them in the warehouse. When Montefusco arrived, the agents lost it.

"What the fuck is he doing here?" Richmond demanded.

"I wasn't aware that my presence here violates any laws," Montefusco answered coldly.

Dirkes interceded. "Representative Montefusco, this is a Federal operation. I suggest you leave immediately."

Montefusco replied, "I will do no such thing. My role as a member of the Intelligence Committee is to oversee the CIA, and that's what I'm here to do." The agents fell silent, left with no choice but cooperation. Once the agents resigned themselves to the fact that nothing would happen until Welding arrived, Montefusco shook Gordon's hand and retreated back to a holiday party downtown.

Daniel Welding, the deputy director, a bookish-looking man, arrived at seven o'clock that evening. When he entered the warehouse, the group of agents began moving toward him in a group. But Gordon shouted, "Hold it right there!" and everyone froze. Gordon continued, "He came all this way to talk to me so he's going to talk to me. I want everyone out of here except for the director and myself." The agents looked to Welding en masse for permission to comply, and he nodded solemnly. Milo and Kathy had risen to leave the warehouse as well. Gordon put a hand on Milo's shoulder. "You stay put. I need a witness for this."

Once the warehouse emptied, Gordon addressed Welding directly. "I'm sure your agents have already given you their side of things."

Welding adjusted his glasses. "They have, Mr. Hicks. I can imagine you have a different take on the matter."

"I'm not going to waste your time by pointing fingers," Gordon replied. "All you need to know is this: we know exactly what our software's value is to the government, and we know exactly how much you need it. We're not going to play any more fucking games with your boneheaded thugs. We could shut down this whole operation today without the slightest scrap of remorse." He paused to light the cigarette that he'd withdrawn from his shirt pocket as he spoke. "I have absolutely no qualms about letting this deal go. I was relentlessly hounded by the government for ten years of my life. I'm sure you know all about that. It cost me $28 million to defend myself against that assault. I'm not going through this type of harassment again."

"What is it we can do to make this right, Mr. Hicks?" Welding asked, his voice weary.

Gordon considered for a moment, taking a long drag on his cigarette. He answered, "I want an apology."

"Mr. Hicks," Welding said, "you have my sincerest apology. I will personally guarantee that you will not be bothered by the agents any further."

"No." Gordon took another drag on his cigarette. "It's not just the agents. It's the whole goddamn thing. I want you down on your hands and knees, and I don't mean that figuratively. If you don't offer me a legitimate apology for this ongoing witch hunt that I've been subjected to, I pull the plug right now. Then, when you get off the floor, you are going to write and sign a letter of agreement, on my letterhead, that says the agency will not make any further attempt to take technology, or any property or assets owned by Hicks Ltd. You will sign this agreement here and now and we will scan your business card onto the record to confirm your assent."

You could have heard a pin drop in the silence that followed. Milo, stunned, hardly dared to breathe. Welding sighed, and then slowly lowered himself onto the floor until he lay prostrate before them. "Please, Mr. Hicks, we need you," he begged, albeit quietly. "I promise that you will be left in peace. Please forgive us for everything that you've been put through. On the behalf of the United States government, I apologize humbly and beg for your understanding."

Gordon smiled, relishing the moment. He looked over at Milo, who couldn't bring himself to meet his gaze. He kept his eyes to the floor, embarrassed by this outrageous display.

Leisurely Gordon said, "Very well, Mr. Welding. You may get up now." Welding lifted himself off the floor. "There will be no negotiation. If you want us to proceed it's going to cost you $100 million."

The director paused before replying, "All right."

"And I want those PhD idiots out of here. Dirkes and the woman agent can stay if they must, but they will keep out of our way. They are not to disturb us."

"Fine."

"And there's one more thing," Gordon continued. "We need greater computing capacity. You've got us working as a commercial enterprise without the proper tools. If you want to expedite this process, and your agents have made it very clear that that is what you want, we need faster servers. And we need them soon."

"I can have them here within 48 hours," Welding said.

As Welding was leaving the warehouse he was met by the lead agents, Walt and Kyla. Walt asked, "What does he want you to do?"

"What the fuck does it matter?" answered Welding cooly. "We do what we have to do until that source code is ours."

Later that evening, Milo accompanied Gordon to where he had hidden the locked safety deposit box that contained the CDs and hard drives. They were dug and buried at a mile marker on an otherwise unremarkable stretch of road leading away from the warehouse. All the way back into town, Gordon was in a foul mood; his temporary euphoria was replaced by a focused frown. As he drove, he chewed a toothpick on one side of his mouth, while drawing on a cigarette on the other. Milo finally got up the courage to ask Gordon what was bothering him. Gordon looked straight forward for a while, thinking. Finally he took a deep breath, drew down the driver's side window and spit the toothpick out the window. Waiting until the electric button had successfully closed the window, he gave it up. "I asked for too little back there. Did you see how quickly he agreed? A classic rookie mistake. I guess I've lost my touch."

They drove back to the warehouse in silence.

CHAPTER ELEVEN

December 2, 2003

✸ ✸ ✸

On Tuesday, a large truck carrying a trailer arrived at the warehouse. The delivery crew began unloading the equipment, following Milo's directions. Each stack stood eight feet tall and contained one hundred of the highest-speed computers available. They also set up fifty additional freestanding high-speed computers that could be used until the blade servers had been completely assembled.

During the unloading process, a car arrived at the warehouse carrying three FBI agents. They introduced themselves and told Milo that it was their responsibility to supervise the equipment setup. The senior agent then saw Dirkes and Taylouni at their desks. Counting five employees instead of three, he called, "May I see your clearance badges, please?"

Dirkes answered, "I should be asking you for the same. This is a Company station. We've been here the past month."

"Not anymore," the senior FBI agent said. "Your agency has no jurisdiction while you're on U.S. soil. While the installation is taking place, we'll be taking over the security and supervision of set up."

"Like hell you will!" Dirkes retaliated. "This facility is Agency property, and if you don't leave immediately I'll have you arrested!"

The FBI agent was not to be denied either, "Well, let's see who ends up on the hind tit!" He turned to his associate, "Get Mueller on the phone."

Each side called its respective superiors, and in the end the FBI packed up and left the building, taking the hired workers with them. Gordon and Milo stood among the unloaded boxes. Milo said, "It's not like these things come with an installation manual. It will take forever to set these blade servers up."

Gordon got on the phone with their Air Force liaison and arranged to have Dr. Sydney Montgomery, an Air Force mathematician, come to Reno to coordinate the server setup. Unlike the nasty bunch of characters they had encountered of late, Montgomery was knowledgeable, professional, and understood the pressure they were under. He calmly asked about the method for using the detection and anomaly software, and agreed that it was a brilliant and impressive program. While he and his team of Air Force technology experts built the new servers, the first week of December buzzed with military personnel. Soon, hearing about the possibilities of the software's capacity, the NSA sent personnel to review things as well. All the agencies agreed that while the CIA took lead on the work, some form of coordinated effort could be possible to keep the program secret, and to still explore what Montgomery thought was an unbelievable software.

By December 7, the business end of the arrangement was set up as a Special Operations Command project. There was a covert budget for this type of innovation; it benefitted from few layers of oversight, and SOCOM always handled the details side of the fiscal process. In another part of Reno, a second company called the Clark Silver Corporation (CSC) was doing top-secret work of their own. SOCOM directed CSC's owner, Steven Kraft, to write Hicks Limited a check each month for $250,000, no questions asked. By Monday, the eighth, they received their first check.

During that same time, Montgomery's team made progress on the blade server installation, while Milo continued to process data on their smaller system. Gordon continued to chain smoke and follow Milo around asking questions. Once Montgomery salved all egos during this first week, Gordon backed down and agreed to have more CIA personnel on the property, provided the agents stayed at arms' length till the first thing in the morning. On the morning of December 9, at 3:00 a.m., Milo began to generate a report on the images he had scanned. That day and each thereafter, the agents would send these images by a dedicated broadband to Langley, Virginia. Milo was told that by 5:00 a.m. each day, Reno time, the Director of the Central Intelligence Agency, George Tenet, had been apprised of the work and that Tenet would regularly brief President Bush.

Later that morning, after Milo had grabbed a nap on his couch, Dirkes approached him with a tape that appeared to be older than all the previous files. The tape was a twenty-minute clip of an Al-Jazeera broadcast that originated from Saudi Arabia. The videotape contained eighteen hundred frames per minute, and this clip had almost 40,000 frames to be analyzed individually. After a consultation, Dirkes directed Milo to pull fifty random frames for individual analysis. He was to use one of the other, older versions of the software to run this scan, while the current files were run on the newer system.

The newscast in question was from July of 2001. Milo began the scanning process: each time he completed a frame, he uploaded the data into a spreadsheet. Most of the frames contained little or no coding, but as he made progress on the assigned frames, he began to notice a pattern developing – a code that repeated itself a dozen times. After the verbal lashing he had received from Dirkes the first time he had noticed such a pattern, he immediately looked up these coordinates. They matched the location of the World Trade Center in New York. Further in the scan, the coordinates began to show up dated for September 11, 2001, repeating themselves.

Milo hurried across the floor to tell Dirkes and Taylouni what he had found. At first they stared at him disbelievingly, without answering. Then Dirkes said slowly, "Are you sure?"

"In the last day and a half I see the same pattern repeated twenty times in nine of the sixteen frames I've scanned." Milo answered.

Dirkes swore under his breath and looked at Kyla. "Suppose we better call the DD's office." He got on the phone and Milo returned to his desk. Within ten minutes both agents' Blackberries and pagers were blowing up with messages. From across the floor Milo could tell that his findings had resulted in all hell breaking loose in Washington. He suddenly felt very claustrophobic and sick to his stomach. He told Gordon he was going to step outside for some air.

In the parking lot he sat on the hood of his car and looked at the chilly desert sky. The sun had just set, and the stars began to show faintly. A bone-chilling wind began to pick up, and he shivered. He was about to go back inside when the front door opened and Kyla came out, holding a cigarette. She paused in the shelter of the doorway to light it. Her hands were fidgety. Seeing Milo, a look of guilt crossed her face.

"I'm not normally a smoker," she confessed. "Only when I get very stressed out. I bummed one from Gordon."

"It sounded like the findings from that Al-Jazeera tape caused quite a stir."

Kyla laughed humorlessly. "You can say that again. Tenet nearly hit the ceiling."

"What is the big deal, exactly?"

Kyla blew smoke into the frigid wind, which pushed it back into her face. She coughed once. "There's a panel on Capitol Hill right now that's trying to determine whether anyone in the CIA could have known about 9/11 before the fact and failed to act. What you found looks bad for us."

"But this detection software didn't even exist in 2001," Milo countered. "Finding the information now doesn't prove anything."

Kyla took another drag. "That doesn't really matter," she said. "Heads will roll regardless."

She dropped the remaining half of the cigarette and ground it into the pavement with her shoe. They went back inside. As soon as they entered the warehouse, Dirkes was on them. "Orders just came down from Washington," he said to Milo. "You're to destroy those results immediately."

Milo was too stunned to respond. Kyla answered, "You can't be serious."

"Orders were from Tenet directly. You will need to act this moment."

Milo found his voice. "But--wouldn't that be destroying evidence?"

Dirkes drew himself up and frowned. "This is not up for discussion, Mr. Caldwell." Milo looked to Kyla for help. She stood shaking her head in disbelief but said nothing further. Dirkes accompanied him to his computer and stood over him as he sat. "You're to delete everything pertaining to this file." Milo thought that Gordon might intervene here, but he too was silent. Apparently, in choosing his battles, this was one he decided to sit out. Milo deleted the files.

What the agents didn't know – and what Gordon and Kathy didn't know, for that matter – was that from the first day, Milo had been generating a backdoor copy of everything he'd worked on. The files he deleted were no exception. At first, he had done it as a technical precaution, should a glitch occur or a virus impact the system. It now dawned on him that he was in sole possession of extremely sensitive and potentially volatile information – and thanks to his incredibly geekish predilections, he might have also become an enemy of the state.

The anxiety of now knowing that two separate terror acts had been communicated beforehand by way of Al-Jazeera pushed the intelligence officers to a new level of ferocity. The next day they brought in dozens of broadcast tapes from days and weeks previous to the months leading up to September 2001. They also began recording the live Al-Jazeera broadcast originating in Saudi Arabia, and put an agent with the tape on a plane from Saudi Arabia to Reno with the day-old footage. Milo was instructed not only to process the September and October 2003 footage, but also to catch up with the most current newscasts.

On Friday and Saturday, the transmissions of the previous week began to show a pattern of the number C4 repeating itself. Milo reported this information to the agents.

"What do you think it means?" Kyla wondered aloud.

Milo didn't say anything. Dirkes, also looking at the spreadsheet, said, "Could it be C4 plastic explosive?" He lowered the document and looked Milo in the eye. "What's your best guess?"

"With all due respect, I don't know anything about this kind of stuff," Milo answered.

Dirkes pressed him. "Well, make an educated guess."

"I can't, I'm sorry."

Dirkes grew impatient. "You've been analyzing this stuff for weeks. How can you really not have formed some opinion of their meaning in all that time?"

Milo's voice rose. "We've been over this before. I've got enough on my hands trying to process these frames as it is! It's two weeks until Christmas and I'd like to get my work done so that I have some hope of getting home to my family, so if you don't mind I'd rather not play your goddamn guessing games and do my job instead!"

This outburst surprised everyone, including Milo himself. Despite the tremendous amount of pressure they had been under for months, he had always maintained his composure, often letting Gordon do the fighting for him. But now, with the end of the year approaching, the possibility looming that he may not have time to spend with his family on Christmas, he felt he was about to snap. The spreadsheet lay sprawled across his desk with the phrase "C4, C4, C4" repeating itself until it sounded like a bell clanging deafeningly inside his brain.

The following Monday, December 15, 2003, the director of

Homeland Security, Tom Ridge, called a press conference to announce that recent intelligence gathering had indicated that a terrorist attack may be imminent on U.S. soil. As a result, the Homeland Threat Level was upgraded to Orange. The following day, an unnamed source within Homeland Security told the press that there was evidence that a terrorist plot was planned for Christmas day. In the days leading up to Christmas, Milo continued to process scans upwards of twenty hours per day. He stumbled home and into bed at 3:00 a.m., and by 5:00 a.m., the data had been sent to Washington and the agency would call him back into work.

The week before Christmas, Montgomery completed the installation and setup of the blade servers. "These are incredible machines," he told Gordon and Milo. "They're going to speed up processing time by twenty-five to thirty per cent." He gave one of the machines an affectionate pat, as though he were the trainer of a prized stallion about to embark on its first race. "The one thing to be aware of in advance, though, is that these things run hot. I'd suggest opening the rolling door to cool things off."

The blade servers were put to use the following day, and the temperature in the warehouse rose to more than 100 degrees. Gordon and Milo cranked open the loading dock door in the cargo area, and the chilly December wind provided some relief. However, they both realized they would have a problem on their hands with the approach of summer. Dirkes got the Air Force liaison, Eric O'Bannon, on the phone, and both agreed to requisition an industrial grade air conditioning unit through fast track channels at Big Safari.

On Christmas Eve, Milo rose just before 3:00 a.m. to head to the office as usual. This time, however, as he was about to get out of bed, he felt Natalie's hand on his arm.

"What time will you finish work today?" she whispered in the darkness.

"I don't know yet," he whispered back. "I'll try my best to be out at eight."

At first she didn't answer. "Milo, it's Christmas Eve."

"Don't you think I know that? All I can say is that I'll do my best."

"I know how much stress you've been under," Natalie responded. "And I know how important this is to you. But I want to make sure you understand that your work life doesn't affect you alone. It affects all of us. We haven't had a meal together, you and me and the kids, in months."

Milo threw back the covers in exasperation and stood up. "Jesus Christ, Natalie!" he said. "You think you know how much stress I've been under? You have no goddamn idea. You couldn't even begin to imagine. I've been busting my ass to support this family – eating takeout every damn night, sleeping in my car; my goddamn hair is falling out. You think I'm doing this just for kicks?"

"All I'm saying," Natalie retaliated, raising her voice to match his, "is that you do have a choice. You're not a slave. And I'm asking you to choose to be with us tonight, on Christmas Eve."

"So you're saying that I choose to work twenty hours a day," Milo shot back. "Just for the fun of it?"

Natalie went quiet, then said steadily, "You gotta live with your choices, Milo."

Milo stood silently for some time in the darkness beside the bed. Then, in a voice filled with bitterness, he said, "Go back to sleep." He dressed hurriedly and left. Natalie listened to him descend two flights of stairs into the garage below. The garage door could be heard faintly laboring open, and soon he had driven off into the pre-dawn blackness and was gone.

CHAPTER TWELVE

Christmas Eve 2003

❀ ❀ ❀

Milo went through the day silent and terse, speaking barely a word to anyone. The agents had a three-day Christmas break, returning home to spend the holiday with their respective spouses. Kathy busied herself at her desk, and Gordon was in a jovial mood, humming cheerfully to himself and smoking a noxious cigar. Finally Milo snapped, "Gordon, do you mind taking that somewhere else? It stinks like hell."

Gordon chuckled, having never been spoken to this way by his partner. "What's eating you, kid?" he asked.

"Nothing." Milo lapsed again into a moody silence.

Gordon looked at the clock, which read ten minutes after three. Then he rapped his knuckles on his desk loudly. "It's Christmas Eve, folks. Let's make a pact to be out of here in an hour."

"Speak for yourself," Milo replied sullenly. "I have too much work to do."

Gordon looked at him closely. "My boy, I never thought in my whole life that I would say this to anyone, but you're working too hard."

Milo shot him an irritated glance. "Well, what am I supposed to do? The 'war on terror' is counting on me."

"Fuck the war," Gordon said. "Why don't you close up shop and get home to your family?" When Milo didn't budge he asked casually, "Everything all right at home?"

Milo grumbled, "Everything is fine."

Gordon nodded understandingly. "In the doghouse, eh? Wives don't understand what it means to have to work your ass off, of course. When Julip can be bothered to notice the hours I keep, she likes nothing better than to give me hell about it." He thought a moment. "Say, Julip and I are going to a show at the Peppermill after dinner. Why don't you join us? Give yourself a break, recharge your batteries, then go home and be with your family."

"Thanks, Gordon, but – "

"Now look." Gordon's tone turned suddenly stern. "I'm not just trying to be kind here. You're the most important asset I've got in this whole operation, and if you're going to be any use to me, I need you to not give yourself a heart attack. You can't keep going this way. It's thirty-six hours off, and then you can throw yourself back into things the day after Christmas. But I will not stand idly by and watch you kill yourself for these bastards in DC."

Milo leaned back in his chair and sighed. "What's the show?" he asked without enthusiasm.

"Hammerhead, that god-awful comedian. Julip picked it; I don't ask questions. We've got front row seats, in any case. It'll be something to get your mind off all this shit for a few hours, at least." Milo hesitated. "Come on, take the edge off," Gordon prodded him. "It won't help things at home to have you acting like a sore sonofabitch on Christmas Eve."

"I suppose you're right..."

"Of course I'm right," Gordon said genially. "Now, get back to work for another hour and we'll head out after."

At four o'clock, Julip picked them up in Gordon's Rolls Corniche. She had a friend with her whom Julip introduced as Michelle. At first Milo was concerned that Gordon had set him up on a double date, but Michelle failed to show the slightest interest in him.

"Hop in back, girls," Gordon told them. "The men want to ride in front." Milo thought Julip might protest, but she and Michelle giggled and did as they were told.

They arrived at the Peppermill and were greeted, as usual, by an overbearing Stagnaro. As he led them toward the theater, he asked what they'd like to drink. Gordon ordered a martini, while Julip and Michelle ordered cosmopolitans. When Milo began to request a beer, Gordon cut him off. "We'll have none of that," he said dismissively. "Staggs, get my friend here a whiskey on the rocks."

Milo protested. "I don't really drink that kind of thing."

Gordon nodded. "Exactly. And that, my boy, is why you are so tightly wound."

Their seats were front and center of the theater. Drinks arrived as they were seated. While they waited for the show to start, people kept coming to Gordon to say hello. Julip and Michelle were engaged in what appeared to be a deep conversation, leaving Milo with nothing to do but focus on his drink, which he finished quickly. Before he knew what was happening, a waitress brought him another.

The lights went down, and the theater erupted into applause as Hammerhead took the stage. His signature wild red hair looked even wilder and redder in person, and his eyes bulged out of his head as he surveyed the audience. "How are you all doing tonight, you bunch of stuck-up pricks?" he asked the room. Everyone laughed and applauded.

Normally Milo didn't find Hammerhead's crude signature style to be funny at all, but as he finished his second and third whiskey he discovered he was starting to enjoy himself. As the night wore on, he heard himself laughing louder than any of his companions. He made a mental note to himself to drink a few cups of strong black coffee before heading home after the show.

Towards the end of the act, Julip and Michelle made a trip to the ladies' room. Hammerhead's eyes zeroed in on them as they walked up the aisle. He pointed to them and hollered into the microphone, "Take a look at these two sluts!"

The audience laughed appreciatively, and the two women paused to smile and laugh along. From his seat Gordon grumbled, "All right, asshole, keep the act moving." Hammerhead continued with his routine. However, later, when Julip and Michelle were returning to their seats, Hammerhead again singled them out. "Take these two bitches, for example," he said. "You can tell by their coked-out faces that they can't tell their cunts from a hole in the ground."

Fewer people laughed this time, and at once Gordon was on his feet. "You take that back, you worthless piece of dog shit!"

People craned their necks to see who was shouting in the front row. Hammerhead yelled into the microphone, "Look everybody, it's their pimp. Looks like he wants me to come down and kick my ass."

"Come and say that to my face!" Gordon yelled back.

"The monkey speaks!" Hammerhead wisecracked to the audience at large.

"Get your ass down here and fight like a real man, you fucking pansy!"

It didn't take much prodding. Hammerhead dropped the microphone and scrambled off the stage, rushing toward Gordon. Julip screamed. Before Hammerhead could reach his intended target, however, Milo stepped into his periphery and delivered a swift punch that hit him square in the jaw. All at once a flurry of security guards was on them, and Milo felt himself wrestled to the ground. As he lay for a moment with his face buried in the carpet, he could hear Gordon shouting, "Do you have any idea who I am? I'll have you all fired!"

They soon found themselves in the casino manager's office, surrounded by a wall of security guards. When the manager heard what had happened, he was furious.

"Don't you shitheads know what an important guest Mr. Hicks is?" He screamed at them, the veins in his neck bulging. He turned to Gordon and beseeched him desperately, "Mr. Hicks, I cannot even begin to express how deeply we regret this incident. I assure you that these gentlemen," here he indicated the wall of security guards, whose eyes smoldered with anger but who stood silently by, "…will be dealt with accordingly."

"Damn right," Gordon murmured, wiping his brow with a handkerchief. "And I don't want to see that so-called comedian within a hundred miles of this town."

"You can rest assured: he won't be welcomed back here!"

"And I want my man here compensated adequately for being tackled by your goons." Gordon put a hand on Milo's shoulder. Milo, for his part, was still reeling from the multiple whiskeys he'd consumed.

One of the guards could not hold his tongue. He burst out, "Boss, we were just – "

The manager silenced him with a warning glance. Then he addressed Milo. "How can we make this up to you, Mr. Caldwell?"

"Just get me a cup of coffee for now," he muttered.

It was well after midnight by the time Milo got home. Natalie was waiting for him. Before she could speak, he said, "No lectures, please.

I've had a hell of a night."

"I wasn't going to lecture you," Natalie said softly. "I just wanted to know if you'd already eaten. There's some leftover meatloaf in the refrigerator."

Milo sat heavily in the chair opposite her. "I'm not hungry. I just need to go to bed."

"Will you have to work tomorrow?"

"At this point, I don't really give a shit." He didn't normally speak like this in front of Natalie. She noticed but said nothing. "Did the kids open their gifts already?"

"No," she answered. "They wanted to wait for you."

He nodded and looked at the Christmas tree glowing softly in the corner of the room, not far from Natalie. He walked over to it, pausing to look at the bright packages neatly arranged beneath the boughs. Normally, decorating the tree was something they did as a family, but this year they'd done it without him.

"Looks nice this year," he commented.

He stood a few feet from Natalie, who suddenly stiffened in her seat. She said slowly, "Have you been drinking?"

He didn't answer at first. Then, "I had a bit at work."

"A bit? You reek. If someone dropped a match near you, you'd go up in flames."

"It's been a rough couple of weeks." With this, he turned and started upstairs to their bedroom. Natalie followed him and watched as he changed into his pajamas and brushed his teeth.

"So let me see if I understand this correctly. You didn't have time to come home and spend Christmas Eve with your family, but you had time to go out and get drunk?"

"For the love of God, Natalie, can't this wait? I've got a splitting headache."

"Well, I've got no sympathy for that."

Milo threw up his hands in frustration. "Fine. Tell me what it is you want me to say and I'll say it."

"I just want to know what you did after work."

"I went to a show with Gordon and Julip."

"How much did you have to drink?"

"I don't know."

"You don't know?"

"I lost count."

They were silent for several minutes. Natalie said, "Anything else you'd like to add?"

He considered his response before answering, "I got tackled by security."

"You what?!"

"It's a long story, and I'm not kidding when I say my head is killing me."

He climbed into bed and settled back with a pained look on his face. Natalie remained standing, with her arms crossed over her chest. When she spoke it was very measured and deliberate. "Sometimes I feel like I don't really know you at all." He didn't respond. "When I think of the way things have been going over the last year..."

"I don't hear you complaining about your new house," he interrupted her. "Or your new car. Or any of your new clothes. Or the fact that neither of the kids will have to take out loans for college."

"Don't put that on me," she countered.

"No, what you're saying is that you want it both ways. You want all the perks of a $200,000 income without the necessary sacrifices."

"Don't lecture me, Milo."

"Then don't be so dense, Natalie."

She recoiled as if she had been stung. Then she said in a hardened voice, "Maybe it would be better if you slept in the guest room tonight."

"Fine," he said angrily, getting out of bed. Natalie watched him leave the room and close the door hard.

Upon entering, he realized that since they'd moved in, he'd hardly set foot in the guest room. Natalie had taken charge of decorating, and she'd given this room a beach theme. The walls were covered with a seashell print. A framed photograph on one wall showed a weather-beaten picket fence on a sand drift with waves in the distance. Milo lay down on the bed, which creaked loudly. It was the first chance he'd had all night to lay down. He soon felt the room spinning. He propped himself up on a pillow and focused on the photograph. The longer he looked, the more certain he was that he heard waves lapping on the beach. Soon he was dozing, and he dreamed of walking on a long and endless beach, seemingly without point of origin or destination.

That same Christmas Eve, on the other side of the country, Kyla

Taylouni drank a glass of white wine and watched the news. Due in part to Milo's findings the week before, the frenzy in Washington had reached a fever pitch. Agency field staff was notified that conflict had arisen between Washington and the French government over a commercial airline flight out of Paris that Christmas morning. The 8:20 a.m. plane to New York already in flight over the Atlantic had a suspected terrorist on board. There was enough scuttlebutt within ranks, that many believed the Air Force would not let the plane enter U.S. air space. Odds were that if the French government didn't direct the flight to turn around, fighter jets were going to intercept the plane and shoot it down short of the east coast. As she pondered the situation, she had the television tuned to CNN to see if anything was coming across the news.

Without warning, the channel changed to *It's A Wonderful Life.* "Allen, I was watching that!" She protested, looking up at her husband, who had snatched the remote when she wasn't looking.

"I know you were, and that's why I changed it," he replied. He was a tall, reedy man with a shock of black hair and round spectacles reminiscent of John Lennon. "Babe, can't you get your mind off work for the next thirty-six hours? I only have you until the morning after Christmas."

"Actually it's more like Christmas night. But it's three in the morning. Why aren't you sleeping?" She took a sip of wine and moved over on the couch so he could sit next to her. He put an arm around her shoulders and she snuggled into his embrace.

No more than a few moments had passed when Kyla's cell phone began to ring. She picked it up from the coffee table.

"Taylouni here."

"Taylouni, it's Walt. Have you heard the news? Welding is having a shit fit."

"Walt, it's Christmas," she answered steadily, knowing full well that this didn't make the slightest difference. "What in the hell are we supposed to do about it?" She shot her husband an apologetic glance. He was shaking his head in resignation, as though he had already accepted already what she was refusing to admit.

"You know as well as I do that it doesn't make a damn bit of difference if it's Christmas or the apocalypse. We're all in deep shit because of this Air France stuff. Welding wants us in Las Vegas by eight o'clock tomorrow morning."

She sighed and hung up the phone before turning to her husband. She began to say, "I'm sorry, but I have to – "

He cut her off. "I knew this would happen."

"I'm sorry, Allen. You know that this is beyond my control."

He nodded and didn't look at her. "I don't know how you expect us to start a family, Ky. Your job might as well be your husband and your child for the amount of time and energy it consumes."

She took his face in her hands and tilted his head until they were looking into one another's eyes. "Please just be patient, honey. It's not going to be like this forever."

"How long is it going to be like this, then?"

Now it was her turn to drop her eyes. "I don't know," she said.

At 5:00 a.m. she met Walt Dirkes, and they were joined by Welding at the CIA's JANET terminal at Dulles. He asked morosely, "Did you have a nice Christmas with your families, agents?"

"Yes sir," they both answered passively.

JANET was the agency's in-house airline service. In addition to the terminal at Dulles, in Vegas the agency maintained a terminal at McCarran to shuttle personnel daily into the Nellis AFB facility at Groom Lake. The agency had been managing a series of joint operational ventures with the Air Force at what used to be known as Area 51, including research and development projects using stealth and drone technology. In 2002, drone attack capabilities were still in the fine-tuning stage. The agency's interests were primarily directed to the intelligence and surveillance gathering potential from a wide range of drone sizes.

Kyla had always believed that she'd been selected for the Reno project on the basis of her first assignment as a behaviorist; she'd been assigned to monitor the team which traveled into Groom Lake. The government was concerned about the level of psychological fitness of workers who commuted into a top-secret job site location in the midst of the War on Terror. The citizen population of Las Vegas who worked in the gaming industry had a significantly higher rate of alcohol and gambling addictions than a non-gaming community. It was an ongoing concern that the same problems might arise for those living under the pressure of clandestine counterterrorism.

Arriving in Las Vegas, Welding and the agents taxied to an

outlying terminal. Other than passing through additional security, the building was indistinguishable from any other at McCarran International. Inside, however, security personnel were armed with semiautomatic weapons.

Inside, they were directed to a conference room where twenty other agents waited. They stood when Welding arrived. He took his place at the head of the gathering.

"Thank you for being here this morning, agents. We appreciate everyone arriving here promptly despite the holiday."

As though we had a choice, Kyla thought.

"We wouldn't have called this meeting had it not been of the utmost importance," Welding continued. "I have no doubt you're all up to speed on the Air France incident. I don't have to tell you this looks bad for us. Now, regarding this Reno project..." Here two assistant agents passed out binders that read CODENAME: HANNAH. "The project has been designated with the name 'Hannah.' Let me introduce you all. Smith, Johansen, Torva, Roberts, and Murphy are from Science and Technology division. Taylouni, Givens; Behavioral. Walt Dirkes and Hank Nordquist, field supervisors."

Roberts raised his hand. "Sir, what about Richmond and his team?"

Welding answered dryly, "Agent Richmond and his team have been reassigned to Eielson in Alaska for some much needed sensitivity training. They will be monitoring Russian hinter-activity for the foreseeable future." He turned his attention to Kyla and Walt.

"Taylouni and Dirkes, you've done great work on the Reno project to this point, given the occasionally strenuous circumstances. We have decided that to alleviate some of the pressure you've been under, we'll be rotating you in and out of Reno on a two-on, one-off basis. We'll be sending you back to Washington tomorrow for the next two weeks. After that we'll have you in Reno for two weeks, followed by Washington for one week. While you two are on your off-weeks in DC, Givens and Nordquist will keep an eye on the project in Reno."

Dirkes leaned over to Kyla, and when Welding directed his conversation elsewhere, complained in her ear, "They fly us all the way to Vegas to tell us we have two weeks' assignment in Langley. Un-fucking-believable."

The meeting ended several hours later. Welding asked Taylouni to hold back, along with Dirkes and Nordquist. As they waited for the room to empty, Dirkes grew progressively more fidgety. It was clear that he had something on his mind. He'd let it be known that he was unhappy at missing soccer and the holidays, and now he was certain Welding saw him complaining to Kyla. He decided to go on the offense and pressed Welding, "Why is the decryption being done by CIA contract and not by NSA?"

Welding answered, "Well, there were two reasons. First, there's enough discovery in the early work to warrant going to Congress and requisitioning a huge budget in decryption. Tenet wants to take advantage of the fear level to get the budget for the agency rather than NSA. At this point, there's enough involvement in Hannah from all the SOCOM partners that everyone is going to vie for the technology. Everyone can see the broader application possibilities, but we're the ones holding the inside track. All we have to do is keep the Air Force in second position over NSA and we'll be fine."

Dirkes nodded and murmured sullenly, "Yes, sir."

"Now then, about these encrypted codes that our Mr. Caldwell keeps turning up," Welding continued. "You should know that embedding the original encryption into the television signal, then decoding through a set-top television box, was an idea the Agency came up with about five years ago. We've suspected that the original sourcing was stolen from a testing outpost in Croatia, and that someone within Al-Jazeera has actually been using our very own invention. While we were able to get the passenger who was a potential threat removed from the Air France flight yesterday, we also have a local embedded at Al-Jazeera who was reported missing this morning."

He was silent for a moment before continuing, "I don't know if these most recent discoveries would cause someone within Al-Jazeera to stop transmissions, or if other broadcasts are being used as well. Our task on the ground now is to buy as much time as possible to find the full extent of the broadcast code's usage, without losing sight of the broader possibilities of the anomaly detection software. If those broader possibilities are there, we need time for our science and tech teams to reverse-engineer the current software that Hicks is using."

He turned to Nordquist. "When you've finished with your first two-week stint in Reno, we'll be bringing you back to Langley so that you can spend some time developing rendition protocols to free the software from Hicks. I don't care what it takes: stealing it outright, disgracing the company, whatever. We need Hicks and that little circus of his out of the way."

The bitterness in his tone surprised Kyla, who had no idea what had taken place between him and Gordon in the warehouse. She and Walt exchanged looks.

Welding addressed them next. "Dirkes, Taylouni… I hope I don't need to remind you that the entirety of Operation Hannah is *sub rosa*. You are not to discuss what transpires in Reno with anyone, inside or outside the Agency. Walt, you'll need to develop an Echelon package on all employees of Hicks Limited, and their family members. I want every phone tapped, every e-mail account hacked, I even want the doghouse bugged. I want to know who these people at Hicks know and what those acquaintances believe is happening at the warehouse. Is that understood?"

After Welding had dismissed them, Kyla and Dirkes walked back to the JANET plane, which was recognizable by the distinctive red stripe painted on the fuselage. As Welding was giving Nordquist instructions, Dirkes sped up to walk alongside Taylouni. He bowed his head as if engrossed in his cell phone, and while he walked, whispered to her in a low voice, "If you have any juice with this Milo character, you'd better ask him to embed our names and phone numbers into the digital records of the footage and the code output."

"Why?" she asked.

"Because we're going to be asked to do some illegal things. If you enjoy your freedom, the only way to keep it is to avoid incriminating yourself. The watermark on the digital record will keep us from a subpoena. Nobody wants to expose agents in the field by publishing digital footprints with phone numbers on them."

The JANET plane touched down in DC at 10:30 a.m. and Kyla caught a taxi home to find Allen sleeping on the couch while a football game blared from the television. She tried to make as little noise as possible, but as she tiptoed to the bathroom she bumped into her suitcase, knocking it to the floor from its standing position. Allen stirred and opened his eyes slowly.

"Hi, honey," she said softly.

He didn't say anything at first. Then he murmured, "This can't go on, Kyla."

"Allen, we've been through this…"

"No, this is different. You told me that you would be home for Christmas, and you weren't even here for 24 hours."

"Allen, you know I can't…"

"I don't want to have this conversation again," he said simply. "We've been through it a million times before. Nothing changes."

She slumped against the wall, suddenly overcome by exhaustion. "What do you want from me?"

He looked down. "My family wants me to move back to Boston. The VP position has opened up at my father's firm and I think I should take it."

She gaped at him. "Boston?"

"It would pay enough so that you wouldn't have to work," he continued. "We could finally start a family."

"I can't just quit my job. I've worked extremely hard to get where I am."

"But you're not happy, Kyla. You've told me this more times than I can count and it's written all over your face every time I see you. Why do you persist in making yourself miserable?"

She couldn't say anything about the importance of the Reno project, so instead she said, "My hands are tied."

"They always have been," he retorted bitterly.

She left the room and went upstairs, stretching out on their king-sized bed. The room was suffused with ink-black winter shadows, and soon she fell into her half world of serenity. Her dreams felt wrapped in the security of her blankets, and that provided an odd feeling of relief. She felt the burden of her marital guilt gone. She was ready to let go. The feeling and the dream surprised her momentarily, but then gave way to exhaustion.

CHAPTER THIRTEEN
January 2004

⊕ ⊕ ⊕

After Christmas, Milo found that the agency eased up on them, which meant that most nights he was now able to go home at 9:00 p.m. rather than midnight. Once the system became more automated, the individual scans of footage took care of themselves. This helped alleviate some of the tension with Natalie following their argument. To his relief, Dirkes was also seen around the warehouse less frequently, which meant that he dealt primarily with Kyla. The introduction of Montgomery, as well as a rotating cast of lower-level tech geek officers into the warehouse environment, helped as well. Friendships developed and the intensity of the intelligence gathering seemed to smooth out. Though it didn't happen often, occasionally someone from NSA or the Pentagon's intelligence operation, DIA, would visit the warehouse and give them a proper commendation.

During this time Gordon, too, seemed to level off. He began to keep regular office hours, from 8:30 a.m. to 6:00 p.m. He also replaced the desk with the black "X" taped on it with the original Grant McKinley monstrosity; a massive wooden desk that was an actual X in configuration. He positioned Milo on the opposite side of this structure and on his side, Hicks laid out several work projects currently underway. He'd recently become involved in several business ventures outside the company, including the purchase of a large plot of land which he envisioned turning into a luxury golf course. Gordon would splay drawings and contracts between the computer screens that maintained stock charts. His habit of smoking four packs of cigarettes each day only intensified, and he no longer bothered to smoke outside. Milo found himself increasingly irritated by this, until at last he would say, "I can't see my screen for all the fog in here. Excuse me while I step outside."

Escaping through the special access door to a small courtyard shielded by the building from the blustery, ever-present Reno wind became a late-morning ritual for Milo. He grew to cherish the moments of mindless relaxation in the wintry sunshine, away from work, away from Gordon and his odious cigarettes, and away from his family. He realized that he hardly had any time to himself anymore – from the time he got up to the time he went to sleep, he was always in the presence of someone else.

One morning, as he leaned up against the wall with his eyes closed and his jacket buttoned tight against the chill, he heard someone coming through the security door. It was Kyla.

She seemed embarrassed at having intruded upon his moment of solitude. "I apologize for interrupting," she said. "I see you come out here every day, and I was starting to get concerned you were planning an exit out the back door."

At first this remark unnerved him, but then he saw the shy smile on her face and understood that she was making a joke.

"I just came out here for a few minutes of quiet," he said.

"I won't disturb you."

He closed his eyes again and turned his face to the sky. For the first few minutes he felt self-conscious, as though she might be watching him. But when he opened his eyes slightly he found that she had moved to the far edge of the patio and stood with her back to him, gazing off towards the east. He relaxed and shut his eyes once more, emptying his mind of all thoughts for several pleasant moments.

Soon this routine became his favorite time of the day. At first Kyla accompanied him, citing security concerns, but before long they established a pleasant habit of using this time to discuss their families, their plans, and to vent about anything that came up in the warehouse.

At the end of her first shift in Reno under the new rotating schedule, Kyla confided in Milo about the situation with her husband. She was anxious about her return home.

"He wants me to come with him to Boston and essentially become a housewife," she said. "But I could never be happy with that, and he should understand that about me."

Milo answered, "I wish I could give you some advice. But the truth is I haven't been a very good husband to my wife since this whole partnership with Gordon started."

"Well, we can start a support group, called the *Confederacy of Married Dunces,*" she joked.

♦ ♦ ♦

Kyla's full week at home in early January was just that miserable. Though she was back at Langley, her work hours continued to be long and tedious. She was asked to compile an in-depth psychological profile of everyone involved at Hicks Limited. Her supervisor insisted on a line-by-line examination of her work and all the personalities on the ground in Reno. She arrived at the office each morning at 8:00 a.m. and often didn't leave until 8:00 p.m. When she got home at 8:30 in the evening, Allen was still at work. For all their talk of living together like a family, Kyla inwardly stewed at the prospect of sitting at home like a subservient housewife, waiting for the man of the house to return so that she could make dinner for him. Nevertheless, she walked on eggshells that week, trying to not upset him once more.

That first week they did not speak of the Christmas argument. In fact, they hardly spoke at all. On Friday night and Saturday morning, they worked jointly on painting their spare bedroom … accomplished with no more than a handful of words exchanged. On Saturday night they had dinner with neighbors, and during these two hours they convincingly played the part of the happy couple. But after they left, laughing and waving and thanking their hosts for the meal, they lapsed into a gloomy silence that lasted through the next morning.

The second week improved slightly when Kyla said gently one evening, "I don't want it to be like this when I'm home. I miss laughing with you."

Allen sighed. "I don't want it to be like this either." They smiled and took one another by the hand.

After that, he was always home by the time she returned each evening. She also made an effort to leave work an hour earlier each night. They finished painting the spare bedroom the second Friday and went to a concert together the following night. On Sunday, she packed her bags for a 4:00 p.m. flight for Reno. Allen drove her to Langley at 3:00 p.m., and though they'd spent several enjoyable days together, the drive was completed in silence. Kyla wondered if Allen had resolved not to provoke the strain between them, or if he might be moving away from her. She couldn't read him either way.

During the two weeks that Taylouni and Dirkes had been at Langley, and Givens and Nordquist broke in the new batch from the Science and Technology team at Hicks Ltd., Gordon and Milo began to meet privately at lunch to catch up on the workflow. Milo was astonished to learn that the SOCOM admin was actually considering giving Gordon a top-secret clearance. "They can't punish me forever," was Gordon's reply.

The fact was that Hicks hardly cared about the fundamental work that the company was doing. He had little patriotic concern for the war. But he did want the money he'd lost in the days of Grant McKinley back – with interest. Beyond that, he was anxious to sell the technology to the government and move on. He revealed his private plan to Milo: use his top-secret clearance to leverage the Nevada Gaming Commission into granting him a casino license. As a person who had felony possibilities in his past, this was denied to him, but he reasoned that once the US government anointed him with the contract and the top-secret standing, Nevada would be forced to acknowledge his good citizenship seal of approval. Milo had no idea whether this was the way Nevada politics worked. But Gordon always planned with confidence.

Since the Peppermill incident, Gordon had managed to get his drinking under control, but in mid-February Milo noticed that Gordon began to keep a bottle of Scotch in his desk again, which he occasionally took a nip from during their lunchtime meetings. He confessed that things had been difficult at home. "I can't seem to keep track of Julip. She just told me the other night that she's twelve weeks pregnant," he told Milo, pouring himself a drink.

"That's great news, Gordon! Congratulations."

Gordon gave a forced smile, "Don't know why she kept it from me this long. Damn little minx has taken to sneaking around behind my back so I never know what in the hell she's up to."

"Is it a boy or a girl?"

"Boy. Julip's got it in her head that we've got to name him Gordon Junior." He sipped his whiskey. "Can't complain about that, of course. And I don't want to say that she's unfit to be a mother – but God knows that woman couldn't keep a cat alive. She disappears for days at a time with her friends, and I never know where she is. And I don't think all of her friendships are entirely platonic, if you understand my meaning. Of course I'm no saint myself. Far be it from me to cast the first stone. But once she has the baby all this damn running around has got to stop, and I can't seem to get it through her skull."

Julip had long envisioned herself as an entrepreneur, and the previous summer, with Gordon's permission, she had purchased a shoe store in La Jolla, California. It soon became obvious that she was more interested in using the store as her own personal shopping station than running the business. Over the course of six months, she ordered more than three hundred pairs of shoes and paid little attention to the rest of the operation. After running up a bill of more than $200,000 for shoes of her own, Gordon shut the store down.

After giving birth to their son, Gordon Jr., in September of that year, she hit on the idea of marketing women's diamond-studded thong underwear. She set up a shop in San Diego's garment district where the diamonds were sewn into the undergarments, and sold them to local luxury retailers. However, the use of real diamonds resulted in not only a costly venture, but necessitated a high-alert security detail to guard the product. A lot of Gordon's folding money was invested in the project, and again, Julip spent most of her energy amassing a collection of precious panties. By the time Gordon shut down this venture as well, she had acquired a small fortune's worth of valuable undies.

Milo noticed the ongoing challenge of the golf course and the home development project in the west Reno hills. Hicks had purchased the water rights to southern Washoe County and had been stockpiling these utilities in preparation for his planned development. Each week another contractor called the warehouse to make sure that Gordon planned to pay his bills. Milo overheard a number of these calls in which Gordon placated the contractors and assured them that their checks were already in the mail. Several months into the project, Gordon indicated that the costs were skyrocketing and that he would sell his Lakeshore home to float the rest of the project. Someone had made a cool $31 million dollar cash offer for the Tahoe property. Gordon took it, walked across the street to the realty office and handed the check to the first agent he saw. The agent took home a tidy fee that day and Gordon plugged the proceeds into the development. Somehow, Milo thought, he always ended up on top of everything he touched.

In late February, an Air Force DIA officer came in, and with Congressman Montefusco at his side, let it be known that the coordinates found in one scan turned out to be a forward US military position near Tikrit, Iraq. The position was evacuated of military personnel, but the structures were left in place. Twenty-four hours later a suicide bomber drove a car into the encampment and detonated the vehicle. The staff at Hicks Limited was told that their work had saved the lives of hundreds of servicemen and servicewomen.

Because of these early successes, the SOCOM/ Hicks contract was quickly routed through another government shell corporation in Reno. Like the Groom Lake project, these black budgets funneled through private corporations as a primary front, and provided a degree of cover for those actually doing the work in counterintelligence and terrorism. That meant that one month Hicks would receive payment from this corporation for digital services rendered to an international coffee company, the next month for monthly digital services for a Phoenix based real estate development company. Ironically, the corporate tagline, emblazoned on every check to Hicks Ltd., proudly proclaimed, "We bring digital to your world!"

As the Hannah project reputation continued to grow, an increasing number of government entities sought involvement. While the Air Force continued to manage the project and the Agency continued to make sure things were running smoothly, the decoding process that had been so laborious in the project's early stages grew more refined and streamlined. Over the course of the first several months in 2004, field agents flew copies of Al-Jazeera broadcasts recorded in Saudi Arabia to the project site daily. They arrived via JANET into the Reno airport and drove the short distance to the warehouse in brown Chevy Impalas. When it became clear that the coding would continue to be a steady practice, the CIA appropriated a local microwave tower and had the Al-Jazeera broadcast routed directly into the warehouse. Milo programmed the servers to automate the deciphering tasks. Now, by midnight, agents sent the data to the Counterterrorism Division at Langley.

The Air Force had made it clear that they wanted to explore other uses for the compression and anomaly detection capabilities, so a steady flow of Air Force colonels began to arrive at the warehouse. Though their interest in coming to Reno was ostensibly work-related, Milo suspected that many had leapt at the prospect of leaving the dismal early spring Washington weather behind in favor of Reno. It seemed that a fresh batch of eager officers arrived every week.

Gordon, ever the willing host, began to capitalize on the steady stream of new recruits by entertaining the colonels each night at the casinos. Since colonels couldn't be subpoenaed by the Congress, they always served as the management and they were happy to oblige. The colonels, as well as their extensive security details, clearly enjoyed these nightly jaunts. As the average colonel earned a salary of around $150,000 annually, and the average intelligence field agent considerably less, they were easily impressed by the magnificent meals and expensive wines that Gordon lavished upon them. He also supplied each of them plenty of gambling chips. Project Hannah became a byword not only for a top-secret government project, but also for a riotous party that showed no signs of abating.

It was during one such celebratory event that Milo was first exposed to a bizarre – and secret – Air Force ritual. Gordon insisted that Milo accompany him to a dinner at Skullduggery one Saturday night, to welcome a new wave of recently arrived colonels. The dinner party included thirty in all, with Milo and Gordon as the only non-Air Force personnel in attendance. The mood was festive, the liquor flowed freely, and the colonels were all in rare form. Suddenly, without warning, the senior ranking officer in the room, Colonel Robert Paulson, stood and shouted, "BUG!"

To Milo's great surprise, the men on either side of him fell from their chairs and came to rest on their backs on the floor. They then proceeded to squirm with their arms and legs in the air like upside down insects. As Milo watched in bewilderment, the men in uniforms lay twitching on the floor, while Gordon and the senior officer laughed and poured himself another glass of wine.

As the night wore on and the men around him grew drunker, Milo suddenly felt a strong hand clap him, on the shoulder. He turned to see Colonel Paulson standing over him, with a steely smile on his face. Gordon stood not far behind, smirking like a naughty schoolboy.

"Son," Col. Paulson said, "your partner Mr. Hicks here has been telling me about all the wonderful things you've done for our country with this ingenious program of yours."

"Thank you, sir."

"Well, I would feel mighty obliged if you'd join me in raising a glass to your outstanding achievement." Col. Paulson put a generous tumbler of whiskey in Milo's hand as he said this. He then knocked his glass against Milo's and said heartily, "To patriots like yourself, boy!" He tossed back the whiskey in a single gulp. Milo did his best to follow suit, and came up from the bottom of the empty glass coughing and sputtering. Both Gordon and Col. Paulson looked supremely satisfied, and Paulson said, "Good man," with a hearty slap on the back that made Milo cough even more.

The first drink made it easier for the second to go down, which was followed by a third and fourth. After that Milo lost count. The red laughing faces of the colonels became a blur, as did the cocktail waitresses in various states of undress who were serving them. At one point, Milo stood from his chair to lurch towards one of the waitresses with the aim of asking for another vodka tonic. In so doing, he caught his shoe on the corner of the tablecloth and dragged half the table settings after him. The men at his table laughed uproariously as glasses of wine and half-eaten plates of food cascaded to the floor.

Later, Milo wound up sitting next to Gordon on a couch, each with an arm around the other's shoulders.

"I know it hasn't been an easy year," Gordon was saying, his face red from a seemingly endless succession of dry martinis. "Lord knows Julip's been up my ass more often than I care to admit. It's probably the hormones and the pregnancy."

"They just don't understand!" Milo shouted, filled with passion.

"Why don't you and Natalie join us on our next cruise?" Gordon asked. "We're bound for the Caribbean. It'll be just what we need to clear away the cobwebs, and just what our wives need to shut them up."

"Natalie will be thrilled!" Milo said. "Maybe then she'll finally get off my ass." He sounded pathetically childish in his mimic of Gordon.

By midnight he was too drunk to walk, much less walk straight. He didn't want Natalie to see him in this state, so the first person he called was Kyla.

She sounded worried when she answered the phone. "Milo? Is everything all right?"

"I need a ride," he said, slurring his words. "I can't go home like this."

She sighed. "Stay where you are. I'll be there in ten minutes."

When she arrived at the restaurant she found him sitting on the sidewalk, slumped against a concrete planter like a forgotten toy.

She parked at the curb and helped him into the passenger's seat. This accomplished, she returned to the driver's side and got in. She said gently, "You're sure you don't want me to take you home?"

Milo shook his head emphatically from side to side. "It's been bad enough already. Now if I come home drunk Natalie will ...well."

"I'm sure it's not as bad as all that."

"You don't understand. My father's a drunk. I'm turning out just like him."

"Now, don't get carried away," Kyla rebuked him. "Everyone makes mistakes once in a while. How about we find you a hotel room?"

Milo shook his head violently once more. "Just take me to the warehouse. I'll sleep it off on the couch."

The warehouse was dark and quiet, save for the soft whirr of the blade servers. Milo stumbled in and collapsed on a couch with Kyla following, carrying his jacket. She watched as he wearily kicked his shoes off before gingerly draping the jacket over the far arm of the couch. Then she asked, "Is there anything I can get you?"

"A time machine," he muttered.

"Very funny. Any water? Aspirin?" He didn't answer. She waited a moment, then asked, "Milo? Are you awake?" In response, he began to snore.

She left the warehouse and went back to her car, letting it idle for several minutes while she thought about what Milo had said about his father. He had alluded to their difficult relationship in a previous conversation, and though she still didn't know much, she felt that what she did know helped to shed light on some of Milo's puzzling personality traits; namely, his near-obsessive workaholic streak. When she had been sitting in the idling car for several minutes, she saw the headlights of another car pull into the parking lot alongside her. The yellow Corvette parked sloppily, and she realized Gordon was driving.

He killed the engine and opened the door, getting to his feet unsteadily. Then, as she watched, he staggered to the front door of the warehouse and spent some time trying unsuccessfully to fit his key in the lock. Finally he succeeded, and fumbled his way in. Despite the fact that he was visibly intoxicated, he managed to remember to lock the door behind him. Kyla chuckled to herself and put the car in reverse. She drove back to the hotel through silent city streets, the only movement that of errant trash stirred by the wind.

CHAPTER FOURTEEN

During the following six weeks Kyla found, much as Milo had, that the working conditions had evened out in Reno. Dr. Sydney Montgomery, who was been instated full-time on the Hannah project following his successful setup of the blade servers, proved to be a steadying influence on the work environment. His enthusiasm for the implementation of the Hannah system into the blade servers was good medicine for Milo. Montgomery heaped praise upon him for the brilliant work that he'd achieved, using the cobbled-together computing arrangement that Milo had frankensteined. Together they relished the possibility of making the new blade servers operate at a previously unimaginable level of speed, power, and elegance. The two of them clicked so well that Kyla, who watched in amusement, said they had great "nerd chemistry." Dr. Sid had acquired the moniker "Sid Vicious" from the field agents because of his straitlaced ways and droll mannerisms. He was anything but the doppelganger for the Sex Pistols' lead singer.

He did, however, occasionally loosen up. As the working hours grew more regular and the difficulties between Milo and Natalie began to lessen, Kyla and Montgomery began to socialize regularly with the Caldwells. Most Friday nights they were invited to the house for one of Natalie's home-cooked dinners, each arriving with a bottle of wine in hand. The four of them discovered that they shared a common love of rescue dogs, and made a group pact to give up their Friday afternoons to volunteer at a local rescue shelter. One afternoon they passed a skeet range half a mile from the shelter, and starchy old Sid Vicious surprised them by announcing that he was an avid shooter. He suggested that they head out to the range to take the edge off.

"I've never shot a gun in my life," Natalie protested.

"Then it's a lucky thing you happen to be in the presence of a professional shooter," Montgomery said. "You couldn't ask for a better opportunity to learn."

Within a month they were rescuing puppies once a week, and following that up with firing shotguns at innocent dinner plates to blow off some steam.

During the weeks that Kyla spent at home with Allen, they reached an agreement to delay the decision about whether to relocate to Boston until the following spring. They fixed up the house in their spare time and kept conversation away from work during midweek. It wasn't a perfect arrangement, Kyla thought, but at least it prevented things from getting worse between them. Allen didn't speak with her parents on the phone, and she made sure to avoid conversations with his.

She learned from Milo that Givens, who had taken her place onsite at the Hannah project during the weeks she was in Washington, was a real buttoned-up type of agent. He had a PhD in psychology from Harvard, and was fastidious in maintaining boundaries between the Agency and the Hicks Limited employees. Milo said that he rarely conversed with anyone on the ground, including the majority of his own colleagues. When he did interact with the staff, he acted more like a therapist than anything else. Milo told her that this had a way of making him feel like he was always under the microscope when Givens was present, and that he looked forward to the weeks Kyla was on site.

Though she didn't want to lose sight of her ultimate responsibilities, which were to track the mental health of all those involved in the Hannah project, Kyla had to admit that Milo was a wonderful, if pathetic, genius in his own way. He was so single-minded in his work habits that he often forgot to eat, and didn't always hear the first time someone spoke to him. She noticed, too, that Gordon proved to be a far less steady presence in the company, and while he managed to keep fairly regular hours, he was clearly letting Milo manage most of the heavy lifting while reaping the financial rewards. Though she didn't know anything about Gordon's side involvements with his various investments, projects, or his wife's ventures, she suspected that the business which bore his name did not have his undivided attention.

The CIA had tasked Kyla with performing weekly psychological evaluations of everyone at Hicks Limited, and these had been routine practice for the past eight weeks. In these face-to-face Q and A sessions, Milo tended to provide a cursory set of fixed responses in answer to her queries. His answers were largely perfunctory, providing just enough information to prove he had a healthy outlook, but never really addressing the underlying tensions about which Kyla had grown concerned. His focus on his work was almost maniacal, but when asked about his motivation, his answer was always the same: to build a secure future for his family. To that end, he seemed utterly incapable of providing for his family in any other way. To Kyla, he seemed to be sixteen years old emotionally, yet almost incapable of truly enjoying himself.

By the first of March, she had forged a closer friendship with Milo and Natalie, and grew better equipped to assess Milo's family dynamic, and therefore his outlook. She felt far more prepared to assess Milo's mental health. She knew she could sway Milo's thinking if necessary.

For the first time in her career, she felt pangs of guilt. Though her primary allegiance was to the Agency and her position in it, she had begun to care a great deal about the project, and about Milo and his family in particular. She secretly hoped that the anomaly detection software's long-term possibilities would be identified, so that Milo might have a fighting chance to secure his family's future. The wild card, however, was always whether he would crack under the strain, or if Gordon's histrionics would sink the whole endeavor.

With every conversation in their weekly evaluations, Kyla and Milo bonded over their outsider status. He began to fill her in on his family's background and his estrangement from his ailing father. She finally asked him about his name, something she had always wondered about. He told her about his father's deep mistrust of the government, and confessed his own skepticism as well. He had, he told her, become disenchanted with the dirty work of the intelligence apparatus. He had also been equally disturbed by both a video of water boarding that he'd watched early on, as well as a video of a beheading orchestrated by al-Zarqawi and broadcast on Al-Jazeera.

What happened next, she had to admit, was completely unprofessional, but after he opened up to her she felt compelled to respond in kind. She confessed the level of contempt she felt for her job. How disappointed she had been in her fieldwork and in the nearly intolerable level of bureaucracy she experienced. She recounted how, on a previous assignment, she had watched a live video feed as a drone strike targeted a mosque where Al Qaeda was holding a summit. To protect the mosque, Al Qaeda – counting on western sensibilities, and with an eye toward PR – had ordered dozens of school children to surround the mosque. The Air Force bombed the meeting, killing those inside as well as the children.

Because she was dark-skinned, married to a Jordanian and because at the time she was often assumed to be Muslim, all eyes in the room slowly fell on her as these events unfolded on the screen. She felt that they were silently awaiting her reaction. It was almost as though they were asking, Are you with them or with us?

She and Milo agreed that they both felt like pawns in some larger game controlled by powerful influences. To that end, a sense of angst visited them, and hung in the air through the early months of the year. Had it not been for the Friday afternoon social time, Kyla would be in a constant state of despondency.

Then it happened that one day, virtually overnight, the encrypted codes disappeared completely from the Al-Jazeera feed. The agents' phones rang off the hook. Dirkes, after getting an earful from his superiors, demanded to know what had happened.

Milo's answer was, "They probably changed their encryption method."

He went into overdrive trying to crack the new code, just as Kyla predicted he would. But it was too late for some. On March 11, 2004, ten bombs detonated simultaneously on four different commuter trains in Madrid, killing 191 people and wounding more than 1,800. Four days later, Milo successfully cracked the code that would have predicted the attack. He reported to the Agency that the information he had uncovered named the date and time that the bombing had taken place, and had it been caught it advance, could potentially have saved hundreds of lives. That night he cancelled his and Natalie's dinner plans with Kyla and Sid, and went home early, overcome by helplessness, anxiety, and frustration.

Following the Madrid incident, Milo went on a binge. In counterintuitive fashion, he put his foot down where his working hours were concerned. He would, he told Gordon, no longer work more than twelve hours in a day. Each morning, he arrived at 8:00 a.m. and left at 8:00 p.m. When he left each evening, instead of going straight home, he went to one of the casino bars for a drink. He didn't hide the fact from Natalie, but told her that he needed an hour to himself each day. She was understanding and respectful, but began to grow concerned.

Milo also became paranoid. One morning, as he and Natalie picked up Natalie's brother from the Reno airport, he noticed a JANET plane on the far end of the tarmac with about twenty people assembled around it. However, when he went into the office later that morning, there were only five Agency members present.

From that day forward, he began to notice black cars with opaque, black-tinted windows. He saw them following him in traffic, and he saw them parked within a few spaces of him whenever he came back to his car after having a drink or going into a store. However, these cars never followed him so conspicuously that he saw them pull into a parking lot after him or follow him home. Rather, they always seemed to be trailing him at his periphery, and when he looked, they faded once more into anonymity.

When he mentioned his suspicion to Gordon, Gordon acknowledged that he felt followed in the same way. His solution to the problem was to get as many of the Air Force colonels on his side as possible – and to capture some of their bad behavior on tape, should such material ever be needed. The restaurant he had leased for the first dinner with the colonels, Skullduggery, served as the regular venue for his entourage. The large back room was converted into a private full service dining room, monitored by a dozen hidden security cameras. He also brought the most attractive female dealers and cocktail waitresses in – even on their days off from the casinos – to support the parties. Milo didn't often attend these gatherings, but when he did, he noticed that Misty, the card dealer from the El Dorado, seemed particularly chummy with Gordon. Since Julip was also in regular attendance, Milo couldn't help but wonder what she thought of all this. From what he could tell, she hardly seemed to notice. She was too busy laughing and flirting with the colonels, who obligingly poured her glass after glass of champagne, even though she was pregnant.

With the influx of SOCOM personnel arriving and participating on the computing advancements, a new floor plan in the main warehouse became necessary. O'Bannon, the Air Force liaison, insisted that the operation be moved into a glass enclosed, sensitive compartmented information facility (SCIF), with no outside phone or data entry into the Hannah computer. The only communications line going in or out was a dedicated server that ran through the highest level of security that SOCOM had at its disposal. Big Safari, the SOCOM black budget source, created a fast track requisition for a high-end air conditioning system that kept the SCIF from heating up like a sauna.

Montgomery had the blade servers running smoothly and the temperature in the SCIF remained steady. The change in the Al-Jazeera encryption code would've taken a month to crack with the old computing platform. The blade servers had it decrypted in two and half weeks, though it was not in time to avert events in Madrid.

At a distance from the SCIF were smaller workstations, and a maze of cubicles constructed for various CIA and Air Force field staff. Dirkes had a desk with a cluster of adjoining stations for his field agents, but these were rarely occupied. The agents rotated throughout the warehouse and provided inside security, while one agent patrolled the perimeter outside the warehouse, and another inside monitored the security cameras that covered the entire complex.

Closer to the warehouse entrance, another enclosed glass structure housed Gordon's massive desk alongside Milo's comparatively humble workstations and phone lines. It was in this little terrarium that Gordon and Milo had their lunches and talked business strategy. They were almost certain the terrarium was bugged, and they therefore made it a policy not to discuss sensitive details inside. If they wanted to discuss something they didn't want overheard, they would head to a lookout on the highway and talk privately.

The final workstation area was Kyla's desk. Situated at the front of the warehouse, she shared the space with O'Bannon and Kathy White. Kathy recorded the entry and departure of every visitor to the site, while O'Bannon monitored the purpose of their visit and review of their accompanying documents. He also scheduled meetings for any conferences on the premises. He performed these tasks while chewing a seemingly endless wad of tobacco, which he would occasionally spit into an empty soda bottle. Kyla tried her best not to look at the bottle, filled with brown liquid, that sat on the far left side of his desktop.

Whenever there was a conference, it was always overseen by O'Bannon with Gordon present. It was Dirkes' job to look out for the agency's interests in those meetings, but most meetings were filled with jostling for access to Milo, and the Hannah possibilities. The majority of incoming Air Force Colonels and their retinues had heard about

Gordon's celebrations and lavish dinner parties. They, therefore, made a concerted effort to sit near Gordon and ingratiate themselves with him in any way possible.

In March, half a dozen Air Force and Navy personnel had managed to arrange a summit at Hicks Limited on Saint Patrick's Day. Milo suspected that this was no accident, as Gordon had made it known that he had arranged with the Atlantis to use their private gaming room. He was throwing a party that, in his words, would make even an Irishman black out.

He got his wish. Following an exquisite meal in which several rounds of rare French wines were consumed, the party took a turn toward hard liquor and high-stakes gambling. After the dinner plates were cleared, and the poker and blackjack tables readied, the waitresses who had served them earlier reappeared, wearing almost nothing. There were two cocktail waitresses for each officer, and they seemed to know their business: hanging on to the officers at all costs and plying them with drinks. Julip, for her part, seemed to fit into the scene rather well, and continued to make the rounds and flirt with one officer after the next. Gordon began to hand out $100 chips as if they were breath mints.

As the night wore on and the liquor continued to flow, the betting stakes grew by leaps and bounds. When the supply of $100 poker chips was exhausted, Gordon began handing out $500 and $1,000 chips. Milo asked if that was such a good idea, to which Gordon drunkenly replied, "Oh Christ, would you lighten up? Anything goes, my boy!" With this he downed a martini in one gulp and slapped a $10K chip on the table, shouting, "Place your bets, you pussies!"

He promptly lost. After a few more rounds and many more martinis, he had managed to get out of the hole, but within forty minutes he was down once more by $1.5 million. It was at this point that he had a stroke of Caligula-like depravity. "Julip!" he screamed across the room. "Get that sweet ass of yours over here!" She promptly peeled herself away from the colonel who had been fawning over her and sidekick Misty, and joined Gordon at the edge of the table. He whispered something in her ear, weaving unsteadily as he did so.

"Oh, Colonel Jones," she purred in her most alluring, faux-Southern belle manner to the man at her side. "My husband has just told me about the most hilarious tradition y'all have. I'm just dying to see it." She pressed herself against him and batted her eyelashes furiously.

The red-faced Colonel Jones, who at this point had consumed half a bottle of expensive brandy himself, grinned and winked at her. He then straightened up and yelled at the top of his lungs, "BUG!"

With this, all the other colonels dropped to the floor and began convulsing, leaving the scantily clad cocktail waitresses surrounding them gaping in surprise. Then they all began to laugh at the spectacle. Julip, too, laughed so hard that she could barely stand. Gordon took this opportunity to seize her roughly and reach beneath her dress. To Milo's astonishment, he came away with a pair of her diamond-encrusted underwear in hand. She continued to gasp with laughter and put up no resistance. After a moment the men began to rise from the floor and Gordon commanded their attention by holding the red thong aloft over his head. When he was certain that all eyes in the room were on him, he slapped the thong down on the table and announced, "Gentleman, the stakes have just increased once more. Please place your bets." There was a hush as the other men complied. Even the cocktail waitresses waited breathlessly to see what would transpire.

In the end, Gordon lost. He snapped his fingers angrily for another martini, and having swallowed this he said to the winner, a Colonel Richter, "You won fair and square, you bastard. Come claim your prize." With this, he shoved Julip towards the Colonel, who caught her in his waiting arms.

Milo had seen enough. He didn't announce his departure, but slipped out unnoticed. At the door, Misty caught him by the arm. "Should we be worried about Gordon?" she asked, sounding genuinely concerned. "Sure, I've seen him get out of control before, but this really beats all."

Milo shook free of her hold. "Gordon's a grown man," he answered bitterly. "Let him look after himself."

The following morning he got a call from Kyla, who sounded disgusted. She had heard from Dirkes that all of the colonels, as well as Gordon, had taken rooms at the Atlantis. "I think it's best that we get Gordon out of there before the security cameras catch his comings and goings," she said.

"But what about the colonels?" he asked.

"We'll let the Air Force worry about them," she retorted. "They know how to take care of their own."

Milo put in a call to Stagnaro and explained that he needed help finding Gordon's room. When he arrived at the hotel twenty minutes later, Stagnaro met him at the front door and said in a low voice, "Follow me." They took a service elevator to the top floor and Stagnaro led him to a set of double doors. These opened to reveal the palatial suite in a state of great disarray, and it took Milo several extra seconds to realize that Gordon could be found in the bed at the far end of the room. And he wasn't alone: both Misty and Julip were there as well. They were curled together in sleep, leaving Gordon to snore on his own at the edge of the bed.

Milo tapped him on the shoulder and said, "Gordon, we need to go." Gordon murmured something indistinct in response. With Stagnaro's help, Milo managed to pull Gordon out of bed and get him into his clothes. Together they half-carried him into the hallway, leaving the two women behind in their spooning embrace, and got him into the service elevator. Somehow they smuggled him out unseen and lifted him into the backseat of Milo's car. At his home in South Washoe, Milo deposited him in bed, thanked Stagnaro, returned him to the Atlantis and then headed to the warehouse.

At noon, Gordon strolled into the warehouse whistling cheerfully. As Milo looked on dumbfounded, he sauntered up to his workstation, did a little tap dance worthy of Gene Kelly, and spun around once with arms outstretched, palms up, as if he were finishing up a performance.

Milo had been prepared to give Gordon a piece of his mind for his outrageous behavior, but after the state in which he had left Gordon earlier, he hadn't expected to see him again that day. Now that he was here, Milo found himself completely caught off guard by Gordon's upbeat demeanor. So he asked the first question that came to mind. "How are you feeling?"

Gordon beamed. "Never better, my boy. Never better!" He performed another dance step shuffle. "At first I was disappointed that the CIA agreed to the $100 million contract so quickly. But then I got to thinking, Gordon, you fool. The reason they agreed so quickly is because Hannah is obviously worth so much more. If a single submarine costs six billion dollars, I don't see any reason why we should settle for less than $500 million." He paused then said, "And with the video recordings I've got of our military elite acting like deranged pagans last night, I'm sure we'll get it."

Milo didn't answer for a moment. When he did, he spoke quietly. "It seems to me that this is a dangerous game you're playing."

Gordon brushed this aside. "You've got to play big to win big," he answered carelessly.

CHAPTER FIFTEEN

Two days later, Gordon informed Milo that they were all going to Miami on the private jet. From there, Milo and Natalie would be boarding a cruise ship with Gordon, Julip, and their entourage. Gordon was going to shut down the warehouse for ten days and have SOCOM stew on the new Hicks demand. He also wanted the military officers to marinate in their iniquity. Prior to their departure, Gordon asked Milo if he still had his red poker chips from the night of the party at the Atlantis. Milo said he did. Gordon told him to bring them along on their Caribbean cruise.

On Friday morning, when Milo and Natalie arrived at the Reno airport, they found Gordon and Julip surrounded by a dozen people. Most were the usual friends and associates but there was one woman that Milo didn't recognize. Gordon introduced her as Sonya.

It wasn't until they boarded the plane that Milo was struck by the realization that Sonya was in fact Sonya Montefusco, the wife of Bob Montefusco, Reno's Congressman. When the plane had landed in Miami where the ship awaited them, Milo cornered Gordon and demanded in a low voice, "Have you lost your mind?"

Gordon, who had had several vodka tonics during the flight, looked annoyed. "What in God's name are you talking about?"

"What is the wife of a congressman doing on our cruise?"

"I can invite anyone I please," Gordon replied snippily. "Didn't the party at the Atlantis prove that?"

Against his better judgment, Milo decided not to say anything about Sonya Montefusco to Natalie as they boarded the cruise ship. Why give her cause to worry at the start of the first proper vacation they'd taken together in nearly five years? He decided that his best course of action would be to simply steer clear of Gordon, Julip, and Sonya Montefusco. He needed time to tell Natalie under the right circumstances.

By the time the ship docked in Turks and Caicos, Milo had almost forgotten breaking the news to Natalie. The cruise was beautiful, and each night they dined on the finest meals they had had in recent memory. The week on Grand Turk passed as if in a pleasant dream. Milo and Natalie spent the days rekindling their marriage, lounging on the beach, swimming, dining beneath the stars, and making love for the first time in months. From the balcony outside their room each evening they sat on a loveseat, Natalie's head on Milo's shoulder, gazing out over the ocean as the stars appeared one by one. Milo began to feel, for the first time since he had partnered with Gordon, that it might turn out to be worth it after all.

But that changed when they docked in San Juan. Milo and Natalie had spent the day roaming the city streets, and toured a now-defunct rum factory. In the early evening, they returned to the ship and changed for dinner. Arriving in the dining room, they found Gordon and Julip seated at a table with Sonya, her son David, and her husband, the congressman. Milo and Natalie looked at one another uncertainly, and then took their seats at the table. Gordon introduced Natalie to Montefusco and said to Milo, "I believe you already know my good friend, Bob, here."

Milo hardly spoke throughout the meal. Neither did Natalie. He was sure that her pointed refusal to look at him meant that she suspected him of having withheld knowledge that Montefusco would be present. After dinner he confronted Gordon once more.

"When were you going to let me know that he'd be coming?"

Gordon laughed. "I wasn't aware that I had to run my social calendar by you first."

"Where the hell did he come from, anyway?"

"After we touched down in Miami, I sent the jet to Washington to pick up Bob. Surely you don't mind him tagging along?"

"I just don't like the position you're putting us in," Milo said angrily. "You're being reckless."

"Well, my boy, sometimes you've got to take a gamble."

"Stop using those empty bullshit platitudes with me!" Milo exploded. "I'm not a fucking child, Gordon. I'm your partner."

Gordon's eyes narrowed. "Then stop acting like a frightened schoolboy and trust that I know what I'm doing, for chrissakes."

"Trust you? I still haven't gotten my half of the money from the government contracts!"

"You've been living on an extremely generous salary."

"Working like a dog while you live like a king!" Milo yelled. "I want what's mine! I want to get paid!"

With this, Gordon immediately rose from his seat and walked away.

They didn't speak to one another for the next week. Milo tried his best to enjoy the remainder of the cruise, but found it difficult to put aside his anxiety about Montefusco's presence. On the cruise's final night at sea, Gordon had scheduled a blowout party in the main ballroom. The morning of the party, Milo awoke to find that a note had been slipped under his door. It read, "Please join me for breakfast in my suite at 10. -GH." Milo went, not knowing what to expect. He found Gordon dressed in a white robe and slippers, reading a newspaper beside a table heavily laden with every conceivable breakfast food.

"Where's Julip?" Milo asked.

"Getting a massage, or a facial, or some damn thing," Gordon answered. "I told her to make herself scarce, at any rate. Please have a seat." Milo sat cautiously. Gordon, for his part, seemed completely at ease. He said, "Have a scone. The almond croissants are excellent, too."

"They're not poisoned, are they?" Milo asked pointedly.

Gordon let out a shout of laughter. "Good to know you've retained your sense of humor, my boy. Please, make yourself a plate. I'd feel much better." Milo did so begrudgingly, but only because the food looked particularly appetizing. Gordon watched, and when Milo had settled into his breakfast, he said, "Milo, I'm going to make things right between us. There can't be any bad blood. Whether the net result of our forthcoming contract is $100 million or $500 million, I give you my word that you'll get your $11 million before anything else is divided up. All I need is for you to tell me that all is well with us."

Milo sipped his coffee. "To be blunt, Gordon, I'm not going to be subjected to the same type of treatment that you got from JJ Singer. I know how much it killed you to watch Singer walk away with the spoils of Grant McKinley, while you were left to scrounge for what you could of the scraps. I don't want to find myself in the same position."

"Fair enough," Gordon agreed. "What we need now is to get this contract signed. Then we can hand over the Hannah source code to those nitwits at the CIA, and wash our hands of all this intelligence industry bullshit and you, my boy, will be rich beyond your wildest dreams. Why, after that we could do anything we like. We could even get back to our first love, and tackle the film work we started so long ago. How would that sound?"

Milo answered, "Let's focus on the immediate situation first. How confident are you that we'll get the full $500 million for the software?"

"As sure as I've ever been of anything," Gordon replied. "Our payday is just around the corner."

Privately, Milo had to admit that it sounded like a good plan – provided, of course, that everything panned out the way Gordon had confidence it would. However, he reminded himself not to get ahead of things. Securing a government contract of that magnitude would be no walk in the park. He further wondered if he wasn't just being paranoid about having Montefusco aboard. After all, congressmen regularly traveled in pursuit of various business enterprises. In reality, he told himself, this was just another way that government and capitalism did business.

Seeing that Milo had relaxed, Gordon turned the conversation to that evening's festivities. "I want to remind you that as stressful and tense as our work is, it's important that we take time to relax and blow off steam," he said. "Though we may not be in hand-to-hand combat on home turf, our part in the fight against America's enemies is just as real. We're on the front lines of something totally unprecedented. And it's taken its toll on both of us. I want you to see tonight as an opportunity to really let loose. Let this cruise be one of the perks for your part in defending our nation. A part that most people will never have any idea exists, let alone truly understand the importance of. We deserve a night to act like party animals. Now then, do you still have those red poker chips?" Milo said that he did, and in fact he had been keeping them in his pocket the whole time. He pulled them out now and set them on the breakfast table. Gordon quickly counted them. "I'm going to convert these into gambling chips for everyone at the party. Of course cruise gambling is small potatoes, so $100,000 should serve everyone's needs easily."

That night at the party Milo decided to take Gordon's advice. Perhaps choosing to believe that Gordon really did have everything under control made it easier for him to relax. He and Natalie enjoyed a sumptuous lobster dinner, and laughed uproariously with the other guests as the cruise comedian performed his routine. By the end of the second course, he had everyone in stitches. Natalie had had enough to drink by the end of the meal, but Milo continued to pour himself glass after glass of wine.

After dessert had been served, Gordon announced that the gambling could commence. He poured $7,000 worth of chips into the hands of each guest and told them to go wild. They moved into the gaming room and started in on their small-time wagers. At one end of the gaming room was a bar, and at the opposite end a karaoke machine stood on a stage. As the evening wore on and the guests consumed one drink after another, they became bold enough to take a stab at karaoke.

Natalie, who had stopped drinking earlier, called it quits early. "I can't take this anymore," she said as Sonya Montefusco belted out a particularly tone-deaf version of "Total Eclipse of the Heart." She excused herself. "I now clearly see why it's necessary to drink before either singing or watching someone else sing karaoke. Milo, are you coming?"

Milo kissed her. "I'm going to stay a little bit longer. Don't wait up for me." When she had gone, he took a shot of rum with David Montefusco. He had decided that he might as well let his hair down for their last night at sea. As he played a few rounds of blackjack, he continued to drink rum, and soon everything grew hazy. He eventually ran out of chips, and it wasn't long before Gordon brought over Montefusco, who was in a similar state, and insisted that they sing a karaoke duet.

Later, Milo could only recall certain details about how the rest of the night unfolded. He remembered tying a napkin on his head like a gangster wears a 'do-rag and insisting that Montefusco follow suit. They joked that they could always share a jail cell if their music careers didn't pan out. They then proceeded to butcher the song, "London Calling" until so many people were booing that Gordon had to come up and escort them offstage. The three of them sat at an isolated table in the corner of the room. Milo took notice that Gordon made certain to seat Montefusco between them, but he was too far gone to say anything about it.

With his back to the party, Gordon said solemnly, "Milo, I want you to be the first to hear about it. Our dear friend Bob here is planning on making a run for the governorship of the fair state of Nevada." He clapped a hand on Montefusco's shoulder. "Bob, I want to personally thank you for everything you've done to help us along, including your help in dealing with those idiots from Washington. Milo here is grateful, too. As a token of our gratitude, we hope you'll take this small gift." With this he pulled out the $100,000 in red poker chips that Milo had given him earlier, and pressed them into Montefusco's waiting hand. Milo, in his rum-induced haze, was thrown into confusion. Hadn't Gordon said that this would be the money everyone would be gambling with that evening? He grew uncertain about precisely what he was witnessing. Somewhere in his booze-addled brain, a signal flashed that something wasn't right here. But he couldn't quite connect the pieces, any more than he could open his mouth and speak coherently to question what was happening. Gordon continued, "You have my full support, Bob."

Montefusco grinned broadly. "You're a pillar of our community, Gordon." With that, he and Gordon rose in unison and returned to the party. Milo, bleary with confusion, decided that he'd had enough for his last night at sea. He stumbled to the stateroom and collapsed into bed without undressing.

It was the morning sun flooding through the cabin window that awakened him, finding its way into his eyes with blinding precision. He became aware that Natalie was moving around the room, packing their things. Each sound she made, from her footsteps to opening and closing drawers, to unzipping the luggage, felt like an explosion in Milo's head. She was clearly unhappy with his behavior the night before, and made no attempts to hide her disdain. In fact, she seemed to be making extra noise to punish him in his current state. He buried his face in the sheets and pulled in the blankets over his head, moaning.

Natalie opted for the silent treatment, though he expected her to say something. After an hour of listening to her slam drawers and clatter here and there, he dragged himself out of bed and made his way to the banquet hall, where a large metal coffeemaker dispensed burnt-tasting coffee from a spigot. He fumbled for a styrofoam cup and filled it, not bothering to add cream or sugar. The coffee, which had repulsed him before now, was bracing and delicious in his ravaged condition.

He found his way to Gordon's suite and knocked. Gordon, as always, seemed impervious to the previous night's debauchery and answered cheerily. When he saw Milo's haggard appearance, he laughed. "It appears that cruise life doesn't agree with you at all, my boy," he said, grinning.

"May I speak to you in the hallway privately?" Milo said in a low voice, fighting a wave of nausea rising inside him. Gordon stepped into the hall and closed the door behind him. Milo said in a whisper, "I've watched you do a lot of crazy things in the time that I've known you, Gordon. I've seen you hand out tens of thousands of dollars in cash and chips to complete strangers. I know that you give cash when it's charity, and chips when you expect something in return. I'm hoping that what I saw last night was just a gesture, rather than a payoff."

Gordon put a hand on his shoulder. "Gesture is the perfect word for it," he answered reassuringly. "I couldn't have put it better myself. As a matter of fact, right as you came by I was getting ready to pay Bob a visit. I'll have to get those chips back from him before we enter U.S. waters; otherwise it will cause him nothing but headaches." Milo nodded and said nothing. Gordon seemed to grow uneasy under his gaze, and continued hurriedly, "If you don't believe me, you're more than welcome to come to his room with me and see for yourself. You can witness the return with your own two eyes."

Milo shook his head. "I trust you, Gordon. If you tell me you're not paying Montefusco off, then I believe you. Besides, I've got a splitting headache and I need to help Natalie finish packing. She's not too happy with my behavior last night."

Gordon put his arm around Milo's shoulders. "Our ship is coming in before too long, to borrow a phrase," he promised. "And once it does, I promise you that your wife will forgive every naughty little thing you've ever done – which shouldn't be too difficult, because you're practically a Boy Scout."

That same morning, in DC, Kyla arrived at the airport only to find Dirkes waiting for her in a car driven by his wife. She exchanged greetings with Angie Dirkes, and promised to call on her for a game of tennis once the weather improved. She had a mind to ask Dirkes why his wife had driven him that day, but her question was answered as soon as he stepped out of the car. His face, neck, and hands had broken out in painful-looking hives, and he trembled with the exertion of the effort required not to scratch them. When Angie had gone, she asked, "Jesus, Dirkes, what the hell has been going on with you?"

"Oh nothing, Taylouni," he snapped. "I just got back from vacation." He caught himself and sighed. "I'm sorry. It's been a stressful week. I'm sure you heard all about St. Patty's Day in Reno."

As they made their way toward the JANET terminal, Kyla asked, "What did Welding have to say?"

Dirkes was grim. "You were spared getting chewed out by him directly? Lucky you. He was so far up my ass that I'm still in pain. He told me in no uncertain terms that Hicks is my personal responsibility, and that it's my job to keep him in line. In other words, not only was the St. Patty's situation my fault, but so was the fact that he suddenly shut down the warehouse to go on vacation two weeks ago."

Kyla stopped walking. "He did what?"

Dirkes shook his head. "My neck is on the chopping block, Taylouni. If this project goes off the rails before we secure the source code, I could very well be joining Richmond in Outer Mongolia before too long." They reached the security clearance checkpoint, and made it through to the waiting plane. As they took their seats, Dirkes continued, "Now Hicks is asking $500 million for the software."

"Is he out of his mind?" Kyla asked incredulously. Then she added, "Well, yes. We already know he's out of his mind."

"Not only that, but because of this little vacation of his, which he declined to tell us about in advance, Givens and the rest of the guys showed up at the warehouse two Fridays ago only to find the doors locked. Welding hit the ceiling. He says what Hicks is doing amounts to extortion, and he's going to terminate the contract when it expires in October. "

"What do we do until then? October is seven months away."

"We've got seven months to keep the operation going and somehow capture the software. God knows how in the hell we're going to do it. I'm sure that's what this SOCOM meeting in Vegas is all about."

Kyla was troubled by the fact that all this information was news to her. "Why didn't Welding bring me up to speed on any of this while I was at Langley all week?" she wondered aloud. "I spent the last five days with the 'Supe' dissecting the Saint Patrick's Day events and discussing the fallout from that. Not one thing was said about Gordon's demands, or his vacation, or any of that. Why am I hearing about this for the first time today? And why did you know about it before I did?"

"Don't know," Dirkes answered, absentmindedly scratching one hand with the other. He realized what he was doing and forcibly clamped both his hands down on the armrests of his seat, gripping the upholstery and gritting his teeth. "What did you talk about, then?"

"Mostly about Milo's behavior and trying to determine whether or not he participated in the hijinks that night. There wasn't anything in the conversation that led me to believe that I should be concerned about the operation." She looked out the window at the cloud covering below. "I always knew Gordon was trouble. Everyone seems to think that if Milo got half a chance, he'd bolt the partnership with Gordon and work for us. I'm not so sure. I've gotten to know him better than anyone else and he's always stood by Gordon. He'll say things like, 'Gordon may be Satan, but he's my Satan.'"

There was a look in Dirkes' eyes that Kyla hadn't seen there before – one of genuine concern. He said, "Truth be told, Taylouni, I didn't want to be on this shit assignment at first, either. It's like they sent us out here to do this crappy job and forget about us, and now that they've realized the significance of the Hannah project, all of a sudden we're in their way. And I'll be honest … I didn't relish the idea of you and I being on this assignment together. I used to think you were too idealistic, and too damn principled for intelligence work." He sighed and looked down at his hands. "Maybe it's me, though. Maybe I've just become too goddamn burnt out and cynical. I'll tell you one thing, though: over the last few months, I'll admit that I've come to appreciate your work. And yes, even your principles. I'm glad to have you on my team, Taylouni."

Kyla smiled appreciatively, genuinely touched by Dirkes' uncharacteristic expression of sentiment. She murmured, "I'm glad we're on the same team too, Walt."

The hint of a smile that had begun to flicker on his face was suddenly and starkly replaced by a dark expression of foreboding. He dropped his voice to a whisper. "You're not as green as I thought you were, Taylouni. But still, remember to be careful. If this goes sour, they plan to burn us both. Make no mistake about that. For me, it just means forced retirement, which isn't so bad. But for you ... this could be the end of your slow ascent within the intelligence ranks. If you still have a job at all, you'll be buried so deep in the bowels of the agency that nobody will even remember you're there."

At this moment a flight attendant bent over their seats and asked, "Would you like anything else to drink?"

"Nothing for me," Kyla answered, slightly shaken by Dirkes' words.

"I'll have vodka on the rocks, with a bit of lime," Dirkes told the flight attendant.

"You know what," Kyla said, "Make that two."

When the attendant had gone to fill their order, Dirkes said, "We'll talk more about this later. But just be sure to watch your back, Kyla."

CHAPTER SIXTEEN

Following two weeks of strategy sessions in Las Vegas and another in Washington, Kyla didn't return to Reno until April 16. In the time since she had last been there, the weather had warmed considerably and the wind had picked up dramatically. She arrived at the warehouse at 7:30 a.m. on Saturday morning, and, of course, found Milo already busy with his work. He seemed simultaneously glad to see her and visibly anxious, as though something was weighing on his mind. He asked if she would like to go out shooting for a few hours later in the morning.

"Cutting work?" she asked teasingly. "This must be serious."

He smiled, but she could still see the concern in Milo's eyes. "Do me a favor, will you? Invite O'Bannon along."

"What about Sid? Shouldn't we invite him?"

"I've got something I need to speak with O'Bannon about."

They made their way to the shooting range at 11:00, where Milo proceeded to tell them all that transpired on the cruise. He confessed to being drunk on the final night during Gordon's exchange with Montefusco, and admitted that he might be slightly foggy about the events he witnessed, but he felt he should share his experience nevertheless. He was clearly agitated at the prospect that he had watched Gordon give a congressman a bribe.

O'Bannon listened thoughtfully while gnawing a lipful of chewing tobacco. Throughout the story, he repeatedly turned his head to the side and spit a trail of brown liquid onto the grass. When he did speak, he sounded concerned but not greatly alarmed.

"We're all of us familiar with Gordon's showmanship," he said slowly after a final spit. "He may be many things, but he's not stupid. I sincerely doubt that he would so blatantly bribe a congressional representative in full view of a room filled with people.

He knows that he's got both the Agency and the Air Force by the nuts because this Hannah project is breaking new ground with each day that passes. None of the higher-ups want to admit it, but short of stealing the technology from him outright, we've got no choice but to bow to his demands. We may not like it, but we don't have any alternative. I think Gordon knows this, and I highly doubt that he's fool enough to jeopardize his position by flagrantly breaking the law." He turned to Kyla. "We should let Dirkes know about this, to be sure. But it doesn't sound to me like there's anything here so overt that we should be launching an investigation." He looked back at Milo. "Our chief concern right now is to keep the project workflow going."

Milo wasn't entirely convinced. "So, you're certain that whatever it was that I saw isn't serious enough to warrant concern?"

"Well, of course I wasn't there myself. But from the sounds of it, what you saw was just another case of Gordon being Gordon – always toeing the line, but never quite crossing it."

It was Milo's turn to shoot. When he had shielded his ears with protective earmuffs, O'Bannon said to Kyla, "The rendition scenarios are already in place? Are you sure we have five specific options for acquiring the code?"

"They are," she answered. He nodded and looked on admiringly as Milo hit the target once, twice, then three times, before missing the fourth.

Within a week, the first rendition scenario had been mapped in its entirety. If the Al-Jazeera transmission station in Qatar was bombed, the Agency reasoned that most of the day-to-day operations outlined in the Hicks Limited contract would be jeopardized. There would be no need for the company's decoding capabilities, and therefore the government could justify drying up the funding. Then Gordon would see quite clearly the harm in pushing for a contract too early. It was a risky move, but by disabling Al-Jazeera they would also be putting a stop to a major transmission avenue by the terrorist network. It was clear that those in the Air Force and Joint Command had wanted to put Al-Jazeera out of commission all along.

Milo's home phone rang at 3:00 a.m. on April 21. He groped in the darkness for the lamp switch, and winced when it lit up. Natalie, who had sat up in a panic on the first ring, said urgently, "What's wrong?"

Milo answered, "Hello?"

"It's Kyla. I'm sorry to wake you, but I thought you should know that the military has commenced bombing Al-Jazeera in Qatar."

"Who is it?" Natalie wanted to know, her voice filled with worry.

Milo put his hand over the mouthpiece and whispered "Kyla" in response. He listened again. She was saying, "We expect that by 5:00 a.m. our time, there will be no further AJ broadcast out of Saudi Arabia, and by 7:00 we should have clear directives in place to close up the deciphering tasks."

Milo tried to make sense of all this, clawing his way from the depths of sleep. He felt like a diver, disoriented by coming to the surface too quickly. "What does this mean for us, exactly?"

"Well, I know the Air Force plans to continue some of the other compression and tracking projects. But it may be that they'll assign someone else from the DIA Behavioral Unit." She paused. "I can't promise I'll be around much longer, but if I do end up leaving, I just want to make sure you know how much I have appreciated our working together."

When he arrived at the warehouse at 8:00, he was met by O'Bannon at the front door and told that the bombing had been called off. O'Bannon had a short, grim-faced man with him that he introduced as Hank Traversi. He said, "Why don't the three of us go for a ride?"

They climbed into O'Bannon's standard issue black SUV, and headed toward the freeway. O'Bannon spit into the empty soda cup that he kept in his car and asked cheerfully, "Who's hungry?" After stopping at the nearest fast food chain for a cheap breakfast, he took them to a neighborhood park in a quiet residential area just off the freeway.

It was here that Traversi spoke for the first time. "First of all, Mr. Caldwell, I want you to know that I've been following your work since day one, and I'm a great admirer. In my office, I have bookcases on all four walls that go to the ceiling. They currently hold more pages than I can count of latitudes and longitudes that you've pulled from the AJ broadcasts over the past six months." Here he pulled a map from his jacket pocket and pointed to a spot that had been circled vigorously. "This is Basra, Iraq. It was here that a joint British and US military outpost was bombed in February. Fortunately, your work pointed us to this location, and we withdrew our forces just in time. When the blast did go off, it failed to injure a single Allied soldier." With this, he reached into his pocket once more and withdrew a silver medal. "I apologize that this has to be done in secret, Mr. Caldwell. But then, secrecy is the nature of our business. It is my pleasure to award you the Central Intelligence Agency Medal of Valor."

Milo took the medal and studied it. It was small but surprisingly heavy. He wondered for a moment if it were made from real silver. He said, "Thank you," and then paused. "I don't suppose I can share this with my family?"

Traversi smiled and shook his head. "Not even the family dog, but I hear he's deaf anyway." Milo nodded. Traversi went on, "I thank you for understanding. Now then: to discuss the matter of your partner, Mr. Hicks. As you can imagine, this is a sensitive issue and you are no doubt in a highly sensitive position yourself. I hope you understand that what I am about to say must be kept among the three of us." Milo said he understood. Traversi continued, "You are, no doubt, aware that Mr. Hicks has demanded a sum of $500 million from the government for your software. The sum is not only exorbitant, but the request for it amounts to extortion. We will therefore be terminating our work with Hicks Limited on October 31. That being said, there are several scenarios that might play out. First and foremost, it is our hope that you would consider leaving the Hicks Limited partnership, and come out to Fort Washington in Maryland to continue the work as a contractor for a new arrangement led by the DIA.

"Before that can happen, however, we have new evidence that Osama bin Laden is close to being captured. We believe that he's in the Tora Bora region of Pakistan, and therefore the deciphering will need to continue to see if there is any confirmation of this on the AJ broadcast."

"Lastly, both Montgomery and I have been assigned to a new project called the Hammer, which is set to get going here shortly. This project consists of hacking into jihadist web sites to trace e-mails and other sensitive information to their point of origin. This is where you would come in. Our thought is that you could use your compression source to launch a cyber attack on the involved routers, using proxy servers all over the globe. Montgomery and I agree that Reno is the perfect place to launch this project – it's just out of the way enough so that we wouldn't arouse any suspicion on a national or global scale."

Milo took all this in. "So you're saying that you want me to ditch Gordon to work for you as a hacker?"

Traversi smiled. "That may be putting it a little less delicately than we'd like, but that's the long and the short of it. You'd also be doing some data harvesting."

"And Gordon would just be left out in the cold."

O'Bannon and Traversi exchanged looks. Traversi said slowly, "Again, I don't know that I'd put it quite that way…"

"Well, essentially what you're asking me to do is to go behind Gordon's back."

O'Bannon spoke up. "Perhaps I'm confused, Milo. You came to us not two weeks ago because you were worried that Gordon was guilty of bribery."

"And you were the one who said that it didn't sound like bribery."

"It may not have technically been the sort of thing we would put personnel into investigating, but nevertheless, I think we can both agree that Gordon is on a dangerous path. It's only a matter of time before he gets himself into another mess like the one at Grant McKinley. Is that the type of person you want to continue to associate with?"

"Well, of course it's not as simple as that…"

"You're just at the beginning of a highly impressive career filled with unimaginable potential. Surely you don't want to jeopardize that."

"Of course not, but – "

"We're not asking you to stab Gordon in the back or anything of the sort. But you've spent the last two years putting his interests and the interests of Hicks Limited before your own. What we're trying to give you is an opportunity for personal benefit as you continue to serve your country. We were so sure that this was the kind of opportunity you'd jump at."

Milo paused before answering. "I have to admit it sounds very enticing."

Traversi smiled. "Then will you at least think about it?"

"I'll give it some thought."

As they drove back to the warehouse, Traversi and O'Bannon

chatted in the front seat, leaving Milo in the back seat to mull over everything Traversi had said. He was touched and honored to have received the CIA medal, even if he couldn't tell anyone about it. He thought about his father, and the way his brother had been so damaged by the war. He couldn't help but feel that the path he'd stumbled upon led to some form of redemption on their behalf. And from the sound of it, the work that needed doing showed promise. But he didn't like the fact that Gordon's demands were being cast aside, and that they were now trying to turn Milo against his business partner. As far as he could tell, they were all hell-bent on their own agendas, and they didn't like the fact that Gordon was telling them what to do. Therefore, while he may have been concerned about the episode with Montefusco, he thought it underhanded that the Agency now wanted to cut Gordon out.

At the end of the day, all Milo really wanted was to be paid fairly to do his work, and to be left in peace. He wasn't interested in the politics of it all. Still, the Hammer sounded like an intriguing challenge, and he loved the idea of hacking on the government's dime.

During the summer months, the pressure on the broadcasts again mounted. Al-Jazeera had changed the encryption keys, and this time the key change was more complex. Furthermore, Dirkes had said that another insider planted at Al-Jazeera had been killed, and that the Hannah work was now the Agency's primary source of information. The Agency began to push once more for greater output and faster processing. The newest code they'd uncovered was found consistently in footage showing either bin Laden or messages from al-Zawahiri. Thus, anytime either showed up in an Al-Jazeera broadcast, the Agency wanted as many frames as possible in the story analyzed.

By the time Milo had cracked the encryption, he had hours of footage to analyze. The field agents pressed for a speedier turnaround, and poor Dirkes began to swell up daily with hives, indicating that he was taking more long distance beatings over the phone. Montgomery and Traversi had set up another SCIF next to the current sweat lodge and begun to build the Hammer, using new Nvidia graphics processors. At the height of the summer, Milo had to hustle between the work on deciphering, being called over to the Hammer SCIF, and then into the terrarium, where Gordon had been recently distracted by the soaring costs of the golf course project.

Secretly, he was also missing Kyla. She had been the only one to whom he could turn when the burdens of the Hannah project and the competing egos assigned to it became too much to handle. Since the morning she had called to let him know about the Al-Jazeera bombing, she had not returned to Reno. Walt had said that she was on another assignment, but when Milo called her cell, she never returned his messages. He was back to working past midnight, and the loss of his Friday night routine with Natalie, Kyla, and Sid depressed him. He began to think that heading home each night wasn't worth the effort. They had recently adopted a dog named Shasta who was blind and partially deaf, so when Milo came home late at night Shasta barked at him, and the rest of the dogs joined in, with deafening results. By the time they had quieted down the whole house was awake. Instead, he began heading to the casino to play a few hands, before returning to the office to get a few hours of sleep on the couch.

It wasn't long before Johnny Staggs got wind of Milo's late night routine and began to make himself available whenever Milo showed up. Despite knowing better, Milo took his appearances as a token of friendship. Since the cruise he'd favored rum drinks, and he had to admit that after a long day it felt good to spend a few hours gambling, and sip a tropical drink that reminded him of the blissful days relaxing at sea. Between the mounting pressures from the project, the secret push by Traversi for him to split from Gordon, and Gordon's own passel of high maintenance concerns, he was at the center of a number of crises; he began to feel himself going down a long slide towards darkness that he felt powerless to stop. Like Dante's ride on Geryon, he rode the back of an imaginary beast all the way down to the nether region. Some nights he placed enormous bets, picturing himself getting rich – cutting Gordon out and becoming wealthy without him. Other nights he sat at the bar, and with each drink could more clearly visualize his work leading directly to the capture of Osama bin Laden, and the ensuing reward of money and fame. Still other times, he fretted over the tenuous partnership with Gordon, and the highly unethical way the government wanted him to stab Gordon in the back. For the first time in his life, he felt paranoid and uncertain about whom he could really trust. He had thought he could trust Kyla, but now she never even returned his calls. Was this by choice, or was there some other, larger force at work? And why should they be kept from communicating? Suddenly he understood exactly where his father's fears had come from. All his life he had thought Ardell was a little off his rocker, going on all the time about ways the government conspired to keep its citizens living in fear and ignorance through a campaigns of manipulation and fear. Now, having witnessed firsthand all that he had, he felt ashamed for casting such aspersions on his own father, even without his father knowing it.

As Milo became more of a fixture at the Atlantis, he began to lose track of his wins and losses. Stagnaro always said the record would be placed on Gordon's account, and that Milo could settle up with him. But in the sober light of day, he found himself unable to discuss what had become his nighttime routine with Gordon. He told himself that even if his bets put Gordon in the red, it all evened out in the end because Gordon owed him. In any case, according to his own admittedly hazy mental scorekeeping, he had won far more than he had lost.

Meanwhile, at the warehouse, the decoding was not proceeding according to plan. The field agents were sure that there was significant evidence pointing to the Tora Bora area as bin Laden's hiding place, but in the codes that Milo turned up there was a consistent reference to coordinates that corresponded with Abbottabad, Pakistan. Instead of a remote mountain area, these coordinates were in the middle of a large urban area. Milo thought that this made sense... after all, wouldn't it be easier for bin Laden to hide in plain sight, in a bustling area with so much activity that one individual would be less likely to stand out? The Agency, however, disagreed. They argued that bin Laden was a calculating and paranoid man, and was unlikely to make himself as vulnerable as he would be living in a tourist city that housed Pakistan's Military Academy. The field agents and their superiors began putting pressure on Milo to alter the results to support their already formed conclusions. Talk about a bias to confirm, Milo thought.

It was around this time that Gordon came up with a new scheme that made everything worse. He reasoned that if code detection could alert them to potential threats, the ensuing threats and actions could be used to play the financial markets to favor an insider. He reasoned that if a bomb were to destroy an oil refinery, going long on oil stocks would see huge gains. Shorting airlines stocks or marketplaces could be done with equally profitable results. He continued to float the idea to Milo, hoping Milo would give him first shot at the information provided to the Agency. Perhaps Milo would even withhold the info that pertained to oil refineries. When the code began showing up for the King's Cross tube station in London for several weeks, Gordon insisted on staying away from the warehouse.

"Do you know something I don't?" Milo asked. "I told you I wouldn't withhold these findings."

"Don't be ridiculous," Gordon answered dismissively. "You know that you have far more access to the information than I do. I agreed with you. Play it safe and all that."

Milo had a foreboding sense that he and Singer had conspired to short the European markets. Sure enough, in September King's Cross was bombed, and all Gordon would say was that it was a shame. Milo was dumbfounded. "We had these coordinates for weeks. Why on earth weren't they sent to the British government?"

Gordon shrugged in an exaggeratedly nonchalant fashion. "Search me. Damn shame though."

Milo stared at him. "Is there something you're not telling me?"

"Like what?" Gordon shot back. There was a clear challenge in his voice. "I've had about all I can take with this damn paranoia of yours. I think this covert work is starting to get to you, my boy."

Milo decided not to pursue the matter with Gordon further. He did, however, ask Dirkes about it. But Dirkes was similarly opaque. "There's a very specific reason, albeit one that I'm not at liberty to discuss," he said. "I know very little myself. My best suggestion to you is to drop the whole matter."

That evening, after leaving work and heading to the Atlantis to play poker, Milo called Kyla once more. It went straight to voice mail. He decided to leave a message, although he knew it was of little use. "Taylouni, it's Milo again. I thought it might be bad luck to leave you an odd number of messages, so I'm calling you again for good measure."

He paused. "I don't know if you're hearing these, or if someone else is hearing these, or what in the hell is going on. But I'm worried that I haven't heard from you. Whoever is listening to this, I just want to make sure that Kyla is okay. That doesn't seem unreasonable, does it?" He stopped and listened, half expecting a response before remembering that he was leaving a message Kyla was unlikely to ever hear. He sighed. "Hope you're staying safe, Kyla, wherever you are." He ended the call.

Johnny Staggs was already waiting patiently at his elbow. "Will you be playing a hand or two tonight, Mr. Caldwell?" he asked genially. He handed Milo a new drink.

Milo thanked him and said, "I think I'll just have dinner at the bar tonight. I'm not feeling terribly lucky at the moment."

Stagnaro smiled. "Well that's the thing about luck, isn't it? You never know when it might change."

He left Milo alone with his drink. Milo finished it quickly, and sat for several minutes looking at his phone. "What the hell," he said to himself and dialed Kyla's number once more. As it rang, he contemplated what sort of a message he would leave. He wasn't even entirely sure why he was calling her again. He was mentally rehearsing his message when the ringing stopped, and was followed by silence. Someone had answered, but there was no sound on the other end. Milo waited in surprise for a second before asking, "Hello?" Whoever had picked up didn't respond. Milo said, "I know you're there." The call ended. He sat stunned momentarily, and then redialed. But whoever had picked up didn't answer again, and in the five subsequent times he tried back, the call went straight to voice mail each time.

CHAPTER SEVENTEEN

The October 31 deadline came and went, and the Agency showed no signs of slowing the workflow to Hicks Limited. With the presidential election days away, there was some fear that jihadist action would be aimed at the polling places or other election-related targets. Security was high across the country, and it translated into immense pressure on the Hannah project.

It also looked increasingly as if Montefusco was going to win his election bid for governor. He strolled into the office one Saturday morning just before the election, and Gordon met him at the doorway of the terrarium. They sat down and began chatting, and Gordon pulled a bottle of scotch out of his desk. He offered some to Milo. Milo said, "No thanks, I try not to drink before noon during the week."

Montefusco laughed. "Are you sure? I'm sure it's five o'clock somewhere, maybe Lisbon?"

Milo excused himself, saying that he had to get back to the blade servers. As he left, the two men poured themselves drinks and sat at Gordon's immense X-desk in the terrarium. As Milo walked back and forth from several workstations, he always checked Gordon and Montefusco as they spent the rest of the morning drinking and laughing. He grumbled to himself about doing all the work, while Gordon reaped all the rewards. Perhaps O'Bannon had been right. After all, over the last three years he had slaved away unimaginable hours keeping Hicks Limited going, while Gordon had all the fun. The more he thought about it, the more he chastised himself for not jumping at Traversi and O'Bannon's offer. But then, after that initial conversation in the car, nothing else had been said of the matter. And now the October deadline had lapsed, with no repercussions. In all likelihood, they were just trying to drive a wedge between Gordon and him so they could take the compression software for themselves, effectively cutting both partners out. He shouldn't have even listened to them, he decided. They thought they had bought his loyalty with their ridiculous medal that he couldn't even show to anyone.

On his way to the security desk, Milo glanced into the terrarium in time to see Montefusco hand Gordon a briefcase. Milo looked around to see if anyone else had caught it. All the other personnel on the floor were occupied, and O'Bannon and Montgomery had convened with a group of agents in an out-of-the-way conference room. Milo watched the two men shake hands, then Gordon showed Montefusco to the door. Montefusco stopped on his way out where Milo sat. He slapped Milo cheerfully on the back. "Don't let Gordon work you too hard," he said with an earnest conviviality. "Say, if you can get away Tuesday night, we're having an election night gathering at the house. We'd love to have you."

Milo managed to keep his voice steady as he said, "I'll try to make it."

Montefusco nodded. "Please do. And please bring your charming wife. I think she and Sonya really hit it off. Sonya has asked, however, that we don't repeat our performance of "London Calling." He chuckled.

Milo watched him cross the floor and exit the building. He reached the door just as Gordon was picking up the phone to make a call. The briefcase that he'd seen change hands sat open on the desktop, revealing several rows of currency bundled and neatly arranged. Milo halted upon seeing it. Gordon calmly raised a hand and shut the lid of the briefcase.

"Was there something you needed to ask me?" There was no trace of panic or guilt in his voice at being caught. He might as well have been in the middle of watching television. Milo shook his head and said slowly, "It's not important. Just wanted to ask if you wanted anything for lunch."

"No thank you, my boy," Gordon answered. "I'm expecting a visitor soon. Do me a favor and close the door on your way out." Milo did as asked and returned to the warehouse floor, shaking his head at Gordon's brazenness.

Early in the afternoon, Steven Kraft, the owner of the CSC, arrived with the monthly check for their government services. He asked if he could take Gordon to lunch, and together they left the building. Milo crossed the floor to the security monitors where O'Bannon sat. He and Dirkes were in the middle of a conversation about the earlier meeting. As Milo stood waiting for Dirkes to finish talking, he saw on the security monitors that out in the parking lot Kraft and Gordon were getting into Montefusco's town car. Montefusco had evidently returned for this lunch, and as he watched this on the monitor, Milo decided he had to say something.

"Do you know who that is?" He asked O'Bannon and Dirkes, pointing at the screen as Montefusco's taillights receded into the distance. He recounted what he had witnessed earlier, feeling himself grow progressively more agitated as he went along. By the time he had finished, he was shouting.

"Enough is enough!" Milo yelled. "Please tell me you're going to do something this time! He's going to get us all thrown in jail!"

"Now first things first – just take a deep breath," O'Bannon said, clearly alarmed by Milo's panic. "We'll get this figured out. Give us a few hours to discuss this with our superiors. We'll bring you up to speed once we know where we're at."

Milo returned to his workstation and spent several minutes trying to sort things out in his head. It was becoming clear to him that he was soon likely to be in the middle of a fight over this work.

The Agency personnel spent the rest of the day engrossed in conversation, but without saying anything further to Milo. He watched them crisscross the floor all day, pausing to speak in low tones, but as the day went on and no one spoke to him, he felt a strong sense of foreboding. The more he thought about it, the more he became suspicious of Traversi and Dirkes. He suspected their plan was to strip the hard drives and sort things out later, leaving him high and dry. So after they'd left for the day, Milo downloaded the files from the hard drives, leaving only the executable software and taking the source code from the operating system. He then established detection and corruption software, and locked the system down for the night. He finished by changing the passcodes, so that Gordon couldn't get in either. At 7:30 p.m. he left the building, and did what Gordon had done in the past. He took the hardware and the software disks, wrapped them in waterproof bags, and placed them inside the trunk of his car. On the way out of town he stopped at a big box hardware store and got a portable lock box. He drove past the skeet range and found a mile marker post along a desert road, and in pitch dark he dug a hole, placing the lock box in its shallow grave.

When he got home at nine that evening, he called Gordon. Gordon, as expected, was in a jovial mood. "How was your lunch?" Milo asked bitterly.

"Couldn't have been better!" Gordon quipped. "Wished you could have joined us."

"Cut the crap, Gordon. I saw what happened today."

Gordon was silent for a moment. Then he said evenly, "I don't know what you think you saw..."

"Don't try to play one of your mind games with me," Milo interrupted. "I'm not happy about the payoffs to and from Montefusco and I don't appreciate the fact that you're playing roulette with my future. You have no right."

"You want to talk about rights?" Gordon asked, his voice dangerously calm. "You act like you're such a saint all the time. News flash, my boy – you're just as much of a sinner and your hands are just as dirty as any of the rest of us. You think I don't know about the generous tab you've been running up in my name at the Atlantis?"

Milo fumbled for an answer. "That's... that's beside the point."

"What about your friendship with that pretty little towelhead CIA agent? From what I hear, the two of you are quite close. How does your wife feel about that?"

"My conscience is clear, which is more than I'm sure you can say for yourself," Milo answered angrily. "I know each and every one of your tricks, Gordon, and I'm not falling for them. And I'm not going to be responsible for keeping your secrets. I've told O'Bannon and Dirkes about what I saw today. As a matter of fact, O'Bannon and Traversi have made me an offer to quit my partnership with you and come work for them."

Gordon paused before answering. "I know," he said.

Milo was momentarily taken aback. "How in the hell could you possibly know?"

"Because they told me." Neither of them said anything for a moment. When Gordon did speak again, it was to scream into the phone. "You can't fucking outsmart me, do you understand? Do you know who in the fuck you're dealing with? You will not betray me more than you already have! If I find out you've been sneaking behind my back with those agents again – and I will find out – I promise you there will be hell to pay. I will fucking ruin you!"

"You think that because you hold the purse strings, you've got all the power," Milo responded calmly. "But you're lost without me, and you know it. If you try to ruin me I'll just take you down, too."

"Don't you fucking threaten me! You're way out of your league, boy, you hear me? Don't ever make promises you can't keep or threats you can't carry out. And as far as I'm concerned, what you've done today constitutes total betrayal. You may need to put that promise to the test very soon." With that, he hung up.

Milo hardly slept that night. After hours spent tossing and turning, he rose wearily and dressed in the darkness. He was at the warehouse by eight in the morning, and when he tried his key card a red light flashed, indicating that his card was not recognized. He tried three more times, but the card failed each time. Finally he tried his keys in the door but they didn't fit. Someone had changed the locks overnight.

He stayed away from the warehouse for the next week. Natalie, while happy to have him at home, was disconcerted by this sudden, unexpected change. When she asked what was going on, he would only say, "I'm staying at home until they call me." Most afternoons, overcome by anxiety and boredom, he would drive to the casino and have a late lunch. But Johnny Staggs, once his attentive go-to at the Atlantis, had made himself scarce. This added to Milo's angst and desire to drink more heavily.

A week after he'd been locked out of Hicks Limited, he received a "Cease and Desist" letter from Gordon's attorney. A hearing had been set for the week after Thanksgiving, regarding Milo's stake in the company. Given that he still hadn't been paid the money that Gordon had promised him, Milo decided he'd wait to hire an attorney until the preliminary hearing gave him a sense of how serious Gordon was about all of this. He knew Gordon well enough to know that he could get a phone call any day saying that they should put this bad business behind them and that he was needed back at the warehouse. But the call never came, and it dawned on Milo that they might be past the point of Gordon forgiving him.

A week turned into a month, and Milo awaited the day in court when he would have to face Gordon again, this time as his enemy. He once again locked himself up in his home office for most of the day, but found that he couldn't make himself sit in front of the computer, and couldn't concentrate on anything. He kept the television in the office turned on to the classic movie channel, but before long the voices and music began to annoy him, so he kept it on mute. He tried to sit at his desk and found he couldn't, so he spent long stretches of time during the day pacing back and forth and gnawing on his nails. He even began to crave cigarettes, though he had never before been a smoker. One afternoon he drove to the gas station and bought himself a pack of Camels. But once he got back in the car and sat looking at the box in his hand, he realized that he had unconsciously bought the same type of cigarettes that Gordon smoked. He immediately got out of the car and threw the box in the trash.

The day of the hearing finally approached, and though he was a nervous wreck, Milo had to face it alone. Natalie had asked if he wanted her to go with him, but he was insistent that she not be present. When she asked why not, he answered, "I've tried not to drag you into this, and I don't want to start now." Once inside the courtroom, he saw that Julip had accompanied Gordon, and she waved to Milo genially as though they were seeing one another at a picnic. Even though she was still carrying the post-partum baby weight, she was dressed to the nines in a tight, short lavender dress and an outlandish hat piled high with silk flowers. Milo thought she looked grossly overexposed. Gordon, however, stared straight ahead and didn't so much as flicker an eyelash in Milo's direction.

His attorney argued that Milo had no right to the intellectual property until the partnership was dissolved. He further argued that until the agreement regarding the ownership of the source code was settled, Milo should not be allowed to work in the technology field. He further argued that Milo should also be compelled to put the source code into escrow while working out a suitable separation agreement. The judge set a hearing to decide the matter three months in the future. In the meantime, he ruled, Milo must observe a stay from all work in the technology sector until the matter had been resolved. When the court adjourned, Milo tried to catch's Gordon's eye. But Gordon swept

Julip from the courtroom without even a glance, with his attorney hurrying after him.

In the weeks that followed, Milo received numerous calls from O'Bannon. These calls were ostensibly to check in on his well-being, but Milo knew O'Bannon's true motive was to get him to hand over the source code. On multiple occasions, O'Bannon tried to get him to say over the phone that he had stolen it when he left Hicks Limited, and that it was legally property of the company. He tried to soften these blatant attempts by sympathizing with Milo's predicament, and agreeing that Gordon had acted rashly. Still, he insisted repeatedly that a partner couldn't just take a company-owned product and withhold it, effectively bringing the business of the company to a standstill. He suggested that bringing the software back and working it out with everyone involved was the best action to take.

Milo also began to receive threatening phone calls daily. Each time his cell phone rang showing a private number, he felt his pulse begin to quicken and his palms begin to sweat. It was always a man's voice, low and slightly mechanical, but unrecognizable. Most said something like, "You and your family are dead if you ever reveal what was going on with Hannah." Or, "Bring the source code in and nobody dies." He considered not answering the calls, but in talking the matter over with Natalie he decided it best to answer them in order to document each one. After two weeks, he had logged more than fifty calls. In response to these threats, he did two things–he hired an intellectual property attorney, and he hired a private security service to watch his family.

The security firm that he hired used ex-Navy Seals on security details, and he arranged for one guard to look after his daughter and her fiancé while Carrie was in her final year at University of Reno. Two others, Bob and Robert, went everywhere with Natalie. The security company recommended Vic Stockwell to be Milo's personal bodyguard. Vic, as he was called, had a hockey player's size and v-shaped torso.

During the evenings, the night shift security came and two members settled in the house while the third would watch from a van on the street.

They tried their best to ease naturally into the Thanksgiving holiday, but with all the extra people around, it felt less like a holiday and more like a bizarrely grave circus. The detail pointed out that the house behind the Caldwells' had recently acquired some new residents. Stockwell thought they looked like the FBI, and everyone began to refer to the anonymous residents as "the Smiths." The house behind them had placed high-end security cameras and microphones on the roofline of the house, directed right at the Caldwell home. The guards also regularly pointed out that the family members were being followed whenever they got into a vehicle. At times Milo felt sure that it was the FBI, but at other times thought it might be the CIA. There was also the possibility that Gordon had hired someone to have him followed.

When he asked his intellectual property attorney what he should do, the attorney said that this aspect of the situation was beyond the range of his expertise, and recommended a high profile attorney from San Diego named Damon Luce.

Milo had an extended phone conversation with Luce, and he pointed out that nothing was going to transpire before the New Year. He suggested that they should just enjoy the holidays as best they could, and after the first of January he would meet with Milo to plan a separation strategy.

It turned into a strange and slightly unsettling holiday, with the security detail sitting down to the family's Thanksgiving dinner, and later, taking turns watching the front of the house while the Caldwells opened presents during Christmas. Natalie tried to keep the house stable, by sewing quilts for the detail's family members. She even, as a joke, sewed matching placemats for the "Bobs."

After the first of the year, Milo drove to San Diego to meet with Damon Luce. Luce was a well-known, gritty advocate for the little guy against big corporate bullies. In the course of their meeting, he made several strategy suggestions for Milo to implement. He pointed out that it might be wise to have a friendly advocate in their corner who could be perceived as a new business partner. He suggested that he knew someone with deeper pockets than even Gordon had, and that a strong financial backer might dissuade Gordon from a prolonged legal battle. Luce recommended a couple he'd represented named Ross and Cassandra Heller. Not only had they expressed a strong interest in investing in technology, but they had the kind of cash reserves that could buy Gordon out. Milo said that they sounded like the kind of people he would be interested in meeting, though he had his reservations following his "partnership" experience with Gordon.

After the meeting he ate a quick lunch and, with Vic, started the drive back to Reno. He hadn't gone far when his phone beeped once to let him know that he had received a text message. It came from an unknown number, and the message contained not words but a phone number: 999.555.6498. He looked for the nearest exit and took it, pulling into the parking lot of a fast food restaurant. Then he dialed the number and waited. He half expected no answer, but instead what he heard was a pre-recorded message. A robot voice intoned matter-of-factly, "The FBI will raid your house on Thursday."

He sat for a moment, his hands shaking, until Vic asked, "Everything all right?" Milo asked him to listen to the message, which Vic did with a straight face. He looked thoughtful.

"What do you think are the chances of tracing this number?" Milo asked.

"In all honesty, not great. I doubt the number is traceable, since it probably got routed through numerous proxy servers before coming through transmission lines to you." He paused before saying, "It's a complicated process."

Milo decided to remain silent and not tell Vic that this was in fact the exact type of thing he'd been working on for the Hammer project. Instead, after a brief silence, he said, "I'm going to give it one more listen and try to record it." He had gotten in the habit of carrying a digital recorder in his briefcase, as he occasionally had ideas for projects or stumbled upon solutions at odd moments for problems he'd faced on Hannah, such as while he was driving or having a drink at the casino. He reached into the back seat and fetched the recorder from his briefcase. But when he dialed the number, there were only a few static beeps, then nothing. He tried twice more. The message had disappeared.

Vic called both Bob and Robert, asking if any of the other family members had received any text messages or phone calls from unidentified numbers. None of them had. He hung up and looked at Milo.

"What's the next move?"

"I guess we'd better book it back to Reno," Milo answered, glancing over his shoulder as he began to guide the car back to the freeway. "But if that message was a legitimate warning, how can I be sure the

FBI will wait until Thursday? What if they come tonight? Or right now, before I can get there?"

"Why don't we check up on your friendly neighbors," Vic suggested, dialing Robert once more. "What's the status on the Smiths? Any unusual activity over there today?" He waited for a moment as Robert offered a response.

Vic responded, "Completely? You're sure?" Then, "Roger." He hung up and looked at Milo. "Looks like the Smiths packed up and moved this afternoon. Not only are all the cameras gone, but the blinds are all open and the house is completely empty."

Despite his best efforts to appear calm, Milo could see his hands shaking where they held the steering wheel. He clutched it tighter to steady himself until his knuckles turned white. Then he said quietly, "Goddammit." He stepped on the gas.

As they accelerated, passing a number of cars in the process, Milo caught sight of a black SUV in his rearview mirror following suit. His heart began to pound. "Vic," he said, his throat suddenly dry. "There's a car following us."

Vic turned in his seat and glanced back at the SUV, which was keeping a measured distance, but nevertheless remaining with them. "It doesn't have plates," he said. "Keep going for another five minutes and then take the first exit you see. Take it quickly. And jump off at the last possible second."

Milo did as he was told. The whole time, the SUV remained at a reasonable distance, but it was always in sight. A road sign told them that an exit was approaching in half a mile. Milo waited until they came up on it, and when Vic said, "Now!" he jerked the wheel and swerved into the exit lane, cutting off another car in the process. The car honked angrily and Milo rode the far right shoulder to let them pass. The SUV slowed slightly, and looked momentarily as though it wasn't certain what to do. But then it sped up and kept going, and as it passed, Milo and Vic craned their necks to in an attempt to see through the windows. They were heavily tinted, and revealed nothing of the passengers within.

CHAPTER EIGHTEEN

When they pulled up to the house at seven that night, there were no immediate signs that anything was amiss. Before Vic could give the appropriate knock of "shave and a haircut," Milo unlocked the front door and yelled, "Natalie!" At once the dogs went crazy in the front hallway, barking and getting underfoot. The noise attracted Robert, who was in the foyer within seconds, his hand on his gun. He relaxed when he saw who it was and told them, "Everyone's having dinner."

Milo and Vic pushed the dogs aside and hurried into the dining room to find Natalie, Bob, Jeremy, and Carrie and her fiancé, Erik, seated around the table. Robert remained in the living room watching the front. Everyone looked up in anticipation as Milo came hurtling in with the frenzied dogs in tow. "Is everyone OK?" he asked.

"Of course," Natalie answered. "We're waiting on you."

Milo looked at the family, then at Bob. "You all need to get out of here," he said. "To a hotel or something. Come on, everybody up."

"What's going on?" Natalie asked as they all rose from their seats. There was a clear note of fear in her voice.

"Dad?" Carrie asked, her voice strained as well.

Vic put a hand on Milo's shoulder and spoke into his ear. "You might not want to get everyone in a panic. I suggest that you calmly explain what's happening. No need to tell them everything, but give them a chance to absorb the news before everyone starts running around."

Milo nodded. "Okay, let's all sit back down and talk this through. There have been some recent developments and we need to get on the same page." The security detail joined them as each one took a seat around the table. "I received a message today warning me that there will be a raid on the house this Thursday." There was a swell of voices as everyone reacted with shock. Milo waited until they quieted down to continue, "We have no way of knowing if this is a false alarm or if it's the real deal, but I don't want to take any chances. Carrie, I think it would be best if you and Erik stayed at his house for the next few days.

Natalie, you and Jeremy had better check into a hotel. I don't want any of you to be here when and if this happens."

Carrie said, "But what about you, Dad?"

"I need to be here and be ready. Vic will still be with me. But if this really does happen, things could get a little hairy for a while." He looked at Carrie. "As much as I don't want to have to tell you this, honey, we need to be thinking ahead. If this legal situation doesn't get sorted out in time, we may have to postpone the date of the wedding."

Carrie nodded and said nothing, but her lip began to tremble and she had to blink back tears. After a moment she couldn't contain it and began to cry. Erik tried to console her, saying, "It's just a few more months, babe." He shot a glance at Milo. "We are talking just a few months, right?"

"At this point, I really don't know," Milo answered honestly.

With this, Carrie began to sob. Shasta, who couldn't see what was happening but felt the extra stress, began to bark, which started the other dogs barking. Natalie looked at Milo as if to say, Do something! Milo spoke up in order to be heard above the din. "Listen," he said, "if you go along with this, sweetie, we'll have the wedding in Maui. If you can just hold out until Easter. I'll even pay for the entire wedding party to stay anywhere you want, and you can get married on the beach at sunset. How's that?"

Carrie quieted down and looked up at him, her eyes wide. "Do you mean it?"

Milo saw immediately that he would have to make good on this promise. He swallowed hard. "Yes."

"Oh, daddy!" She threw her arms around him. Natalie had been looking at him sideways this whole time, but said nothing.

"Now, I need you guys to get your things together and get out of here. I'll call you in a few days when this is all over."

When they left the room, Natalie said, "It'll be nice to get a Hawaiian vacation out of the wedding at least."

"Please don't give me a hard time right now. I'm trying to keep the family safe and still make everyone happy."

Natalie nodded and turned to Jeremy. "Go pack an overnight bag. Sounds like we're going to be away from the house for the next few days. No texts or cell phone calls to any of your friends, either."

Milo and Vic drove them to a hotel on the far side of town while the Bobs followed closely behind in a second car. Milo had planned to drop them off at the entrance, but Vic said gently, "Maybe you'd better spend the night with your family tonight."

"But what if the raid takes place tonight?" He found that his teeth were clenched as he said this.

"We can have one of the Bobs stay at the house and give you a call if anyone shows up there. But if it does happen tomorrow, there's no telling what might happen after that."

"You mean there's no telling when I might be able to see them next."

Vic nodded grimly. "Try to get a good night's rest, at least. Give yourself that chance."

They checked into a suite with a set of sliding doors that closed off the common area. Vic and Robert set up a pair of cots in the next room while Natalie and Milo slept in the bed and Jeremy slept on the sofa bed. Bob had gone back to the house to keep watch, promising to call Milo the second one of the dogs so much as barked. Milo slept fitfully that night, waking at least once every hour to check his phone. But it never rang.

At nine the following morning he drove back to the house. He was half a mile away when Bob called. "They're here," was all he said.

When he pulled up to the house, the driveway was blocked by three FBI vans and three more black Ford Crown Victorias. Half a dozen men and one woman in FBI windbreakers exited from the vans. Another half dozen agents were climbing out of the cars – two from each, wearing jumpsuits and sunglasses.

The lead FBI agent was Bradley North, whom Milo had met previously when the blade servers had been delivered to the warehouse. When he walked up after parking his car halfway down the block, North shook his hand solemnly. "Mr. Caldwell, Agent Bradley North. I recall meeting you last year on the premises of Hicks Limited."

"I remember," Milo said.

North took a folded bundle of papers from the breast pocket of his suit. "We have a warrant to search your home. If your family is present they will need to remain during the proceedings."

"They're not here," Milo answered. "I didn't want them to be here to have to see this."

North stared at him for a moment. "Am I to understand that you knew about this in advance?"

"I did."

North was clearly taken aback, but did his best to retain an air of control over the situation. He continued forcefully with the mandate, as if Milo had not spoken. "You will comply with this search or you will face arrest. It is likely you will be arrested today regardless."

In keeping with the instructions Luce had given him, Milo asked to see the search warrant. North handed it over. Milo scanned it for a specific listing of what they were after, but it read simply, "Open Warrant, Classified." Milo looked up. "What are you searching for, exactly?"

"We believe you have stolen classified materials and government property, Mr. Caldwell," North replied. As he said this, the other agents began to stream up the driveway toward the house. They positioned themselves in a semicircle around the front door, ready to break it down. Then one of the agents turned and walked down the drive to ask Milo for the key.

He put his hand in his pocket and clutched his keys. "I'd like to be present for the search, to ensure that nothing gets damaged or broken," he said.

North crossed his arms. "I'm afraid I'll have to refuse that request."

Milo handed over the keys. When the agent opened the door, the dogs went nuts, spilling out in a blur of teeth and fur and tails. Milo started forward to calm them but North clamped a hand on his shoulder. A chaotic couple of minutes ensued until one of the agents shouted that Milo had better get his mutts under control or they would be shot. At this point Milo lost his cool. "How in the fuck do you expect me to control the dogs if I can't go near them? The whole point is that they're protecting the house you won't let me go inside!"

After several adrenaline-fueled minutes, the agents calmed down and let him collect the dogs. He escorted them to the backyard, followed closely by one of North's men the entire way. After he had sealed them off with the sliding glass door, the agents instructed him to pull his car into the garage. When he asked why they said, "We don't need to answer your questions. Just do it or you'll be placed under arrest."

The FBI cars were backed out of the driveway, and Milo did as he was told. Once he exited the car, the agents swarmed it. One of them pointed at him and said, "Get him out of the garage." He was escorted back to the driveway and watched as a small detachment of agents thoroughly combed the car, checking every pocket and tray, opening the glove compartment and examining it thoroughly for hidden doors or spaces, taking everything out of the trunk and inspecting it inch by inch. Milo learned later that the warrant didn't cover the vehicle unless it was parked in the garage. He had been tricked into helping them with their search.

The agents spent the next five hours searching every square inch of the house. The closets, furniture, and dresser drawers were ransacked. Early in the afternoon the agents found the safe in Milo and Natalie's bedroom. One of them came outside to where Milo stood and said, "We'll need you to open the safe, sir."

Milo looked at North, then back at the agent. "And what if I refuse?"

"Then we'll have to torch it."

Milo handed over the keys. Knowing the raid was happening, Milo had already moved the valuables from the safe. This included around $150,000 in cash, Natalie's jewelry, and the family's passports. He had placed them in a storage unit several miles away that housed all of Natalie's quilting fabrics. He looked carefully at the warrant and noticed nothing was said about those premises. He was relieved.

After several hours of placing calls, Milo finally reached Damon Luce by phone, and Luce began filing motions to stop the seizure. However, they soon found that it was worse than they had initially imagined. When Natalie tried to order a pizza that night and her debit card was rejected, they learned that the FBI had frozen their bank accounts and credit cards.

When the search turned up very little at the residence, the FBI obtained a second open warrant that evening; and while the Caldwells cleaned up from the day's mess, the search team headed to the storage unit company. They threatened the owners of the private storage facility with arrest if any employees from the facility dare call the Caldwells. While sorting through the quilting materials, North's team found the bundled cash, jewelry and passports, and took them all into evidence.

Next to the quilt storage was a second unit that Milo had rented and which housed long-unused computer equipment from Milo's earliest work at Hicks Limited. At length, word came back that they had found several disk drives but Milo knew that there was nothing of significance on them. Until the FBI could cite specifically what they were looking for, he reasoned, he couldn't trust anything that he heard. Nor could he believe that whatever they found hadn't been planted.

With the credit cards cancelled Milo had Natalie and the security detail go over to the storage unit the next morning to secure some cash to hold them over for a while. When they arrived at the storage lot, the owners described the activity of the previous evening. Natalie was distraught when she reached the quilting locker and found the money and valuables missing. She called Milo and delivered the bad news. Immediately he got on the phone to Luce to ask for some help.

Luce sprang into action when he saw the extent of the FBI's tenacity. He contacted the Hellers and arranged for the whole family, as well as the dogs, to stay at their compound in La Quinta. Natalie, Carrie, Jeremy and the dogs—as well as the Bobs—flew out of Reno the next morning, which was a Friday. In the process of gathering clothes and cleaning up, Natalie found an FBI business card sitting atop her pile of folded lingerie. Unlike the rest of the drawers, it was obvious that the drawer had been searched and all of the intimates had been refolded. Upon realizing this, Natalie immediately threw the whole pile into a plastic bag and resolved to take them to the drycleaners when they landed in La Quinta.

In the days that followed, it looked as if the Air Force would be throwing its support behind Gordon. O'Bannon continued to call Milo throughout the weekend, trying either to have him admit he had taken the source code, or to convince him to patch things up with Gordon as quickly as possible. "Be reasonable," he said. "Surely we can find a way to put all this bad business behind us."

"I'm just trying to protect myself and my family," Milo replied. "So far you haven't given me much of a reason to trust you."

Meanwhile, the CIA was absent. Except for the occasional

anonymous text warning him against divulging information about Hannah, he didn't hear from anyone. Not Dirkes, not Givens, and not anyone else at Langley. Certainly not Kyla.

For the next week, neither Milo or Natalie slept much. Often they lay awake in separate cities, and one would eventually call the other and ask whether they were awake. Each would be awake when the other called; they would then turn on the lights and spend several hours talking. "Why aren't Kyla or Sid around to help us?" Natalie wanted to know. "We spent so much time with them. Here I thought they were our friends, and it's like they've completely disappeared."

"I doubt whether they were ever our friends," Milo scoffed. "It's all so clear to me now. They were probably trying to just get dirt on me to use against us."

"But that doesn't seem like the type of thing they would do," Natalie insisted. "They seemed like good people, really. I just don't understand. Maybe they were ordered to stay away."

"At this point it doesn't seem to make a difference whether they were our friends or not. The bottom line is they can't help us now, whether or not they want to."

Natalie didn't say anything. The sleepless nights were taking their toll on her and she described the dark circles that set in under her eyes. Milo got up and went into the bathroom, where he looked at himself in the mirror. He looked worse. In fact, he realized he had put on a good ten pounds in the last year, without even noticing, likely due to the stress and drinking more regularly. He switched off the light so that he wouldn't have to look at himself anymore.

Gordon's attorney continued to call, but Milo repeatedly directed him to Luce. Then, on one Saturday morning, Milo and Vic stopped at a deli to pick up lunch. Vic offered to come inside with Milo, but Milo said, "I'll only be a few minutes." He went in. There was only one other person, a woman, waiting at the counter, and the proprietor was engaged behind the deli case making a sandwich. Milo took a number, and stood gazing absentmindedly at the meat selection behind the glass. Suddenly he became aware of someone standing next to him. He looked up into the face of a tall blond man with sharp gray eyes. The man seemed to have materialized out of nowhere. Before Milo could say anything, the man spoke in a low voice. "If you don't make it right with Mr. Hicks, then your family is dead." he whispered, looking

Milo dead in the eye. Then he turned and walked calmly out the door. Milo watched as he crossed the parking lot and climbed into a car that appeared to be driven by Johnny Staggs. He found himself momentarily frozen, unable to move or make a sound. His mouth went dry and all he could do was shiver, which he did uncontrollably. The car drove away. He looked at the woman waiting for her sandwich to see if she had heard. She apparently hadn't, absorbed as she was in a gossip magazine.

Milo left without ordering his sandwich. Vic could tell by his face as he approached the car that something was wrong. He opened the passenger side door and got out. "What's going on?" he asked.

"Did you see that man?" Milo asked, his voice sounding strangled coming from his suddenly parched throat.

"The one that just left the store?" Vic asked. Milo nodded mutely. "What happened?"

Milo gradually found his voice and recounted the incident. When he was finished, Vic was furious. "Milo, you need to get a goddamn grip!" he yelled. "First you hire us, then you insist on directing us. I can't believe I let you take charge like that. You're making me look like I served in the French fucking foreign legion! If you're going to step out on your own, against my advice and expertise, you've got to pay attention! I can't help you and still give you your personal space if you don't signal me when something like that happens!"

"I'm sorry," Milo murmured passively, still deeply shaken. "I was caught totally off guard."

Vic called the Bobs and let them know what had happened. They agreed that they all needed to be extra vigilant, and not let any of the family members out of their sight in public for even one moment.

On Monday morning Vic drove Milo to the Reno airport, where the Hellers' private plane was scheduled to pick them up. It was a warm, cloudless day and a dry desert wind sent tumbleweeds bouncing across the runways until they caught on the chain link fence surrounding the airport perimeter. Vic parked the car and they entered the terminal, almost entirely empty except for a few senior citizens who were traveling in a group. The TSA guards stood at their posts looking bored, and processed Milo and Vic through the security checkpoint without much interest.

They walked through to the tarmac, heading for the waiting jet. As they made their way, Milo cast a glance toward the temporary JANET hangar. There was no sign of the larger planes that brought hordes of eager colonels in Hicks Limited's heyday. The area surrounding the hangar looked almost deserted, except for a small turboprop plane with the distinctive red stripe painted on its fuselage. From where he stood, Milo could see three people milling about the plane, and he strained to see if he recognized any of them. He didn't even see the person approaching from the periphery on his right until Vic stopped her and said, "Can I help you, ma'am?" Milo turned to see that he was addressing Kyla.

The first words out of his mouth were, "Taylouni, where the hell have you been?"

Vic looked momentarily perplexed. "Do you know her?"

"We used to work together at Hicks," Milo answered. "She's not a threat." He paused. "I hope."

Kyla smiled apologetically. "I'm sorry, Milo, but you've been SSPed." With this, she handed him an envelope containing a document. She looked around once and then leaned in to speak in a low voice. "Follow the rules and I promise I won't let you down." Before Milo could say anything, she turned and began to walk briskly back to the JANET hangar.

Milo stood staring after her until Vic put a hand on his shoulder and said, "Come on, let's board before this thing takes off without us."

Inside the plane, they took their seats and Milo attempted to gather his thoughts as the engines roared to life. Once he had buckled his seatbelt and settled in, Vic said, "Let's have a look at that."

Milo was still holding the envelope in his hand. He opened it and spent a moment pondering the affidavit. "This is all Greek to me," he said.

Vic took it and looked it over. "It's a States Secrets Privilege."

"What does that mean?"

Vic answered flatly, "It means that the government is cracking down on you. You'll have to forget about being a regular guy. They've got you now."

Milo turned and gazed out at the window. He was silent for several minutes. At last he said slowly, "So my life as an ordinary citizen is gone forever."

"I'll put it this way," Vic said, "you must be somebody pretty important for them to give this big of a shit about you."

CHAPTER NINETEEN

The Caldwells spent the next several weeks living at the carriage house on the Heller's private compound. A great granite "Grey Wolf Creek" sign stood outside the gates, and from there it was a half-mile drive on a winding road leading to the majestic main house. The carriage house, several hundred yards behind the pool, with a driveway of its own leading up to it, was bigger than most houses that the Caldwell family had lived in. It was kept in immaculate condition by daily visits from cleaning staff, a fact that Natalie found disconcerting at first. "It doesn't feel right to ask someone else to clean up after us," she told Milo, after he found her one morning helping one of the slightly confused maids clean the kitchen.

By the beginning of March they found a house to rent on Toscana Way and relocated there, determined to begin their life anew. They celebrated Easter Sunday a week after moving in, the dining room still crowded with boxes pushed to one side to accommodate the table and chairs. Milo said a prayer over the ham. "Lord, let us learn from you when you rose up again. Let that be our example."

He and Natalie talked late into the night each night about how best to handle the pressure they were under. They both wanted to use this opportunity to create a fresh start, which in part meant changing their lifestyles. Natalie said that it was important to her that she begin going to church, and Milo figured it was as good of a place to start as any. The Episcopal Church of La Quinta was a large congregation whose membership included many notable people of influence, so the fact that the new attendees would have their own security retinue was not the first time such a thing had occurred.

Each Sunday, beginning with Easter, the security detail dropped them off at the beginning of the service and was ready to pick them up when it ended. This continued without incident until the second month, when the detail noticed a man seen hanging around the church while the service was in session, but never going in. Several of the ushers had noticed him, too, and said that none of them had ever seen him before. As soon as the Bobs began to keep an eye on him, they noted that he was always present to watch Vic walk Milo and Natalie from the front door to the waiting car. After three weeks of this, Vic advised that he felt it was in their best interest to let the pastor know what was going on. Natalie was adamantly against the idea, and in the end, they shelved the practice of going to church just as quickly as they had taken it up.

With the decision to postpone Carrie's wedding and to relocate it a year from now in Maui, Erik joined them in their La Quinta house. He quit his job as a loan officer in Reno, and began working alongside Milo at the Hellers' tech company, called Cassander Technologies. Cassandra supervised the day-to-day operations, though as far as Milo was concerned she didn't do much supervising. She essentially checked daily with their Palm Desert office, and got a report on the work plan. After that, they didn't hear from her again until the next morning.

Meanwhile, Milo and Erik got the Palm Desert office up and running. They set up several workstations, and a secure room where they could download the daily Al-Jazeera broadcasts and systematically back them up with the most recent, state-of-the-art business blade servers. These weren't as powerful as the ones Milo used on the Hannah project, but the hope was a government contract would be forthcoming, so that they could upgrade. Their plan was to scan the footage to detect anomalies once the proper equipment had been secured, but for the time being they focused their efforts on simply copying the incoming transmissions.

At home, Natalie and Carrie poured all their efforts into planning the wedding in Maui. Since the initial scare with the stranger at church, Natalie seemed to be settling into their new life in the desert. In many ways, Milo thought, she had adjusted much better than anyone else in the family. She joined a quilting circle and joined a women's church group; always, of course, with Robert in tow. She took up the planning of Carrie and Erik's wedding with a gusto Milo had seldom witnessed in her before. Though Milo didn't relish the idea of her and Carrie planning how they would spend the money on the wedding before they actually had it, he kept his mouth shut to keep the peace.

The Hellers had promised an advance on future salary until the court cases with Gordon and the FBI could be sorted out. Once the

Hellers saw the cash flow that had been part of Hannah, they were more than willing to take a gamble on Milo's software and skill set. Cassandra advanced them a $50,000 line of credit, and assumed the costs for Damon Luce against the total salary arrangement of $100,000 per month for a one-year contract.

Luce, for his part, had taken over both court cases. He first challenged the injunction for the non-compete agreement on his own, then brought in his partner, Bill Schnellenberger, to challenge the FBI's search and seizure actions.

The strategy of bringing in the Hellers proved well-advised. Brennan Royals, the judge in the non-compete hearing, was unsympathetic toward Gordon. It quickly became clear that as far as the judge was concerned, Gordon's history at Grant McKinley was a relevant factor in the present case. When all was said and done, Judge Royals ruled against the injunction, but placed a 180 day stay on the use of the source code for either party until a suitable separation agreement could be hammered out.

Cassandra Heller tried to convince Milo that simply buying Gordon out was his best option, as galling as it might seem. She reasoned that if the Hammer project took off, he would easily recoup his initial eleven million in no time. After all, she said, wouldn't it be worth it just to make Gordon go away?

The search and seizure hearings proved to be more complicated. Once the State Secrets Privilege was invoked, Milo was prohibited from using any information derived from the Hicks Limited contract as argument for his appeal. Each party, the FBI, and US Attorney's office were compelled to produce documents to the Pentagon and CIA attorneys before presenting them in court. Both governmental entities redacted anything that even remotely represented a state secret, so that those sections could not be presented in court. Similarly, Milo was not allowed to call any Hannah team members as witnesses for rebuttal.

Each hearing was conducted in chambers and besides the participants—Agent North, Milo, and their attorneys – there were three clandestine-looking men in suits who sat silently alongside the court reporter. Occasionally the topic would move toward some of the specific details; then one of suits would request to speak to the judge privately. The judge would return and redirect the proceedings.

Finally, after three months, Judge Royals presided over the 41 (g) hearing in which Luce argued for a motion to return illegally seized property. Royals agreed with Luce's argument that many of the documents used for the initial warrant were inconsistent with what was presented in the hearing. He further ruled that Agent North and his team had used their authority, albeit directed by the US Attorney's office, to go after a private citizen without probable cause. The judge came about as close as anyone could to suggesting that the US Attorney's office had used its resources to political ends. Judge Royals ruled that Milo was to receive in return everything taken in the raid, and the FBI was given a hands-off, "scorched earth" mandate barring them from, in his words, harassing Milo Caldwell and his family again. The judge then turned to Milo and personally apologized for authorizing the warrant in the first place.

"There really is no remedy for what has taken place and what you and your family have been put through, Mr. Caldwell," he said, "but I am glad that you had your day in court to rectify this gross oversight."

Two days later, President George W. Bush fired the US Attorney for Nevada.

❀ ❀ ❀

May gave way to June, and the desert heat began its steady ascent in La Quinta. At night, Milo took long walks with Vic through the warm, empty streets of the subdivision. He felt strangely unnerved when on one such walk a coyote dashed across the street a hundred feet in front of them.

"Let's turn back," he said in a panic.

Vic laughed. "That thing is more afraid of us than we are of it. No need to be on edge."

"I'm just ready to go back." He turned and started walking quickly, leaving Vic to catch up with him.

A week later, as he let the dogs out before bed one night, he thought he saw movement in the back yard. He flicked on the patio light and saw a mountain lion crouched beside the pool, recoiling from the light. It slinked away and leapt to the top of the barrier wall before disappearing into the darkness beyond.

Everything seemed well on its way to resolution with Gordon, but Milo felt instinctively mistrustful of this. Gordon's attorney had worked with the Hellers' business attorney to reach an equitable settlement, and they were close to an agreement. It didn't seem like Gordon's way at all. The developing arrangement seemed to contain none of Gordon's hallmark vindictiveness. The Gordon that Milo had come to know hated to lose, and wouldn't settle for even a marginal win.

But when both rulings came down the death threats ceased, and he allowed himself to exhale. Still, the security detail remained vigilant. As they prepared to make an offer to Gordon, the Hellers continued to discuss the compression software possibilities with Milo. As wireless transmission continued to grow in popularity in a variety of business applications, Cassandra asked if the compression utility could be used in other fields besides military application. They hit upon an idea that Milo had begun to formulate the previous year: a wireless cardiac device that could transmit to a central business hub. Similar to the emergency wireless services on automobiles, if an emergency cardiac situation arose, the patient would have the ability to send the output of their cardiac rhythm to a central monitoring hub. The hub would connect to the nearest enrolled emergency hospital or doctor's support system to render a protocol based on the monitoring. The Hellers thought the idea was promising, and suggested that if things with the government didn't work out, or if Gordon became difficult in the negotiations, the company could look at alternative research and design.

As the summer temperature climbed steadily, Milo was tasked with booking a minister for Carrie and Erik's wedding. He decided to contact an old friend from his high school days who had been ordained. David Holden had a reputation as a wild and irreverent Youth Director. Soon after Milo had fallen out of touch with him,

Holden had returned to seminary to become an Episcopalian priest. When they spoke on the phone in early July, Milo was startled to hear that his formerly screwball friend had toned down his ways.

"I think it's been more than ten years since we last spoke," Holden said when Milo called. They spent some time catching up and Milo marveled at the change in his friend.

Holden laughed at his bewilderment. "I suppose you've got to put your rebellious streak behind you at some point."

Milo chuckled as well. "Sounds like we've both settled into a steady life of stubborn conventionality."

"It was bound to happen sooner or later," Holden agreed. "In any event, I'm very glad to hear from you. What's on your mind?"

"I wish I could say that I'm just calling to catch up, but I really need to ask two favors. The first is that I'm looking for a minister for my daughter's wedding in Maui towards the end of the year. The second… to be honest, my father hasn't been doing well health-wise. When the time comes, I hoped I could ask you to perform his funeral."

"Well, yeah, I guess, congratulations are in order for your daughter's wedding, and I'm sorry to hear about your father's condition." He paused and added morbidly, "though I hope I won't have to perform the wedding and the funeral in the same ceremony." The joke was perversely cryptic and seemed to Milo to summarize his life in Reno and his time spent working with Gordon and the government. Milo went quiet, then suddenly choked up, unable to speak.

Holden quickly realized what he'd done and apologized. "I'm sorry, Milo, that was a tasteless joke. I guess I worked with crude teenagers too long."

"It's not that," Milo said, his voice heavy with emotion. "So much has happened in the last two years. Sometimes I feel as if I've lost my way. I've tried to do right by my family, and in the process I've lost sight of what's important to me." As he said these words, he immediately felt ashamed. How long was he going to invoke his family's welfare as a justification for his actions? He now felt, for the first time, that he had simply let everything happen, without having the moral fiber to change the course of events. He felt certain that his voice betrayed him; that Holden could see through his weak defense even over the phone. For the first time, he felt exposed for what he really was — a coward.

"Would it help to talk about it?" Holden asked.

And so, Milo found himself divulging the whole of his story as Holden listened attentively. It was as if a dam had broken inside him. He found himself unable to spare even the more lascivious details of Gordon's ways and doings, though the pastor made no remark on these points. He talked for two hours, with Holden putting in a word here or there. When the story brought them to the present he said, "David, I've told you things that I wasn't supposed to."

"Of course everything you've said will be kept in confidence. But does this put you in danger?"

"I don't know," Milo answered. "The government can't possibly prosecute me for my confession to a priest." He had no idea whether or not this was true. Rehashing his tale from start to finish had left him exhausted and emotionally spent. "Do you think I'll ever escape hell?"

"My friend," Holden answered, "that is entirely between you and God. It sounds to me as if you want to change, and that is the first step. But you must act on what you know to be right."

Milo was silent. Then he said, "Once, on one of our private flights from New York to Reno, Gordon hired a priest so that he could confess his sins before we landed. I can't remember what happened to prompt this, but somehow or other his conscience had gotten the better of him. The priest looked the other way while Gordon poured himself a few drinks, and when he was ready he just poured out a flood of confessions. And I sat through the whole thing. I heard him spill every detail of this sinful life he'd led into the priest's ear. The flight was five hours and Gordon wept and moaned and confessed the entire time. When the plane landed, we disembarked, and the plane turned around and took the priest straight back to New York. And the next day, Gordon was back to his old ways. It was as if, in his mind, his slate had been wiped clean, and he had free range to do whatever he pleased.

"Late that night I got a call from his wife, telling me he was at the Atlantis and he was in trouble. She demanded that I go help him. As soon as I got there, I found him in a private gambling room surrounded by naked women, lying on the floor too drunk to stand up. But still he kept betting. He was a million and a half dollars in the hole and digging himself deeper by the minute. I took over his hand and within an hour I had played him out of the hole. Finally I got him out of there and poured him into a suite, and as I left I could hear him sobbing from his bed. The next morning he came to work on time at 8:00, as if the previous night had never happened. He never thanked me, never apologized, never mentioned it again." He took a deep breath. "Dave, the reason I'm telling you all this is because I don't want to live the life of hypocrisy and selfishness that Gordon has. But I'm afraid I've followed him down the rabbit hole, and I think that it might be too late to get myself out."

Holden didn't speak for a minute. Then he said, "Do the right thing, Milo, and God won't let you down."

After they ended the call, Milo sat gazing out the bedroom window at the dancing shadows cast against the side of the house by the underwater pool light. Holden's statement had been almost word for word what Kyla had promised when he had last seen her on the airport tarmac in Reno.

CHAPTER TWENTY

July brought Milo's and Natalie's birthdays, and with it a sense that the family's prospects may be improving. The FBI had dropped their pursuit following Judge Royals' decree, and the talks with Gordon's lawyer seemed to be progressing smoothly toward an amicable conclusion. Luce believed that they would have a fair separation agreement in place by the end of summer, and in his conversations with the Hellers, Milo was fairly certain that soon thereafter he would have the capital necessary to buy Gordon out entirely.

As all things appeared to be coming to a peaceable end, the planning for Carrie's wedding took center stage. She and Natalie made several trips to Los Angeles to look at wedding dresses, and Natalie became consumed by the assorted details to be tended to: the invitations, the flowers, the catering, the reception. Milo couldn't help but laugh when he came to bed after a long day at the office and found her still awake, propped up in bed and poring over her laptop with her brow knit in concentration. "You're working harder than I am," he teased, "and you're not even getting paid for it."

"No rest for the mother of the bride," she sighed.

Recently the death threats had ceased as well, prompting Milo to reevaluate the necessity of the security detail. Though he had to admit that it gave him extra comfort to have them around, keeping them on had begun to take a toll on the family's finances. When eight weeks had passed without a threatening text message or phone call, Milo told Vic that he felt their services were no longer necessary. After all, Judge Royals had effectively scorched the Feds on their search, and the matter with Gordon looked to be resolved shortly. Vic listened as Milo had his say and then answered, "I certainly hope for your family's sake that this is over and done with, Milo. And I won't say I'm not sorry to go. You're as good a guy to work for as I've ever known. I just want to caution you against being lulled into a false sense of security."

"I appreciate your concern," Milo said, "and if I had the money,

I'd rather keep you on until it was all completely behind us. But things have been tight, and this is the hard decision I've had to make."

They shook hands. Vic said, "Just be sure to look after yourself, okay? Keep an eye out. And if things change, don't hesitate to call me and the Bobs."

When the Caldwells had first hired the security detail, they all felt strange being accompanied by the imposing men everywhere they went. Now, without them, Milo felt suddenly vulnerable. He found himself being extra cautious, and paying almost obsessive attention to the details of his surroundings. He even got in the habit of keeping his digital recorder in his pocket to capture audio notes about anything strange he happened to notice.

In the first weeks following the dismissal of the security detail he saw cryptic, potentially threatening signs everywhere: a car with tinted windows stopped behind him at a red light; an indistinguishable solitary figure taking a walk through the neighborhood at night; a satellite dish on a neighbor's roof that seemed to be pointed at the Caldwell household. But as the weeks stretched on without incident, Milo began to feel that he had become as paranoid as his father.

The most pressing issue at hand was the matter of cash flow. The $150,000 returned to them following the FBI raid served as their primary reserve in addition to the loan from the Hellers. The Reno house had sat on the market unsold for several months, and the lease-to-own costs on the La Quinta house were proving astronomical. Furthermore, Milo had agreed to help Erik and Carrie with a down payment on a house, and when the time came for him to deliver on this, he found himself unable to renege on his promise. Carrie had learned early on that her father's way of expressing sentiment was through cash offerings, and she used this lesson to spare no expense in planning the wedding. She selected the Four Seasons at Wailea in Kihei, the most expensive hotel on Maui, and booked two dozen rooms for the week-long festivities in April. Milo saw that his ill-conceived promise to pay for the wedding in Hawaii had been taken full advantage of, and was now getting out of hand. When he tried to broach the topic with Natalie one night as she sat in bed with her laptop, researching favors for the guests, she snapped, "It's a little late to change your mind."

✹ ✹ ✹

July 15 was Natalie's birthday, and to celebrate Milo took her out for dinner and birthday cake. After they returned, the visit that sent the dogs into a frenzy and the arrest followed.

His nine days in jail over, Milo emerged ready to erupt. The cab dropped him off at his house at eight o'clock in the morning, and by nine he was yelling hoarsely into the phone at Cassandra Heller. "How is it that you couldn't bail me out sooner?" he demanded. "Do you have any goddamn idea what I've just been through?"

"Of course I didn't know that I was getting into business with a compulsive gambler, now did I?" she shot back.

"Now wait just a minute." Milo was indignant. "Those gambling debt charges are completely phony. I don't know anything about them. My suspicion is that Gordon used his influence to mobilize state forces against me since the Fed action didn't get the results he wanted. You know as well as I do that now with Montefusco in the Nevada governor's mansion, Gordon has a powerful ally to do his bidding for him."

Cassandra seemed dubious. "That doesn't even make sense, Milo. Why would Gordon go to such lengths with all this when we're so close to cutting a deal?"

Milo was silent. At length he said, "Because he's spiteful."

"Give me a break. You're saying that he would risk this whole deal crashing down just to get back at you?"

"You don't know Gordon like I do. He won't stop until he's ruined me."

"Do you know how paranoid that sounds?"

"Look, Cassandra, I don't know what's going through Gordon's head right now. Maybe he thinks it's better to burn something to the ground than let somebody else profit. I don't know. What I do know is that if you and Ross are getting cold feet on this deal, I'm not going to be left with any choice but to go crawling back to him."

"What you decide to do is immaterial at this point. I'm not going to continue feeding the company any further money until I know what the hell is going on. That means there will be no more salary for you, do you understand? You can live on the line of credit until this mess has been cleared up."

Milo felt as though the wind had been knocked out of him. "Just like that, is it?"

"I'm your employer, not your keeper. I will do as I see fit when it comes to the interests of my company." She paused before continuing, "Things will have to change regardless. Ross and I are getting divorced and he's moving up to Seattle."

Milo was at a loss for words. "I'm... I'm sorry to hear it," he stuttered awkwardly.

She continued as if he hadn't spoken. "He'll be handling our joint real estate interests in Washington, Idaho, and Montana. I'm staying in Palm Desert, but it remains to be seen what this will mean for the company." She spoke almost casually, as though she were discussing the dissolution of someone else's marriage and not her own.

Following the abrupt departure of his partner, Gordon had shown no interest in divesting himself quite yet from the contract with the Air Force. With the CIA out of the building he seemed to lose his inclination towards extreme behavior, and as a result, the Air Force personnel renewed their commitment to staying on with Hicks Limited. They had been successfully convinced that the rest of the Hicks staff was re-engineering the Hannah software.

Each week, Hicks personnel provided output from the Al-Jazeera broadcasts. It was, however, the result of an elaborate sham. Gordon had secretly paid each of his employees a $50,000 bonus to fabricate the results that Milo had so painstakingly managed to achieve. This was done by randomly generating dates and coordinates, and Gordon could rest easy that it would take the Air Force months, if not years, to unravel the randomly generated data, should they ever take the time to go through it all. The employees, for their part, had reason enough to go along with the lie, especially Kathy White. Kathy was a single mother whose young son had a degenerative nervous system disease requiring extensive medical care, and Gordon had promised her ongoing support for his needs if she went along with the fraud. He also hinted at the prospect of ruining her reputation in the tech world if she didn't.

Furthermore, Gordon had a cash flow problem that required the Hannah project to move forward. The ongoing golf course and housing development project had hit snag after snag, and none of Gordon's screaming, threatening, or tantrums could get it to move as quickly as he wanted it to. The real estate boom had hit the area and contractors were getting prime prices for their work, which meant that most demanded payment right away. If someone failed to pay immediately, the contracts simply moved on to the next project. Demand was so high that they were in a position to operate this way. As a result, Gordon had to keep the money flowing for the graders, the golf course experts and the first hundred custom homes planned for the prime locations around the course.

Julip Hicks, meanwhile, had decided that she needed a reputation makeover following several uncomfortable incidents among the Reno elite. She and Gordon had recently attended a fundraiser for children's leukemia where they had rubbed elbows with some of the city's old money; "Blue bloods," Gordon had muttered begrudgingly. It was the first time Julip felt that her taste in fashion had steered her wrong. In a room filled with conservative necklines, modest jewelry, and sensible yet formal shoes, Julip's tight, fire engine red dress and elaborately winking diamond necklace seemed ostentatious. Heads turned, but not in the way to which she had grown accustomed. She could swear that she heard various people muttering under their breath about her getup, and more than once she caught someone staring at her before quickly averting their eyes when they saw she'd caught them looking. She tugged at Gordon's coat sleeve. "Can we make this quick? These statues are giving me the creeps," she hissed.

"Just have a drink and relax, will you?" Gordon had snapped in response.

It turned out to be a bad suggestion. Julip's nerves got the better of her, and by the end of the evening she had consumed so many Greyhounds that she couldn't walk or stand without weaving. Gordon, red-faced, eventually had to call a cab to take her away. But the cab didn't take her home, and he didn't see her for several days after that. When she did return home, he asked what had become of her lavish diamond necklace and she answered, "I don't wear tacky jewelry like that anymore."

She felt that if Gordon was going to become a stakeholder in Reno's larger community as a developer and potential casino owner, she needed the profile of an entrepreneur and civic minded socialite. It was necessary for her to wash herself clean of her former life as an exotic dancer and call girl. She began by hiring a publicity firm to customize her reputation in the community. She also hired an etiquette coach to guide her through the process of changing nearly everything about her: the way she spoke, the way she dressed, the way she ate. Following the incident at the leukemia gala, she stopped drinking in public altogether and regularly made visits to local charities, delivering contributions. It became a regular retinue, with Gordon Jr., in tow, strollered by an innocent looking nanny, and Julip's publicist and photographer.

Two weeks after he had posted bail, Milo paid a visit to the King and Prince, his criminal lawyers in Vegas, to learn what he could about the circumstances surrounding the arrest. He was told that the markers in question were apparently signed by him at the Atlantis in Vegas. "But that's not possible," he protested. "I never took out markers in Vegas. Whatever gambling debt I had was in Reno."

David Abram clasped his hands together and nodded. "Did you sign something, perhaps? A bill that could be attributed back to you?"

Milo thought long and hard. "I suppose I could have signed off on a bill or two when Gordon was too drunk to do it himself," he answered doubtfully at length. "But frankly, I can't recall any specific time that ever happened. At one of the Pentagon parties maybe... but it seems far-fetched." He looked out the window and became thoughtful. "Is it possible that Gordon was able to have Johnny Staggs switch the positive balance I had at the Reno casino with the negative balance that Gordon held in Vegas?"

"When your friend is the governor of Nevada," his attorney

answered, "a great deal is possible."

"It would be in keeping with Gordon's vindictive personality that he and Montefusco created this fabrication to ruin our proposed deal, or to at least to strong-arm me into dropping the allegation that I saw Montefusco take a bribe."

After the meeting Milo drove the long road home from Vegas, wondering how he could possibly get out of the mess he found himself in. He knew that he would be unable to defend himself without the support of the Hellers and their deep pockets. He also knew that he couldn't let this matter go to trial, but the only other option seemed to be prison, and from his nine days in county jail he knew he would never survive prison. And how could he go on facing his family? Following his release from Riverside County Jail they had treated him gingerly, like someone with a debilitating disease who was on the verge of death. They tiptoed through the house quietly and spoke to him in gentle voices, and there was an ever-present look of fear in their eyes when they looked at him. What were they afraid of? Were they afraid that after his harrowing experience something had permanently broken inside him? Was it concern over his fate? Or did they let themselves wonder if the charges against him may have some merit? He had always gone to great lengths to keep his work life separate from his private life. None of them had ever asked what it was, precisely, that he did for a living... how it was, exactly, that he earned the money to pay for the roof over their heads.

Nor did they know the details of what had gone on in the hours of his day. He winced as he thought of the long hours he'd put in at the height of the CIA's decoding push. The family seemed to take it on good faith that he'd been working the whole time. They didn't know about the occasional lavish parties with the Air Force colonels, with cocktails served by naked women. They didn't know about the recent days when Milo had capped his working hours by heading to the casino to spend some time "decompressing," as he called it. For all they knew, he could be precisely the scoundrel that these scurrilous charges made him out to be. He realized with a heavy pang of regret that if he'd spent less time trying to make money for his family to spend, and more time enjoying what they had together, they might know him better as a person and know that the accusations leveled against him were baseless. But they didn't know him, really. He had turned himself into a provider for them, but in so doing he had failed to be a good father or a good husband.

It was at this moment that his cellphone rang. He answered it, "This is Milo."

"Milo! Hank Traversi."

"Hank... it's been a while." The last time he had heard from Hank was when Gordon had locked him out of the Hicks Limited building. "I'm a bit surprised to hear from you, frankly. What can I do for you?"

"Truth be told, I'm a little concerned. Things around the warehouse seem to be going downhill since you left. I'm concerned that Gordon has been providing false output to the Air Force in your absence."

"Duh! Didn't see that comin'," Milo answered.

Hank began to laugh. "At least you haven't lost your sense of humor. Now listen, I have a proposal for you. I wonder if you'd be amenable to coming to Fort Washington and perform a scan on 300-400 frames of footage. I can offer you $2,000 a day. We're operating under Sid Montgomery's Hammer set-up, but you're welcome to bring your own source code and take it with you when you're all finished."

"But what about the injunction? Isn't it your guys who are preventing me from doing business with the Hellers? They're hanging me from a string."

"Look, let's be honest. I know you're going to ignore the injunction anyway. In spite of the fact that things have been tough on you, you're still free, right? Kind of makes you think someone's looking out for you."

Milo answered doubtfully, "I suppose. Anyway, let me think about it." His phone began beeping, which meant another call was coming through. He looked at the screen. "Hank, I'll have to get back to you. Natalie's calling me. I'll be in touch within the next week."

He hung up and switched over to Natalie. He could hear at once that her voice was strained. "Where are you?" she asked.

"Near Lake Havasu heading into Parker. The news from my lawyer was not great. The meeting didn't leave me feeling very hopeful."

Natalie was silent for a moment. Then she began to cry.

"Honey, we'll get through this," Milo said, trying to make his voice sound reassuring. "Don't give up on me yet. We'll find a way of beating this."

"It's not just that," she sobbed. She inhaled and attempted to collect herself. "Your mother just called. She said that your dad's health has taken a bad turn, and he's not expected to last more than another day or two. She asked me to tell you to come straight to El Cajon."

Though his father's health had been in decline for a long time, Milo still found himself stung by the news. He realized with a pang that he hadn't once called or visited his father since Ardell had left the hospital the year before. In many ways, he had treated his father as though he were already dead. Now he had to get to Ardell's deathbed before it was too late.

"Call Mom and let her know I'm on my way," Milo said. He hung up and pulled into the nearest gas station to look at a map. Before long he was on I-95 headed south. His father's words of warning about trusting the government echoed in his head, and he now realized that the last person whose advice he had trusted and the last person in the world he had ever listened to was the one who had been right all along. When the government had needed Milo they made his work their top priority, but when things came undone he found himself left holding the bag. He heard himself whisper aloud, "You were right, Dad. You were right. I'm sorry that I never listened to you. And now I'm in over my head." In many ways, Gordon had acted as more of a father to Milo than Ardell ever had, and Milo had gotten so caught up in the whole act that he had ignored all of the warning signs from the start. He hadn't been an innocent bystander by any means — he could have easily blown the whistle on many occasions, long before things had gotten so far out of hand. But greed had an evil twin, and it was power. To that end, Gordon and the government deserved each other.

He arrived in El Cajon at 10:15 that evening, and drove straight to the nursing home where Ardell had been convalescing for the last nine months. As soon as he approached the building, Milo had another heavy pang of guilt that he had never visited his father in this place. Ardell had been moved there after several months of home hospice had proven unsustainable. It was a dismal, low beige building with blinding fluorescent lights that cast a sickly pall on everything within. He entered and asked at the front desk where his father could be found.

The room was dark, save for a small lamp on the stand next to the hospital bed, and the flickering across the screen of the machine that monitored Ardell's vital signs. An IV hung from a stand on the other side of the bed, and the thin tubes fed into Ardell's emaciated arm. His breathing was heavy and labored, and he was asleep. A strange rattle emitted from his chest with every ragged inhale. The sound set Milo's teeth on edge, as it had many years before. He knew from his days as a medical technician that his father had only hours, if not moments, left to live.

Milo sat in a chair beside the bed and took his father's skeletal hand in his own. The hand was cold and almost transparent. The warmth of his son's touch wakened Ardell from his slumber, and he roused himself with a loud and painful inhalation that turned into a bone-rattling cough. He stirred with a grimace on his face, and his sallow eyelids opened slowly. He said with great difficulty, "My boy."

Milo started. Ardell had never called him that before, while Gordon had never called him anything else. He said gently, "Hi, Dad."

Ardell's eyes took a moment to gain their focus, and when they did, he turned his head to look at his son. "How is the world's greatest decoder?" he asked, his voice no more than a whisper.

"Okay, I guess, Pops. How's the world's greatest carpenter?" Ardell let out a chuckle, which immediately turned into a racking cough. Milo at once regretted being so frivolous and put a calming hand on his father's damp forehead, saying, "Sorry, Pops. Take it easy."

It took a moment for Ardell's breathing to return to normal. Once he managed it he said, "Looks like I'm headed for glory, unless there's any chance you have some medical magic in that computer brain of yours."

Milo felt the tears stinging in his eyes. "No, Dad, I'm fresh out of magic. For you and for me."

Ardell slowly lowered and lifted his eyelids, which was meant to signify a nod. "Son, you have one more thing that I need. Would you give it to me?"

Milo held the frail hand tighter. "Anything you need, Dad. Just name it."

"Stay here 'til the angels come to take me, will you? I want them to see the world's smartest son."

"Of course, Dad. Glad to." There was no holding back the tears now. They flowed freely down his face and dripped from his chin. He kept his father's fingers interlaced with his own and lifted his free arm to wipe his nose with his sleeve. Ardell said no more. Milo sat gazing at his father's form beneath the blankets, his crushed and twisted hand hidden at his side. If it weren't for that hand ruined in the machine, Milo wondered, would things have turned out differently? Would his father have followed his dreams, made a better life for himself? Would we have been a happier man, a better husband, a kinder and more patient father? Would he have married Sarah at all, in whose lap he had laid his head and cried? Would she have fallen in love with him and given him a son? Would their daughter have been conceived... would she have been born? Would Ardell have gone forth into the world, married a different girl, and would Milo never come to be? Or would everything have been the same, despite the hand? Was Ardell destined to be an angry man and a frustrated drunk, one way or the other? Milo didn't know.

He remained at Ardell's bedside for another hour, listening to the labored rattle of his breathing. He had just begun to drift off to sleep, holding his father's hand with his own and propping his head up on the arm of the chair with the other, when Ardell let out a sudden gasp that startled him awake. He said, "Dad?"

Ardell's fragile grip had suddenly become intensely strong. His knuckles were white. He said in a clear and forceful voice, "God graciously hear us." And with that he was gone.

CHAPTER TWENTY-ONE

The service was held six days later at the Camellia Gardens Memorial Park in San Diego. It was a smoggy, unpleasantly warm and still early September day. The attendees shielded their eyes from the blinding yellow sky with dark glasses. The women fanned themselves with their paper programs, and the men tugged at collars saturated with sweat. The air felt heavy and dense and everyone, without exception, stuck to their folding chairs. David Holden wiped his brow with a handkerchief before tucking it back into his inside breast pocket. He surveyed the small gathered crowd sweating and fanning themselves before him. They were eight in all, including himself.

He dropped his eyes to the small Bible in his hands and continued reading aloud from the book of Psalms. "He who dwells in the shelter of the Most High will rest in the shadow of the Almighty." He closed the Bible and looked once more at the small crowd before him. Everyone was silent. He lifted his hand and gestured toward the St. Peter and Paul mausoleum wing of the marble building across the lawn. "Let us put Ardell Caldwell to rest," he said.

They walked across the lawn in pairs: Holden with Natalie; Milo with his mother; Carrie with Erik; and Jeremy with Ardell's one and only friend, a bent and cantankerous man in his early eighties named Lou Figgs. Though they had apparently regarded one another as friends, Milo had never witnessed a single interaction between Ardell and Lou that didn't involve a shouting match. It might be about anything... politics, sports, the best place to eat pork ribs. They seemed to disagree on everything. Yet as long as Milo could remember, Lou came over to the Caldwell house every Friday evening to sit with Ardell in the living room and smoke a cigar. Lou didn't drink, so Sarah always brought him a glass of Diet Coke on ice. His cigars stunk up the house and Ardell never failed to complain loudly to his friend about his disgusting habit; yet he always allowed Lou to smoke indoors.

There came a collective sigh of relief once the group had reached the shade of the mausoleum, but once inside, the air felt clammy, and after several minutes they had all begun to shiver. The smell of the burial tombs was one that Milo would not soon forget. Midway down the hall seven chairs faced a small pulpit. The group took their chairs and Holden took his place at the head. To the pulpit's right was the open crypt where Ardell's casket had been placed. On the floor below the opening lay a granite cover for the crypt. On tracing paper the words "Ardell Wayne Caldwell" had been penciled in.

Milo sat with his mother in the front row, and listened as Pastor Holden read aloud from the Bible once more. Milo stole a glance at his mother, who seemed lost in a fog. Since the time of Ardell's passing she hadn't shown any outward signs of significant grief; instead, she seemed perpetually lost in a daze. She often failed to hear when people first spoke to her, and had to be prodded gently to pay attention. She now sat staring off into space, with a look of vague worry on her face. She repeatedly clasped and unclasped her hands in her lap almost compulsively, and her thin lips moved slightly as though she were reciting something to herself. Milo reached over and took her hand. She submitted to the gesture but continued to gaze off at something no one else could see.

Then Pastor Holden said, "Milo, would you like to say a few words?"

Milo let go of his mother's hand and went to the pulpit. Everyone waited in respectful silence as he took a sheet of handwritten notes from his jacket pocket with shaking fingers. "It's been a long and difficult journey," he said, reading aloud from the page. Then he stopped and took a deep breath. Without entirely realizing what he was doing, he refolded the paper and returned it to his pocket. "My father was not an easy man to be around," he continued, not quite knowing where the words came from. "We all know that. Was he a good man? It's difficult to say. I know that I, for one, can't pretend to know what it is that makes a man good or bad. Someone who wants to do the right thing but doesn't, either because they can't or they don't know how, may not be any better than someone who doesn't care either way. In the end, neither of them do the right thing, so why should the intention count? I know my father didn't always do right... in fact, he rarely did. But I also know that he always wanted to. He believed in truth, and justice, and even if he had a difficult time living by those standards himself, they were important to him just the same. And isn't that worth something? Shouldn't our values mean something even if we don't always measure up to them?"

He became unconsciously aware at this point that his face was wet with tears, but he didn't pause to wipe them away. "Even if we fail to live up to the standards we set for ourselves, we've got to have them. Even if in the end it doesn't make a difference, I believe we've got to have them. What else can I think? What else even makes sense?" The small audience listened with solemn attentiveness. Only Carrie wept heavily with youthful abandon. "My father may not have lived up to his own values or his own standards, but he made certain to impress them on me. I can only pray that my children have absorbed the values I've tried to raise them with, even when I fail. And I fail every day. I can only pray that they'll do better than I have. I understand now that that's all my dad ever wanted for me." Here he had to stop speaking, overcome by emotion. He turned his head and broke down.

Pastor Holden waited for a moment to see if he would continue before stepping up to the pulpit and laying a reassuring hand on Milo's shoulder. Milo took his seat, crying brokenly. He listened distractedly as Pastor Holden offered up a homily about the living and the dead, perishable and imperishable, resurrection and life in the world to come. He finished by reading Psalm 23.

Quietly, as the family recited "The Lord is my Shepherd," the memorial park staff took their places next to Holden. When the recitation had come to an end, they placed temporary hand clamps to all four corners, and prepared to place the granite cover over the mouth of the crypt.

It was a moment for which Milo had been preparing himself since his father passed from this life into the next, clutching his son's hand in an iron-like grip. Up until the crypt cover had been lifted from the ground he had not known whether he would be able to go through with it or not. But now, in a split second, he found himself acting without thought, his body moving of its own accord as though compelled by some power or sense of resolve beyond his own. He stood, reached into his pocket, and withdrew the six computer discs that contained the source code for Hannah. Standing before the casket, he put out a hand and touched the lid of the mahogany box containing his father. He whispered, "God graciously hear us." And with that he slipped the discs into the crypt alongside the coffin. He also found himself pulling the CIA Medal of Valor from his hip pocket, though he couldn't remember having consciously put it there. This he laid alongside the discs before he stepped back to let the men seal the tomb.

That night, Milo set out for a walk from his mother's house. Natalie had offered to go with him, but he told her that he needed to be alone. He wandered aimlessly through the neighborhoods, hardly sure of where he was going, but he didn't care. The air in his mother's house had seemed suffocating, and the small talk between the family and few friends who had come over after the funeral made him want to scream. After a few hours of enduring this, he felt he had to be alone or else he'd go crazy.

The muggy day had settled into a warm and pleasant evening, and the insects began to sing in the jacaranda trees. The neighborhood bordered a canyon and he walked along the edge, looking down into the pit and wondering vaguely if his problems might not be solved by simply throwing himself in. He had been walking for about fifteen minutes when he felt his phone begin to vibrate in his pocket. It was a number he didn't recognize, but nevertheless he answered it.

"My boy," said a voice out of the past.

Milo was too stunned to answer immediately. At length he found his voice. "What the hell do you want, Gordon?"

"Now now, easy there. I come in peace. I heard about your father's passing and I'm calling to offer my condolences."

"How did you hear?"

Gordon wouldn't be put off guard. "Let's just let bygones be bygones, shall we? I'm deeply sorry for your loss and I wanted to extend a hand to offer your family anything you might need in your time of grief."

"I said, 'how did you hear?' Are you having your friends at the CIA tap my phone?"

Gordon sighed. "Let's just say I heard it through the ether. Let's leave it at that, shall we?"

"I don't have anything to say to you, Gordon. And my family certainly doesn't need anything from you."

"Milo, Milo," Gordon chided him. "As high-strung as ever."

"Can we just cut the crap for once? I know you well enough to know that everything you do has one or more hidden motives. So just tell me why you're calling."

"All right." Gordon's voice reverted to its normal brusqueness. "You're not interested in niceties. I can't fault you for that. So I won't beat around the bush. I want you to come back to work for me."

"And why in the world would I ever do that? You're the one who put me in this position."

"And I can make it all go away." He paused. "This can't be easy for you, can it? The financial strain. The emotional toll on your family. No stable income and no prospect of anything stable in the near future. The possibility of jail time. The legal fees piling up. I understand that in addition to everything else you've promised your daughter a wedding that you can't afford. And now on top of it all, you lose your father. There's the funeral to pay for, your mother's well-being to think of now. Am I painting an accurate picture?"

"You forgot to mention the car repairs I have coming up," Milo answered dryly.

Gordon chuckled pityingly. "My dear boy. You're in over your head, anyone can see that as clear as day. We can put this all behind us and continue what we started together."

"Forgive me if I don't jump at the opportunity. You might remember that you still owe me a lot of money."

"You're absolutely right, and right to be cautious. Here's what we'll do. I'll instruct my attorney to cut you a check for the full amount you're owed, no strings attached. You can cash it immediately, take care of all these obnoxious little things hanging over you, and then you can decide whether you want to take my offer."

"After everything that's happened, why would you want me back?"

Gordon sighed once more. "At the risk of sounding corny, I need you. I've been hard-pressed to find anyone capable of replacing you. And if you want to know the truth, when I heard about the loss of your father it touched me. In many ways you've been like a son to me. Fathers and sons are bound to have disagreements at times, but that doesn't mean we can't heal and move on."

"And why should I trust you, Gordon?"

"My boy, at this point, can you afford not to?"

Milo considered this. On the face of it, he knew he would be a fool to believe that Gordon wouldn't put him through the ringer all over again. He knew that Gordon wasn't really capable of changing, and that he would just be using him like he had before. Then again, if Gordon really needed him as much as he said he did, that gave Milo the upper hand. He could dictate his own terms. After all that had transpired, Gordon must be even more desperate than he was willing to admit in order to call his old partner up and ask him to come back. Milo stood at the lip of the canyon, looking out and parsing all of this in his mind. When he had not spoken for some time, Gordon said gently, "You don't need to decide at this moment. At least let me pay you what I owe you so we can wipe the slate clean."

"You know what, Gordon? You keep your money. I don't want anything that has your name on it, and I never want to hear from you again."

Gordon protested, "Now, be reasonable… " But whatever argument he intended to make was lost to the wind as Milo brought back his arm and hurled the phone down into the belly of the canyon. He watched with a sense of momentary exhilaration as it bounced several times on the way down, shedding bits and pieces at it went, before coming to a shattered halt forty feet below.

He stood looking at it for a while, then turned and made his way back to his mother's house. As he came through the door, Natalie looked up from her place on the couch. "Oh, there you are. I was starting to wonder when you were coming back. I tried calling you a minute ago."

Milo realized that he was shaking from head to toe. "I threw my cell phone into the canyon."

Natalie took this in stride. "Really? Any particular reason?"

"It seemed like the right thing to do at the moment. I was trying to make a dramatic gesture."

"Was it at least cathartic?"

Milo considered. "Yeah, it was," he answered.

Milo and Natalie returned home two days later, on September 11. The first part of the drive from El Cajon was completed in near silence. Natalie had attempted to make some semblance of conversation in the first hour and, finding herself met with only monosyllabic answers, she eventually gave up. She assumed that her husband was upset over the death and burial of his father, but this was only partially true. Milo had said nothing of the conversation with Gordon, nor did she know about the internal struggle he'd experienced since that time over whether he had made the right decision. He could see no way out, and he even found himself growing irrationally angry when he remembered Holden's platitudes at the funeral about difficulty breeding character. "I've had enough character lessons to last me a lifetime," he thought irritably. It was becoming increasingly clearer that Cassandra was not going to move forward in the negotiations with Gordon, and that meant that Milo stood a good chance of going to jail for theft.

They stopped for gas at the halfway mark. Natalie watched as Milo climbed out of the car, put his credit card into the gas pump, then removed the nozzle and fitted it into the gas tank chamber. As he waited for it to fill he stood looking off into the distance. He wasn't aware that he was being watched, and allowed himself to slump in exhaustion against the side of the car. Natalie sat quietly, regarding his back pressed up against the driver's side window. She was struck suddenly by how much his physical demeanor had changed since they had first met in high school. Back then he had been sprightly, almost to the point of annoyance. He had never seemed to be able to sit still. He often leapt to his feet and propelled himself forward in quick, sometimes almost violent bursts of movement. They had met in their sophomore year English class, where the teacher had reprimanded Milo for his inability to go an entire class period without suddenly jumping out of his seat and asking to be excused to go to the restroom. In their junior year chemistry class, another teacher had castigated Milo for incessantly drumming the tabletop with his pencil. He had seemed, in those days, to be in a permanent state of agitation, and from afar Natalie had interpreted this as an impatience to go forth into the world and do something. After watching him from a distance for two years, she couldn't bear not finding out what it was he wanted to do that was so important he couldn't sit quietly.

She asked him one afternoon early in their senior year if he wanted to get a hamburger after school. His evident shyness at being asked had surprised her. She had assumed that someone so visibly bursting with energy wouldn't be so timid.

Over the years, she came to understand that his agitation had not come not from a sense of needing to go forth to do something in particular; rather, he wanted to do something, anything, but he could never figure out quite what, and this troubled him. As time passed and the compounded effects of working, buying a house, and raising children made themselves felt, he lost that physical restlessness that had once so intrigued her. Only his mind continued to spin frenetically. Now as she watched his tired frame lean against the side of the car, she was overcome by a sense of what had been lost over the course of the last thirty years as a result of life's many frustrations, unexpected detours, and disappointments.

Milo replaced the gas nozzle in the pump and climbed back into the car. They pulled out of the station and back onto the freeway. After a moment of silence Natalie said, "You know, I've been thinking about Carrie's wedding…"

"Honey, I'm sorry but I don't think I can handle talking about that right now."

"I don't mean I've been thinking about any of the planning stuff. I've just been thinking about how wrapped up in it I've been." She looked out the window. "Sometimes I feel like I get so caught up with what's right in front of me that I lose sight of the bigger picture. I get carried away. Like with this wedding. I've been thinking about how it's gotten a little out of hand. I know you tried to tell me that, but I was so much in the thick of it that I didn't want to hear about it. And now that I'm taking a step back from it I'm feeling a little bit overwhelmed by how carried away I've gotten… we've all gotten." Milo didn't answer, so she continued, "I guess that's how life goes, isn't it? You get tunnel vision and then you forget about what's really important."

Milo nodded, but still didn't speak.

Natalie went on, "I think it's been easy for all of us to enjoy the spoils of how hard you've worked over the last couple of years, but I also sometimes think that it's caused us to give up something else. Of course I've loved moving into bigger houses and having a pool and all that, but right now I would trade any of it for the simpler life that we had in Lodi. I mean, just playing board games as a family on a Friday night. I can't even remember the last time that we did something like that."

"I miss that, too," Milo said.

"I don't want you to think that I'm blaming you, or anything like that. It's not anybody's fault. It's just the way things have gone. If anything, I feel like I'm the one who should have been happier with what I had, rather than wanting more." At this point Natalie stopped speaking abruptly. Though she didn't make a sound, Milo could tell without looking at her that she had gotten choked up. She turned her head away from him, and didn't say anything further.

Milo, for his part, felt the same sense of claustrophobia building up in the car that had pushed him out of his mother's house after the funeral. The artificial cool of air conditioning became suddenly oppressive, and he found himself feeling parched. His teeth began to chatter and he turned the A/C down. I'm trapped, he thought. I'm caught in quicksand. He felt helpless, overcome by a sense of futility. It didn't seem to matter in which direction he attempted to move. He had gotten in too deep. The more he struggled, the more it pulled him in. The icy blast of the air conditioning still chilled him, and he turned it down further. He set his jaw in an attempt to stop his teeth from rattling. He felt himself descending into self-loathing. It's all been a lie, he realized. All the talk about morals, values. All my years of pretending to have religious convictions.

Going to church, praying. It's all been a crutch for me in times when I've needed it. And then when I don't need it I toss it aside and do whatever I want. I'm no better than my father. His teeth clenched.

Once home, he dropped Natalie off at the house and drove to the kennel to pick up the dogs. As he waited at the chain link gate for the keeper to gather them from their respective quarters, the sounds of barking echoing through the halls, he realized glumly that the animals that had so often brought him joy suddenly seemed more of a burden. He winced as the pack advanced toward him, yelping with excitement at seeing their master.

Later that evening, he took Shasta for a walk. The fiery sky of the Indian summer evening had burned down to a palette of pinks and purples, and here and there an errant star began to flicker overhead. Milo walked without noticing where he was going, preferring instead to let Shasta lead the way. Shasta happily obliged, taking full advantage of his master's distracted manner to pause at length to sniff whatever interested him. Milo glanced absentmindedly at the houses they passed, and the street-facing windows that began to light up one by one as the darkness deepened. Certainly the people in those houses and on the other side of those lighted windows had troubles of their own, he mused, but it was difficult to imagine that any of those troubles could possibly match his own. It made the walk difficult, feeling as keenly as he did that he had little of the security so many here took for granted.

As night fell in its entirety, he suddenly woke as if from a dream, and realized that he had allowed the dog to lead him much further from home than he had intended. He turned and began the journey back, tugging at Shasta, who was clearly resistant to Milo's recently awakened sense of authority. He kept trying to lead in a different direction and Milo would yank at the leash, protesting, "Come on, boy. We don't want to be dinner for coyotes." They were crossing Pienze Way when Milo noticed a black car parked at the curb, ten yards ahead of them. As they approached, the passenger side door opened and he paused, at once thrown back into the agitation that he'd known in the days when Vic accompanied him. Instinctively, he reached into his pocket for a cell phone that was no longer there. But the figure emerging from the car surprised him so greatly that he immediately withdrew his hand. It was Kyla.

A beat passed before he could speak. When he did, all he managed was, "I'm a little surprised to see you, Taylouni." She smiled in response. At that moment the driver side door opened, and out stepped Dirkes. Milo was taken aback again. Dirkes' hives had completely cleared up. "Walt, you're looking better," he found himself saying.

"It's good to see you, too, Caldwell," Dirkes said shortly, though with an unmistakable grin. Milo had never seen Dirkes crack a smile before.

"How did you find me?" Milo asked.

"We stopped by your house, and Natalie told us you'd gone out for a walk," Kyla answered. She crouched down to let Shasta cautiously sniff her hand before he allowed her to ruffle his fur.

The moment of initial surprise had passed, and now Milo felt his blood begin to boil. "Where have the two of you been? You know how much shit I'm in, so why isn't the agency helping me?" Kyla rose to her feet but said nothing. "Why did you put the 'SSP' on me? Do you want to see me go to jail? Do you even care if my family is ruined?" With each question his voice grew louder and more insistent.

Kyla maintained a Mona Lisa smile through this onslaught, cryptic and infuriating. When he had finished she said gently, "Do you remember what I said to you the last time we saw each other?"

"Of course I remember. You said to do the right thing and you wouldn't let me down. I hate to tell you, but that's not exactly the way things have gone."

She didn't let the remark derail her. "Well, you have done the right thing, and I haven't let you down. These are for you." With this she took two file folders from the front seat and handed one to him.

"What's this?" he asked.

"Can you handle a bit of backstory?" She frowned as Milo rolled his eyes. "Hey, you're always telling one to me. So just indulge me for the time being, would you? It could very well help you to listen more than you talk." She took a deep breath. "Not too long ago Allen and I were at home watching *Chinatown*. It's about water rights in Los Angeles. Have you seen it?"

"It's one of my favorites."

"Well, it reminded me of one of my father's favorite ancient Chinese sayings.

My father would always tell me, "He who owns the water controls the world." So this got me thinking about Gordon's development project, and how much it depends on the water rights he purchased from the equity company that wanted to build casinos in south Washoe County. I know that's quite a kettle of fish because I read about things like this all the time while on my first assignment in Vegas."

"Okay..." Milo prodded her to continue, hardly able to understand the point.

"So I asked Allen to do some research on groundwater in the state of Nevada. He found that prior to 1995, the control of rights and deeds was kept on the county level rather than at the Nevada Department of Water Resources. Well, here's the point. Often the rights or deeds in formerly remote areas were cancelled for non-use. These cancellations never made it into the records at the NDWR. When those cancellations occurred, the deed reverted to the previous owner. It was always the responsibility of the purchaser to investigate, both at the NDWR and on the county level."

"And?"

"And in the case of south Washoe County, those deeds for water rights were purchased in 1981 by a junk bond equity company. But nothing was ever done with them. Once they placed the pumps into the wells, the equity company simply kept them maintained. When Gordon purchased these deeds from the equity company in 2002, he apparently only checked the records at the NDWR and not at the county. The county had the deeds reverted back to the previous owner, which was the Department of Interior, Bureau of Land Management. Up until 1981, those lands were used for cattle leases."

In spite of his desperate need to believe that Kyla had something that could help him, Milo found himself losing his ability to follow. "I guess I'm not really understanding why any of this is important." Shasta was becoming anxious that they'd been standing in one place for such a long time, and had begun to whine. Milo petted his head and shushed him.

"Well, when Gordon goes to turn on the water, the county won't give him permission. First, because each groundwater well has been issued a 'cancellation of water rights for failure of due diligence.' Secondly, he'll have to purchase them all over again from the original owner, the BLM."

Milo sighed. "Kyla, I'm really happy to hear that Gordon royally screwed up. It couldn't have happened to a nicer guy. But I still don't see what any of it has to do with me."

With this she continued with a smile, "When Gordon shut down the warehouse, made his insane demand for $500 million, and headed for the cruise, I had been given a suitcase from the black budget for the next stage of the Hammer. I was supposed to bring it with me the next time I saw you. But the AJ bombing plan put me off track and Gordon's ridiculous effort to manipulate things with Montefusco was so pathetically transparent, I wasn't about to credit him with the money. So then when he started turning on you, starting with the payoff to Montefusco on the cruise, I figured there'd be a time when you could use it. What I did was get Allen to help me purchase the deeds for the water rights in south Washoe County under your name with the black bag money, which wound up being almost $2 million.

We've been quietly making the purchases from the BLM over the past year, with the help of one of Dirkes' buddies in Interior."

Milo's jaw dropped. "How can that possibly be legal?"

"It's a black bag budget. Dirkes and I figured that our agency has run a drug business in Nicaragua and has paid off tribal leaders in Afghanistan. The least we could do was help one Boy Scout in Reno get his merit badge. Allen tells me that the law on water rights is first owned, first right. The Interior Department did the Agency a favor and got us out of further work with Gordon. But Dirkes and I knew we couldn't take the last step, putting your name onto the deeds of conveyance, until the FBI was neutered by Judge Royals. Those guys don't exactly like us, and no one wants us messing around in domestic affairs. But as you've experienced, that's kind of a fuzzy line. That envelope contains your deeds of conveyance."

Milo could hardly take it all in. "I really don't know what to say."

Kyla continued, "But you need to hear me on this. Do not, under any circumstances, keep these deeds. If you do, you'll be in court against Gordon for the rest of your life. Use them in the only way possible, and turn them over to him if he promises to use his influence to drop the charges that stand in the casino. Then you'll be free to proceed with Cassandra. Oh, and by the way," she reached into her suit jacket pocket and handed him a second envelope. "As I said, the deeds were just short of two million. The last fifty thousand should just about cover the rest of those crazy stupid wedding costs of yours. Really, Milo." She shook her head chiding, "Maui?"

Milo shrugged helplessly and replied in a tone of resignation, "Anything for my little girl."

Kyla's mischievous look turned softer. "Do the right thing, Milo, and move forward."

Milo nodded and said, "Thank you."

They smiled at one another. From inside the car Dirkes called out, "Come on, Taylouni, let's get out of here."

She turned and climbed back into the car. The engine started as she closed the door. Shasta was, by this time, tugging impatiently at the leash, and Milo turned to rein him in. By the time he turned back the car was pulling away from the curb, and he stood watching until it disappeared into the darkness, the twin red taillights swallowed by the night.

CPSIA information can be obtained at www.ICGtesting.com
Printed in the USA
LVOW07s0203260913

353854LV00002B/2/P

9 780989 685016